Derek never wished to inherit his title as a result of a bloody battle. With the old count dead and the truce dependent on his marriage to the rival duke's son, Derek has no choice but to agree to the victor's terms in order to bring peace to his homeland. When he learns of the sinister rumors surrounding his intended groom, Derek begins to have doubts—but there can be no turning back from saying I do.

After the death of his wife, Callan of Mulberny never expected to be forced into another political marriage—especially not to someone like the new Count of Camria. Seemingly soft and meek, it's only fitting that Derek's family crest is a flighty sparrow, worthy of nothing but contempt.

Another war with the seafaring people of the Outer Isles looms on the horizon, and the reluctant newlyweds must team together to protect those caught in the circle of violence. Derek and Callan slowly learn to let go of their prejudices, but as they find themselves enmeshed in intrigue fueled by dark secrets and revenge, their tentative bond is all that keeps their world—and their lives—from plunging into chaos.

THE WOLF AND
THE SPARROW

Isabelle Adler

A NineStar Press Publication

Published by NineStar Press
P.O. Box 91792,
Albuquerque, New Mexico, 87199 USA.
www.ninestarpress.com

The Wolf and the Sparrow

This is a work of fiction. Names, characters, places, and incidents are either the product of the author's imagination or are used fictitiously. Any resemblance to actual persons living or dead, business establishments, events, or locales is entirely coincidental.

Printed in the USA
First Edition
November, 2019

Print ISBN: 978-1-951057-91-6

Also available in eBook, ISBN: 978-1-951057-89-3

Warning: This book contains sexually explicit content, which is only suitable for mature readers, depictions of violence, battle scenes, physical injuries, mentions of torture, allusions to domestic abuse, dealing with grief, and the death of secondary characters.

Chapter One

"DEREK, YOU LUCKY devil," Macon said. "A marriage proposal the minute you inherit a title. How propitious."

Derek ignored the note of bitter mockery in his brother's voice. Instead, he focused on the letter lying on the table in front of them. Words were scribbled across thick paper in an almost careless hand, with nothing to indicate its earth-shattering contents at a casual glance. The red wax seal bore the emblem of a wolf's head, and an unpleasant jolt went through him as he recalled the same sigil splashed over black-and-silver banners streaming above a bloody battlefield. Pain flared in his injured shoulder, as if in response to the memory, and Derek shifted uncomfortably in his chair, adjusting the sling that held his left arm. He made himself focus on the words again, tracing them as if they could somehow magically rearrange themselves into a different message upon rereading.

"Macon, this is not helping," Lady Casea chided.

Macon threw their mother a sullen look that clearly indicated he wasn't there to help. He was sixteen, the age when everything was painted black and white, right and wrong, with nothing in between. Both Derek and their mother knew all too well how washed-out those colors became with time.

They were all sitting at the round table in Lady Casea's drawing room. The upheaval of the last few days hadn't seemed to reach it, unlike the rest of the keep. Embroidered tapestries lined the walls, displaying flowers in fanciful patterns, and the chairs were lined with soft cushions. A familiar scent of lavender and sage permeated the warmth from the fireplace. How strange it was to discuss the grim future of their family in this cozy room, with the only reminder of the presence of death in the gray mourning ribbons tied around their sleeves.

"Let us go through this again," Ivo said, picking up the letter. His tone was neutral, as if he were discussing a passage from a recently read book. He was the scholar among Derek's siblings, but Count Johan had long refused to send him to one of the royal colleges in Oifel, the capital. Father hadn't approved of bookishness, especially not in a nineteen-year-old man who was perfectly capable of holding a sword.

"Duke Bergen offers Lady Casea condolences on the passing of her husband, and asks for Derek's—the new Count of Camria's—hand in marriage to his eldest son and heir, Callan, 'to secure the recently signed truce in hopes of reaching a standing peace treaty between our fiefdoms and show goodwill.'"

"'Passing,'" Macon sneered. "'Goodwill.'"

"Derek, have you even met Callan?" Ayleen asked, turning to him. "I had no idea he was interested in you."

"I doubt he'd know me from a signpost," Derek said dryly.

He'd only ever seen Callan in passing while visiting the Royal Palace a few years ago, and they had paid each other little heed. Undoubtedly, Callan had been in the field along with his father, Duke Bergen, when they fought Camria's forces, but fortunately, Derek hadn't encountered them directly, and neither of them had been present during the signing of the truce, delegating it instead to their field commander.

Ayleen was only twelve, and still somewhat charmed by the notion of romance. Derek was a little sorry to disillusion her, especially so soon after all the other shocks she'd had to endure in the past few days, but it was better if she knew exactly what was going on. Ignorance and pretense weren't going to help any of them when their situation was so precarious.

"The proposal isn't coming from Lord Callan, but from his father. There's nothing to it but politics."

Ivo looked up. "I fear Bergen's essentially trying to annex us. Derek would keep the title while he lives, but with him being a lower noble, it'd eventually pass to his husband or to their heirs. Not to mention that his spouse—whoever they are—would be an equal ruler of Camria while Derek lives."

While he lives. The words sank into Derek's mind, laden with meaning. The marriage contract would still be valid, even if he were to die, effectively passing the fiefdom of Camria to the duke's family. And with Derek out of the way, they'd be free to do what they wished with it.

He said nothing aloud.

"Can we possibly refuse? Find some pretext to decline the offer?" their mother asked.

Ivo shook his head. "I cannot see how. This is not exactly an offer. More like an order, if courteously worded. The letter continues on to stipulate that the wedding take place as soon as possible. In fact, as soon as it would take Derek to arrive at the duke's ancestral castle at Irthorg."

"What about postponing it, then?" Lady Casea turned to Derek in concern. "You're badly injured. Surely, they cannot expect you to stand at the altar, still bleeding. At least a few months, until you're well. It will give us time to petition before the High Queen. This is nothing short of coercion under duress."

There were fading bruises on her neck peeking above the collar of her dress, a yellow imprint of fingers that had nothing to do with the recent battle. Not for the first time, Derek thought that perhaps their father's death was more of a blessing than a tragedy. It felt treasonous to entertain such notions, as though he was betraying his father's memory, but he hadn't imagined the relief in his mother's eyes when the messenger delivered the awful news. He was ashamed to admit, even to himself, that he'd felt the same relief.

But it also meant he was now the head of the family. It was his duty and his responsibility to protect them after Count Johan had failed to do so. Even if it meant marrying a man he'd never met, who'd nearly destroyed everything he held dear, who might still want him dead.

"I'm not hurt that badly," Derek heard himself say. "Besides, I hardly think they'd care—or if the Queen would see it quite the same way. The truce expires in a week. If I don't give an answer by then, I'm afraid there will be no long-standing treaty."

Casea frowned and was about to say something else, but Derek forestalled her.

"I don't see any solution other than conforming to Duke Bergen's wishes. I'd rather not aggravate him while his troops still have free rein within our borders. There would still be an opportunity to do something when we're not in such dire disadvantage. A marriage can always be annulled should the Queen prove sympathetic to our case."

"So, we just roll over and give the duke our land?" Macon said. "That's what he's really after, isn't it? He basically threatens us with another war, and he has the audacity to call it a gesture of goodwill!"

"It *is* goodwill," Derek said quietly. "He doesn't need this union to take the land away from us. In fact, nothing is stopping him from storming the keep and killing us all when the truce ends. It would be his right to do so since he was provoked, and frankly, we've already seen that Camria cannot hold its own when it comes to military strength."

As a warrior himself, Derek was loath to admit it. But Camria was a small fiefdom, and its contingent consisted of the Count's Guard, which numbered only two hundred men, while the rest were mostly peasants who had been hastily called to arms and had little to no fighting experience. That was hardly a match for Mulberny, a much larger and more prosperous domain with a long and bloody history of fending raiding sea pirates off its shores. But of course, these considerations had meant little to his father in the face of a perceived slight.

"You seem very eager to go through with it," Macon sneered. His eyes were rimmed in red and recessed in deep shadows. "Can't wait to become the bed toy of our father's murderer?"

"Macon!" Casea said sharply. "Watch your tongue."

"I will not!" Macon slammed his hand against the table, making everyone save Derek jump. "He's only trying to save his own hide while his new husband turns us out of our own home!"

"Will you stop that?" Derek said levelly, fixing his gaze on Macon. He kept a tight rein on his anger. There was no point in getting into a shouting match with his brother, whose grief was perhaps the most acute of all of them. "No one said anything about turning you out. I'm trying to keep all of you safe, and it would be much easier to do from within the duke's castle than from the chopping block."

"Yes, much easier for *you*! You'd be the duke's lapdog while the rest of us are reduced to beggars!"

Derek's patience, already frayed, finally snapped.

"Maybe Father should have thought about that before he waged war on Bergen over a fucking river dam and got himself killed!"

Macon rose to his feet so abruptly he knocked over his chair. Without another word, he stormed out of the room, slamming the door with enough force to rattle the flower vase on the side table.

There was an awkward silence while everybody avoided looking at one another.

Derek sighed and ran a jerky hand over his face. "I'm sorry. I shouldn't have said that."

Lady Casea got up from her seat. "I've had quite enough of this squabbling. There are still soldiers' wages and widows' allowances to be distributed, and I have work to do. Ayleen, come."

With an apologetic glance at Derek, Ayleen followed Casea out the door.

Derek slumped on the table, propping his head with his right arm. He wasn't used to being in his mother's rooms without her there; however, he was in no hurry to leave. They were all tired, hurt, and confused. Derek had barely slept since signing the temporary truce between

Camria and Mulberny. The nagging ache in his shoulder had worsened, and now his head was throbbing as well. But he welcomed the pain. It was the only thing keeping him from numbness—and he couldn't afford to sink into it at the moment.

This was not how he'd imagined coming into his inheritance. Shouldering responsibility was not unfamiliar to him. His father had been more than happy to let Derek handle the more mundane affairs of daily life in the keep and the surrounding villages—though Derek sometimes thought it was so he'd have someone to criticize. But this...this was almost too much to take on. He was good with a sword and possessed sound common sense, which was perhaps enough for a minor ruler of a small fiefdom, but now he had to admit he was in over his head. Despite trying to present a solid front to his family, he had no idea what to do to prevent more harm coming to them.

Ivo coughed delicately, drawing his attention.

"I didn't want to say anything in front of Mother, but there is something you should know before you make a decision."

Derek raised his head. He didn't like the sound of that, but what could possibly make this entire affair worse than it already was?

"What is it?"

"Did you know that Lord Callan was married before?"

"No." Derek straightened in his chair. He didn't like the look on Ivo's face, the one that said he was troubled. It was a bad sign. Unlike Macon, Ivo was rarely visibly upset over anything.

"Well, he was. To an Agiennan clanswoman, no less. I don't recall her name, but it was about two years ago.

Apparently, the duke has a thing for offering his son in marriage to secure his peace treaties."

"What happened to her?" Derek asked, already knowing he wasn't going to like the answer.

"She died. Some sort of accident, but...there were whispers about something not being quite right with that story."

"And you know all of this how?"

Ivo smiled faintly.

"Unlike you, dear brother, I pay attention to rumors. Most of them are nothing more than idle gossip, but some contain a kernel of truth."

"All this might be just that—nothing more than gossip," Derek said.

"I'm absolutely certain he was married," Ivo repeated. "Accidents do happen even to the most lofty, but you'd better be careful. Some people have an unfortunate tendency to bury their spouses all too often."

"What are you saying?"

"You should consider why Callan wants to marry you—or why his father wants him to. Camria is a well-off fiefdom, but it's hardly of much strategic importance. The duke's heir could set his eyes on a much more advantageous match, striking a union with a foreign noble, or even marrying into the royal family. Your nuptials could be nothing more than a stepping stone for whatever larger scheme he envisions."

"He can't subjugate Camria based on a marriage contract alone, not until Callan and I either unite or produce heirs. The law is clear—if something should happen to me, the fiefdom would pass to my next-of-blood kin. To you."

"I am not yet of age to inherit. Your husband could be legally appointed regent, and if that is what they're after, they don't need you for any longer than your wedding night." Ivo shrugged. "Once you say your vows and the marriage is consummated, he could contest the inheritance of your fiefdom at the Queen's Court if you happen to die under tragic circumstances. And then Callan is once again free to take another spouse. Maybe someone more lucrative."

It appeared Derek had not been the only one to have thought of that, but again, Ivo had always been the smartest of his siblings, and the most astute, despite his age.

"You make him sound like some sort of fairy-tale villain," Derek protested, out of some stubborn determination to refuse to be intimidated, whether by Ivo or by his own apprehension.

But he couldn't help feeling there was something odd about the proposal. It seemed entirely extraneous. Whatever treaty Bergen wanted to sign would have been achieved without a marriage contract to strengthen it, given that Camria was at a dire disadvantage. And Derek entertained no illusions about being so desirable a match as to be of particular interest to the other party. Moreover, while arranged marriages were par for the course among the aristocracy, nobles of similar rank (in this case a newly minted count and the heir apparent of a duchy) did not usually enter such unions for precisely the same considerations of seniority of inheritance Ivo had voiced earlier. If this was all about upholding the peace, it would have been much more reasonable for Duke Bergen to ask for Ivo's hand in future marriage for his son, as he was the only one of Derek's younger siblings close enough to the age of maturity.

"I'm saying that by agreeing to accept this proposal you might be placing yourself in danger," Ivo said.

"And if I don't, I'll be risking all our lives," Derek said sourly. "Macon might not understand it, and Mother might not accept it, but you do. Bergen is blackmailing me with this treaty. I have no choice but to agree to his terms."

"I do understand. I just don't want you to step blindly into a trap."

Derek reached out with his good hand and squeezed Ivo's arm.

"I know, and I'm grateful for your concern. But there's nothing to it. Our best hope would be for me to marry this Callan and bide my time until we figure out how to convince the Queen to issue an annulment."

"Unless you end up falling in love with your arranged husband," Ivo said with a wry smile.

"You know," Derek said, getting up with effort, "I think there's a better chance of him murdering me in my sleep."

BY THE TIME Derek reached his father's study, he was ready to pass out from the pain. The doctor would most certainly be cross at him for exerting himself after being shot with an arrow through the shoulder. To be honest, Derek wanted nothing more than to lie down on his bed and sleep for several days.

But he knew he wouldn't wake up to find all his problems to have magically disappeared. This unfortunate and untimely marriage proposal was now the top item on Derek's long list of obligations, as if he wasn't under enough pressure already to secure the peace treaty as soon as possible. His anger flared, as it always did when he thought about his father's brazen attempt at using brute force to solve the long-standing disagreement between the fiefdoms over the Sevia River dam. Derek had tried to warn him, plead with him, make him see how disastrous the move would be, but his father had refused to see reason, as he'd often done of late. Count Johan hadn't taken well to being opposed. He hadn't dared hit Derek, not anymore, but he'd had no qualms about spilling his ire verbally on the son who was "as cowardly as he was useless."

So Derek had stood by as his father attacked the Mulbernian garrison that guarded the dam which stemmed the flow of water needed for the newly dug irrigation canals the count had commissioned for the fields of northern Camria. The count's victory had been short-lived: Duke Bergen, who was a seasoned warrior, a veteran of the bloody Seven-Year War with Agienna, the realm of the Outer Isles, had not taken the offense lightly. Just as Derek had predicted, his forces crushed whatever meager defense Camria had to offer in a battle that had cost Johan his life, and which Derek had been lucky to escape with only an arrow wound—and a new title that weighed heavier than a mountain.

The room he entered served as a stark reminder of that weight. Derek rarely spent time in his father's study, and never when the count wasn't there. Without him, the small, cramped room felt empty and stale, like a tomb. Mementos of his father's presence were still strewn everywhere—the ledgers and the letters piled haphazardly on the carved redwood desk, the dried quill discarded in haste, the faded tapestries adorned with the Camrian coat of arms with its heraldic sparrow that had graced the walls for as long as Derek could remember. A map of Camria and the neighboring fiefdoms—which belonged to the Great Realm of Ivicia, along the shores of the Sevia River—was half-unrolled at the corner of the desk, catching Derek's attention.

He traced a finger along the winding line of the river, upward, contrary to its course, past the village of Laurel Falls where the battle with the duke's forces had been fought, until he came up to a large dot that marked Irthorg, the capital of Mulberny. It was hardly more than a castle surrounded by a small town and a few farmsteads. Derek had never seen it in person, and he wished he never would. Now, with Count Johan gone, Camria needed him, even if he couldn't quite measure up to everybody's expectations of a strong ruler. He lacked his father's ruthlessness, a trait as necessary for a fief lord as the ability to breathe. People liked him and sometimes listened to him when he used reasonable enough arguments to sway their opinion, but it was hardly enough. It certainly hadn't been enough to impress his father. It hadn't been enough to protect his people.

But there was something he could do now to amend his failures. Perhaps he was a coward for giving in to Duke Bergen's demands, as Macon seemed to believe him to be. And he was afraid, so afraid he was making the wrong move, the wrong decision. So much depended on it, and yet he couldn't think of any other way to secure the peace they so desperately needed. Camria had grown soft, placid in years of quiet and relative prosperity. A single battle had sent the entire fiefdom reeling; a war would be nothing short of devastating. If he was a coward for scrambling to prevent it, there was nothing he could do about it.

He rolled the map and sat at the desk, pushing the books and papers away to clear some space with one hand. The dull gleam from the heavy signet ring that now adorned his finger caught his eye, and he splayed his hand to study the silhouette of a flying sparrow engraved deeply into the green stone's surface.

This had been his father's ring, his seal, the token of his office. It felt foreign on Derek's hand, weighing him down, and he tore his gaze away from it with a twinge of guilt.

Taking out a fresh sheaf of paper, he dipped the quill in the inkwell, and began penning his letter of acceptance.

Chapter Two

UNDER DIFFERENT CIRCUMSTANCES, the outing could have been a pleasant one. The last breath of summer still lingered in the air, scented with the smell of grass and wildflowers, and the southward road wound its way around steep hills that gradually gave way to green plains and meadows dotted with grazing sheep.

Callan loosened his grip on the reins and lifted his head toward the caress of a warm, gentle breeze, so different than the gales that swept the high walls of Irthorg Castle. They weren't so far from the sea that he couldn't smell its salty freshness on the wind, but the scenery was a welcome change from the barren cliffs of the shoreline.

The road Callan and his party were currently taking was by far the most traveled, as it connected Mulberny and Camria and continued on south through Urgan and Hundara, where it met the old King's Road to Oifel. Usually, it saw heavy traffic—farmers' carts, merchants' wagons, lone travelers or messengers hurrying along their business—but following the conflict between their neighboring fiefdoms, the trade had trickled down to an almost complete standstill.

Callan scowled at the thought. Count Johan must have been out of his mind to challenge Mulberny in such reckless fashion, over something that could have been easily solved with careful negotiations and amendments to trade agreements. And now Callan was effectively being punished for the old count's folly by having to marry his eldest son.

He had railed against his father's decision, of course. After Idona, he had no desire to be wed to anyone, even if the union was merely a political one. This marriage of convenience was neither really convenient nor necessary, and he couldn't understand his father's sudden desire to strengthen the ties with Camria in this manner. After the beating they've received, he hardly thought the Camrians would rise again against them. A simple treaty would have been enough, but for some reason his father had been adamant that he marry the new count. Derek.

In the end, Callan had no choice. He couldn't defy the duke—not when presented with a direct order. And so now he was on his way to meet his intended and escort him to the castle as a gesture of courtesy.

Callan would have rather take on a ship full of rogue Agiennan pirates bare-handed.

Sensing his seething anger, Arrow, his gray gelding, tossed his head in agitation, and Callan pushed down on his irritation. He could do this. He could be civil to his future husband, at least, even if the thought of once again taking another person's hand in his in front of an altar made him want to vomit.

His lieutenant, Leandre, rode up to him, her sun-bleached flaxen hair pleated in a tight braid around her head, her black cloak snug around her shoulders.

"There's an armed company coming up the road toward us," she said.

"Finally," Callan muttered. He'd enjoyed the ride so far, but every mile that brought him closer to the Camrian delegation soured his already lousy mood, and he yearned to be done with the welcome. For all he cared, he'd rather only to show up for the ceremony and forgo all these fake niceties altogether.

Now he could see it too—about two dozen men on horseback cresting a hill and descending into a narrow valley, where the road widened as it skirted the side of a small lake. Green and gold banners, tiny at this distance, flapped over their pikes. When the Camrians reached the bend, a man in the lead, whom Callan assumed to be the new count, lifted his hand, calling the company to halt, and waited for Callan's party to approach.

As far as Callan could remember, he hadn't met Derek before, but he was told the man had fought alongside his father, apparently in full support of the count's foolhardy ways. Seeing him now, Callan could well believe it. Derek had a good seat, controlling his horse with little effort despite having his left arm tied up in a sling. A sword hung below his saddle, its simple leather-wrapped hilt worn with use, and he was dressed in plain riding attire fit for traveling rather than finery. While not strikingly handsome by any standard, he was trim and had a pleasant enough face, framed by mousy-brown hair that curled just above his ears. He had an air of competence about him that Callan had learned to recognize over years of campaigning, but there was also a youthful softness Callan was hard-pressed to pinpoint. It lurked somewhere in the depth of Derek's brown eyes, in the curved line of his lips, in the way the man waited docilely for him to draw near.

Callan didn't like soft men—or women, or those who were neither. It was a liability for any warrior, however young, a weakness that endangered not only themselves but also those who were under their protection.

Mulberny, especially, could not afford a weak ruler, even if he was a joint one by right of marriage.

He rode out as his followers hung back, and Derek did the same.

"Count Derek," Callan said. He was trying for polite, but his voice was probably about as warm as the bottom of the nearby lake.

The other man guided his horse to stand abreast with Callan's, and they clasped their hands together in greeting. There was a wary look to Derek's eyes, which had dark circles beneath them, suggestive of long nights without sleep, but even so, Callan couldn't help but note how beautiful they were, dark and deep, framed with long lashes. He'd never seen eyes like that on a man before, a doe's eyes filled with lively intelligence.

Derek's horse shifted nervously when he let go of the reins. Encumbered by having his other arm pressed close to his body in a sling, he wavered for a split second, and Callan instinctively tightened his grip on the man's hand, steadying him.

Derek flushed in what was most likely embarrassment, a blush spreading from his cheeks to the tips of his ears. The faint tinge of color unexpectedly made him appear almost pretty. Equally unexpectedly, Callan found himself wondering what Derek might look like without the distorting veneer of anxiety and fatigue, with his eyes glinting and his lips tugged in a smile rather than set in a hard line.

The young count nodded curtly and withdrew his hand. Callan let his own hand fall as if nothing had happened.

"Welcome to Irthorg," he said. "Did you have a nice journey?"

Derek, whose injury was clearly hurting him a great deal if the stiffness in his shoulders was anything to go by, nodded.

"Yes, thank you, it was fine. It's a beautiful country," he added with a touch of something Callan could almost mistake for sincerity.

"It is," Callan said curtly and gestured for Derek to follow him.

Pleasantries safely concluded, Callan turned his horse around and fell in beside his guest, leading the way back without another word, his men flanking the Camrian contingent on either side at Leandre's sign. The nervous glances the Camrians cast at his men told him they felt more under an armed escort than a welcome cortege. Now, he could make out the Camrian ruling family's crest on their banners, a gold sparrow in flight on a field of green.

A vapid bird. How fitting.

Occasionally, Callan risked a glance at his groom when he was sure Derek wasn't paying him attention, inexplicably curious despite his earlier aversion. Callan didn't know what he'd been expecting, really—maybe someone haughty and entitled, somebody much like Count Johan. But Derek seemed none of those things. He kept quiet and didn't try to strike up a conversation, which suited Callan just fine.

A man of about forty or perhaps a little older followed the count closely. Like almost every other person in their little group, he bore the evidence of the recent battle etched into his face in the form of a fresh red scar by his hairline. Callan assumed he was the Captain of the Count's Guard, judging by the unfamiliar insignia on the pins of his cloak and the tense, hostile looks he was giving both Callan and Leandre. Farther behind rode two youths, so very like Derek in appearance as to leave little doubt who they were. The older brother gazed around curiously, while the younger, little more than a child, stared gloomily at the road ahead, refusing to acknowledge anyone else's presence.

The noonday sun burned high in the sky when they reached a knoll that placed them within seeing distance of Irthorg. The ancestral home of the Dukes of Mulberny stood on sheer white cliffs overlooking the sea, the foaming waves crashing incessantly far below. Its stone walls darkened with age and weather, the dwelling had been built as a fortress against invasions of sea raiders, and served this purpose to this day. But the recent generations of occupants had expanded on it, adding new structures, gardens, and walkways, softening its otherwise severe appearance. A small town had sprung up around the foot of the hill, encircled by a sturdy wall, with several roads leading into it from different directions.

Derek's mouth tightened at the sight, and Callan suppressed an irrational flash of resentment. Despite his polite words, this newcomer was probably too cosseted to either appreciate the stark, rugged beauty of this land, where the cold sea met the sky, or to weather its dangers. What was he to do with such a one for a husband?

After about an hour, they reached the main gates of the town, which stood open during the day but were nonetheless guarded. The watchmen saluted Callan as he rode past, and he nodded back.

Inside the town, the road merged into a narrower street that wound its way upward, going past the large market square, bustling with activity, and the two- and three-storied townhouses, which grew larger and more affluent the higher they climbed. People gathered along the streets and hung out of the windows to watch their procession, and small children ran behind their horses, laughing.

The main keep was separated from the rest of the town by a drawbridge that spanned a natural fissure in the bedrock. As they passed over the bridge, the Camrians glanced down uneasily at the tips of jagged gray rocks far below.

They rode into the lower bailey, where they dismounted. Derek slid off his mare with such graceless stiffness that Callan almost lunged to catch him, but stopped himself at the last moment. Derek had managed the dismount himself, and Callan would rather not cause further discomfort by extending help that wasn't asked for.

Thankfully, one of Derek's brothers—the older one—came to his side, no doubt to offer discreet support. The youngest sibling threw the reins of his horse jerkily to the stable hand. The boy was about Adele's age, but Callan had a feeling his sister was by far more mature than the spoiled brat.

In any case, their guests were now safely inside the keep, and his duties were thus concluded. Medwin, the castellan, was already waiting to show them to their rooms. Callan headed for the stairs to the gallery, ignoring the surprised look his future husband shot his way, but was stopped by a servant when he reached the passage to the family quarters.

"My lord, His Grace requests your immediate presence."

Callan's gut lurched unpleasantly. He had a hunch his father's desire to see him had nothing to do with idle curiosity. With a nod to the servant, he turned and hurried down a different hallway.

CALLAN STRODE RIGHT into his father's study without bothering to knock, still wearing his riding clothes. Neither of them stood on ceremony—especially not when the summons had been so urgent.

The duke's study was, for the lack of a better word, austere. The only furnishings, aside from a huge fireplace, consisted of a large writing desk, a few chairs, and shelves stacked with rolled maps and a selection of books. The duke was seated at the desk, writing a letter. The only item of luxury in the room sat on the desk in front of him, filled with water—a silver goblet etched with minute images of bloodhounds chasing a fox. Callan remembered playing with it as a child, sitting by the fireplace on the wolfskin rug while his father conferred with his lieutenants or received messengers from the more distant provinces.

"What happened?" he asked without preamble.

Bergen raised his head and waved him in. Callan closed the door and lowered himself into a chair opposite his father's desk. The tall narrow windows of the study looked out over the cliffs, letting in the early afternoon light along with a chilly breeze and the hum of the waves, a sound that had permeated his life with such constancy he barely registered it anymore.

"There have been reports of more raiders pillaging the villages north of Bryluen," Bergen said, his words clipped. He indicated a stack of letters sitting neatly on the edge of his desk.

"Again?" Callan frowned.

Pirates attacking the coastal regions was hardly a rare occurrence, but this year saw an abnormal increase in raids throughout the last weeks of summer. This hadn't happened since the signing of the peace treaty with the Outer Isles following the Seven-Year War—a truce which Callan's first marriage had been meant to solidify.

How exceptionally well *that* had turned out.

"The survivors' accounts speak of pirate ships, but it's not hard to guess who is really behind those attacks," Bergen said, his eyes boring into him. Callan resisted the urge to fidget in his chair, reminding himself he was a twenty-six-year-old man, not a timid child, and took the letters to occupy his hands and avoid the duke's icy gaze.

"We don't know that," he ventured, skimming the uneven handwriting on a half-torn piece of paper.

The reports were bad. They always were, but some of these new ones contained details of excessive brutality. Farms and entire villages burned, their inhabitants raped and slaughtered, their bodies left behind in pieces as an offering for the carrion birds, which the Agiennans worshiped as the messengers of their gods. Callan gritted his teeth. It was no wonder Bergen wasted no time informing him of these, despite the wedding preparations.

"They wouldn't be half so brazen without someone backing them up," the duke said. "The Danulf clan is by far the strongest in Agienna. It is why you—"

"Yes, I remember," Callan said, a little more harshly than he intended.

Bergen raised an eyebrow, but otherwise showed no indignation at his insolence, and continued:

"The Danulf have been grasping for ways to exact revenge on Mulberny ever since they broke the treaty. The other clans have no desire for another war, which is why they've refrained from open conflict so far. But I've no doubt the Danulf are the ones sparking trouble along our coast."

Guilt stirred deep inside Callan, a familiar pang that never failed to manifest itself whenever the subject of the Danulf was brought up. Whenever Idona's name was mentioned. It never really went away, merely slept beneath his breastbone as a lump of dull ache until it was called out to the surface.

"But why now?" he asked. "Why would the Danulf act against the will of the other clans if they were reluctant to do it in the past?"

"Who knows? Inner politics? Opportunity? The timing hardly matters. Whatever the case may be, I want you to take your men and head up north," the duke said, his fingertips tapping on the polished desktop for emphasis. "Find out who's behind the raids and give those pirates a proper bashing. It'll have to do until the rest of our troops are called back from Camria."

Callan couldn't hide his surprise.

"What about the wedding?" he asked. It was telling that he'd rather fight a bloody battle than stand before the altar with the Count of Camria by his side, but he couldn't quite hide his enthusiasm at the idea.

"We'll hurry the wedding," Bergen said, effectively dashing Callan's tentative hope for reprieve. "I'm sure the count and his family wouldn't mind."

There was a hint of mockery in the way he uttered "count." Despite the marriage contract, the duke didn't consider the young heir of Camria his equal, that much was certain.

"You've met him. How did you find him? Is he an amiable man?" the duke asked, changing both tone and subject.

"I'm not required to like him, only marry him," Callan said curtly.

Bergen leaned back in his chair. "I suppose that's true."

The concession unexpectedly stung. Callan and his father had never been the overly affectionate sort, but hearing him dismiss Callan's feelings as inconsequential still hurt. It was all the more surprising considering that despite his reticent nature, Bergen had been there for him in the aftermath of Idona's death.

Why are you doing this to me? Callan wondered, but said nothing aloud.

"Take him with you to Bryluen," the duke continued. "It wouldn't be much of a honeymoon, but he should learn what life in Mulberny is like for us, even if he ultimately chooses to reside in Camria most of the time. The sooner, the better."

"I can't take him on a campaign," Callan said, not bothering to keep the incredulity from his voice. He recalled the stiffness with which Derek held his injured arm pressed against his body, the way he nearly toppled from his horse at the end of what must have been a wearying sojourn. Even if the man hadn't issued a single word of complaint, he was in no shape to travel again so soon, let alone fight. "He needs to recuperate."

Bergen huffed dismissively.

"He's not a baby to be coddled. He's a warrior, a lord of his own fiefdom. As your husband, it's nothing if not his duty to accompany you."

"Remember what happened last time my spouse wanted to accompany me," Callan said sharply.

The duke's expression softened.

"I remember," he said gravely. "But it wasn't your fault then, and it wouldn't be your fault should something happen to this new count. It's a risk we all have to take. A title is an obligation as much as it is a privilege. I don't have to explain that to you, but perhaps I should have a talk with your groom, if you feel he's the sort to balk at assuming responsibility."

"No." Callan shook his head. "I'll talk to him myself."

His acquaintance with Derek had been too brief to adequately judge the quality of his character, but he didn't strike Callan as someone who'd shirk his duty. The last thing he wanted was to be cordially accommodating to the man who'd been practically foisted on him. But as the son of a duke he wasn't supposed to indulge his wishes. Marriage was merely a political tool for the likes of him, not a matter of personal choice.

What he'd had with Idona was pure luck, a blessing from whatever deity that had favored them. When she died, his heart died with her along with all his dreams and hopes for a family of his own, and all he was left with was the guilt he carried like a stone around his neck. His father could try to absolve him of blame all he wanted, but Callan knew the truth. And so it didn't matter if it was this Derek he married now or someone else. They were all but pawns on a vast board, striving to serve their purpose until they were taken off of it.

Chapter Three

THE GUEST QUARTERS, where Medwin, the duke's castellan, had taken them upon arrival, faced east. In Derek's opinion, they presented a much nicer view than the bleakness of wild gray-green waters breaking upon barren rocks. His window offered a vantage point over the entire town of Irthorg spread below them, and beyond that, a vast expanse of fields and grassy hills punctuated with small lakes at the bottom of narrow valleys. The sky just above the horizon was stained with ink as the sun had already begun its descent into the sea.

Even though the destination wasn't one he'd choose willingly, Derek was glad the journey was finally over. The pain in his injured shoulder had gotten worse with every passing day in the saddle, to the point where Derek could barely move the fingers of his throbbing arm. As much as he hated to admit it, he needed rest, even if it was in a strange room, on a strange bed.

At least it was a comfortable one. Hamlin, the Captain of the Count's Guard, had insisted on searching it before Derek had the chance to settle, going as far as sniffing the water in the washing pitcher, but had found nothing out of the ordinary.

Derek walked away from the window and sat on the edge of the bed with a poorly suppressed sigh of relief. With the help of his servants, he'd already washed and changed into something more suitable for a social gathering—black pants, crisp white shirt, and a somber gray wool coat with just a hint of green and gold threads running around the collar, elegant but still appropriate for mourning. But there was still plenty of time before the formal dinner they had all been invited to. Ivo and Macon had gone out into the town almost as soon as they'd arrived, eager to explore a new place, but Derek had stayed behind with the mind to take advantage of the few hours of repose.

He was a little apprehensive about his brothers going off on their own, especially Macon, but he trusted Ivo to keep them both out of trouble. And they could all use a bit of a distraction from worrying about the future of their family and their dubious standing as the guests of someone who had very recently considered them his enemies. Lady Casea had pleaded the excuse of mourning to remain in Camria along with Ayleen, which Derek thought to be prudent. Not that he really thought the duke would assault his own son-in-law and his family while they were staying in his home, but he'd rather spare his mother the humiliation of being a supplicant to her husband's killer.

Derek sighed, chiding himself for being so overdramatic. This kind of mindset was hardly helpful if he wanted to approach the matter with any semblance of good faith. He was here for a wedding, not (hopefully) an execution.

He lowered himself on the coverlet, mindful not to disturb his shoulder, and closed his eyes, but his mind kept drifting back to his earlier meeting with Callan in the middle of the dusty road by the lakeside. He'd seen the other man in the past, but Derek had been too young then, and the memory was worn, faded. Now, Callan's image was painted with new colors, impossibly bright. Tall and broad-shouldered, he boasted exceptional good looks accentuated by an air of casual arrogance. His short hair was the exact shade of a raven's wing, his blue eyes as sharp as shards of ice.

Derek appreciated male beauty, and Callan was nothing short of striking, a veritable picture of masculine perfection, whereas Derek himself could never aspire to be called anything more flattering than "average." Brown eyes, hair the color of mud falling in short waves over his ears, medium height, and almost bland features—nothing about his person would inspire a potential suitor to swoon at his feet, aside from his lately inherited title. And even that asset was currently hanging in the balance. He couldn't shake off the persistent feeling that one of them was getting the short end of the bargain, but who it was still remained to be seen.

His thoughts began to scatter. He meant only to shut his eyes for a few minutes, but he must have fallen asleep because he was startled awake by a loud rap on the door.

Blinking owlishly, he sat up on the bed, the stiffness in his joints slowing his movements. If anything, he felt even less rested than before his impromptu nap. The room was now completely dark, and significantly colder. There was no escaping the damp chill that seemed to haunt the castle.

He couldn't waste time lighting the fireplace, however. Suppressing a yawn, Derek hobbled across the room, wincing with every jolt to his arm, and opened the door. He was expecting to see the castellan or a servant come to fetch him to dinner, but instead came face-to-face with Ivo, who was wearing similar clothes and an uncharacteristic scowl. Derek's heart sank a little.

"Did something happen?" he asked, glancing up and down the hallway. But Ivo was alone.

"Macon is drunk, and he's making an ass of himself," Ivo said curtly.

Derek sighed and ran a hand through his hair. "Did you *have* to take him to a tavern?"

"I didn't. He slipped out of my sight as soon as we got into the city. I've been running around searching for him up until about an hour ago."

"Where is he?"

"The stables. I tried to talk some sense into him and help him get to his room, but he wasn't particularly amenable," Ivo said, trailing after Derek as they found their way into the main courtyard. "You know how he can be."

Derek knew enough to imagine that conversation hadn't been pretty. Macon was never particularly courteous, and drink made him even more brash. Derek reminded himself to be patient. Macon was just a boy, whatever he thought, and not used to dealing with real anguish.

"Macon was close to Father," he said. "He's taking the loss hard. I can't blame him for lashing out."

"We're all grieving," Ivo said, "in our way. But this isn't the time or the place for making a spectacle of it."

Derek couldn't argue with that. He was beginning to regret letting his brother come along. He'd take being all alone at his own wedding over trying to keep Macon from doing something reckless to jeopardize the shaky agreement the duke had strong-armed them into.

Surely enough, they found Macon at the back of the stables, retching onto a stack of hay. The stable boy who was unsaddling Macon's horse shot them a disapproving glance before leading the animal into its stall.

Derek put his right hand on Macon's shoulder, but the boy threw it off, straightening and wiping his mouth on his sleeve with a hateful look. It seemed the ale had done nothing to dull his resentment.

"Come on, let's get you to your room so you can rest," Derek said, doing his best to sound coaxing rather than irritated.

"Don't tell me what to do. You have no right!"

"Yes, I do," Derek said, still grasping for patience. "I'm the Count of Camria now, like it or not, and you're shaming me in front of my future husband's family. Shaming all of us."

"You don't know the meaning of shame," Macon spit out, his eyes glinting defiantly in the dimness of the stable. "Spreading your legs for the victor, like some whore."

Ivo's sharp sucked-in breath sounded too loud in the sudden silence. For a moment, everybody went very still, waiting for the imminent blow, before Derek took a deliberate step back. Holding his anger in check required no small effort, but he refused to let Macon provoke him, not after reprimanding him for being an embarrassment. He would not resort to their father's ways of dealing with exasperation, and besides, initiating a brawl in Duke Bergen's keep wouldn't help anything.

"I might not know the meaning of shame, but I know the meaning of duty," he said instead, his voice low and hard. "I'd spread my legs for all of Irthorg if it meant keeping my family from becoming homeless. Now go to your room. I've had enough of you."

Macon muttered something less than flattering, but this time, he let Ivo take him by the arm and lead him outside. Derek followed them in silence.

Macon swayed and dragged his feet all the way into the guest quarters. Once or twice, Derek was afraid he would pass out in the middle of the hallway, but at length, they found his room without further incident. Ivo reached for the handle, but Macon stopped abruptly, making him miss a step.

"You know he murdered his first wife, right? Everybody knows," he said with a strange sort of satisfaction. His speech was a bit slurred, but otherwise, his words were perfectly coherent. "You reckon that'll happen to you too? I think there are bets being placed on how long you'll last."

Ivo yanked open the door and shoved Macon inside with surprising force before Derek could respond. They both ignored the muffled curse and the sounds of shuffling that came from the other side.

"What did he mean by that?" Derek asked, feeling silly acknowledging such a puerile remark. But Ivo's expression told him it wasn't simply a figment of Macon's alcohol-addled brain.

"It's nothing."

"Ivo." Derek didn't mean for that to sound as harshly as it came out, but he was suddenly too tired. Tired of making sure everyone was on their best behavior, tired of shouldering the responsibility he didn't want in the first place and being blamed for it, tired of the constant physical pain he had to endure because of someone else's poor choices. He had no patience for this evasiveness.

"All right, fine." Ivo glanced to the side. The hallway was empty and silent save for the distant creaking of the hoist pulleys that allowed for easier access to the upper levels. He lowered his voice anyway. "It's like I've told you. They all say Callan killed the Agiennan girl he'd married.

They say he hates the clansmen of the Outer Isles, and that having to take an enemy as his spouse was a slight to him."

"Who says?"

Ivo shrugged noncommittally.

"Macon probably heard it around town, or from one of the servants. No one seems to know exactly what happened, but a lot of people believe Callan did away with her. Some even say he's cursed for it. The Agiennans are known for their dark witchcraft."

"This is becoming ridiculous," Derek said. He turned on his heel and strode down the corridor back to his own guest room. Ivo followed him after a heartbeat. "And that's a pretty serious accusation to be throwing around on hearsay. He doesn't look like a murderer."

"What do you think a murderer looks like?"

Apparently, Derek was paying too much attention to Ivo recounting titillating gossip and not enough to where he was going, because as he rounded a corner, he collided hard with someone coming their way. The impact shook his arm, and he hissed in pain, recoiling.

"Sorry," Callan said. "I didn't mean to startle you."

For a second, Derek fumbled for words, caught up in momentary mortification as he gazed upon his groom. From Callan's blank expression, it was impossible to say whether he'd heard what they'd been talking about. The moment stretched, until Callan cocked his head to the side, the look in his blue eyes taking on an expectant quality.

For some reason, Derek's brain latched on to the most ridiculous details. He noted absently the sensual curve of Callan's mouth, the way his thick lashes cast long shadows on his high cheekbones, and remembered the feel of his touch against his palm, firm and reassuring. The light of the torches gilded his dark hair, making it appear luminous.

"It was my fault," Derek said, a blush creeping up his cheeks. "What are you doing here?"

The question came out harsher than he intended, and he winced internally. Callan blinked and took a step back.

"I was going to invite you to dinner," he said. "Half an hour, in the great hall."

Without waiting for a response, he turned and strode off the way he had come. His footsteps echoed in the narrow hallway until he reached another turn and was out of sight.

"That was...intense," Ivo said under his breath.

"It was wrong of us to discuss him like that," Derek said. It seemed no matter what he did and how hard he tried, he couldn't avoid embarrassing himself in front of his hosts in some way or another. "Anyone could have heard us."

"Do you think he really came all this way just to issue a personal invitation? He could have sent a servant to fetch you," Ivo said, despite Derek's admonition.

"Why else?"

"Maybe he wanted to talk to you in private."

"If he did, I doubt he'll want to do that now, after I've called him a murderer behind his back." Derek sighed. "Do me a favor and make sure Macon is presentable for dinner, all right? Or better yet, let him sleep it off and come by yourself. Let's save face while we can."

Ivo nodded. "I'll meet you there," he said, turning away.

Derek stepped up to his own door, but hesitated for a moment, peering down the hallway in the direction Callan had taken. Was it just his imagination, or had there been a flicker of hurt in Callan's eyes? It seemed unlikely, considering Callan's cool attitude toward him. And yet, he'd come to deliver an invitation in person—only to be met with rudeness on Derek's part, however unintentional.

Coming to a spur of the moment decision, he hurried after Callan. The castle was still a maze of drafty hallways and passageways to him at this point, but after inquiring a few servants, he was able to eventually track him down to the library.

It was a small one, to be sure, smaller even than the one they had at home—none of the Lords of Camria, save Ivo, had been voracious readers. A casual glance at the titles confirmed the collection was mostly centered on history, warfare, and hunting, but Derek didn't have the opportunity to examine it closer. Callan stood by one of the small reading tables, leafing through an open book by the light of a three-stick candelabra. At Derek's approach, he turned and simply stared at him in silence.

Derek halted, shifting uncomfortably under his heavy gaze. The black coat, rich with silver embroidery around the hem and the tall collar, didn't make Callan seem any softer than his riding attire, but accentuated his perfect figure even further. Other than that single concession to lavishness, Callan wore no jewelry, and his hair was carelessly tousled, as if he couldn't care less about his appearance despite his station—or maybe because of it.

"I'm sorry," Derek blurted before he could think of a more diplomatic way to broach the subject.

"For what?"

He wasn't going to make it any easier for him, was he? Well, Derek couldn't really blame him. If Callan wanted honesty, he had no problem with that.

"For discussing sordid gossip about you out in the open," he said, unflinching.

Callan's eyebrows shot up. He closed the book and placed it back on the table.

"Don't fret about it."

There was an awkward silence.

"Were you the one who killed my father at Laurel Falls?" Derek asked suddenly.

It was a stupid question, and it was all Macon's fault for planting it in his head. Not like it would make any difference one way or another; he wasn't going to storm out in righteous indignation even if Callan were to give an affirmative answer. Whether he'd be able to live with himself afterward was another matter, but no one cared about that anyway.

Callan didn't give any indication he was outraged by the question, but it clearly wasn't the one he expected.

"No," he said after an infinitesimal pause. "I wasn't the one."

He didn't offer anything else, and Derek didn't press further. And of course, Callan might be lying. But something eased in Derek's chest at the answer.

Callan grimaced.

"For what it's worth, I'm sorry it had to come to this. Fighting against fellow citizens of the realm is not a choice I would make of my own accord."

This was as close as Callan would come to criticizing his father's decision to a stranger, Derek realized. He felt an unexpected surge of sympathy for him. Count Johan had been a difficult man, but from everything he'd heard, Derek suspected his father's obstinacy couldn't rival Duke Bergen's iron will. As the heir, Derek had always known he'd marry for political gain rather than love. Considering his personal tastes, he supposed he was lucky to be matched with a man, but Callan might have thought very differently about this entire ordeal.

"I'm sorry too," Derek said softly, and he meant it. The punishment was the same for them both—saddled with a husband neither wanted.

He wanted to ask more. Of course he did. The notion that the man he was going to marry in just a few days' time might be a cold-blooded killer was nothing if not disturbing. But while Derek had the right to demand the truth about Callan's role in his father's demise, he couldn't inquire the same about Callan's late wife, whom he knew nothing about, not even her name. And while the other man's presence, imposing as it was, didn't make Derek feel threatened, he wasn't sure he wanted to hear an honest answer to that particular question. Although, if he was looking for grounds for future annulment, an admission of guilt would go a long way toward getting him out of this mess.

The silence was becoming uncomfortable. Derek should have probably headed out to find the main hall and leave Callan in peace, since he gave no indication of wanting to continue the conversation. But he'd intended to meet with Derek before, so he must have wanted something beyond broody staring.

"Did you...want to talk to me earlier?" Derek asked hesitantly.

"Yes." Callan's gaze raked over him, pausing on his sling for a long moment before locking on to his eyes. "My father wishes to expedite the wedding. It's to take place tomorrow."

"Tomorrow?"

Derek realized he was gawking and closed his mouth. He had expected to have at least a week to prepare, to familiarize himself with the duke's family, get to know his intended a little better—which, all things considered, was perhaps a foolish endeavor. This came as a blow, though he hardly expected to be somehow fortuitously excused from his commitment even if he had extra time. "Why?"

"There's some trouble along the northern coast," Callan said curtly. "Nothing that should concern you, but it must be seen to as soon as possible, and the duke doesn't want to delay."

"All right," Derek said slowly. Any matter which required cutting short the festivities surrounding the wedding of the duchy's heir apparent certainly didn't sound like "nothing." But Derek was in no position to object.

At least Macon wouldn't have as many opportunities to put him out of countenance, he thought, still digesting this new turn of events.

"Come. We'll be late for dinner," Callan said, rousing Derek from his reverie, and headed to the door, brushing past him in the narrow space, so close Derek caught a whiff of the sage-scented soap on his skin.

He had no choice but to follow. Before exiting, he threw a last glance at the book Callan had left on the table. The gilded lettering on the worn leather binding read *The Customs, Dialects, and Sorcery of the Outer Isles.*

Chapter Four

THE MAIN HALL was decked out in preparation for the grand wedding feast, but signs of haste were visible upon closer inspection. The roses that had been commissioned from the orangeries at Reithen hadn't yet arrived, and instead of live garlands, the pillars were wrapped in stark white draperies, which lent the space a somber look. Smells of roasting pork and venison wafted through the entire keep, and the carts heaped with produce hastily acquired from the surrounding farms were coming through the gate in an incessant procession under Medwin's watchful eye. Callan had never seen the castellan so harried, but he managed to weather the enormous undertaking of orchestrating a stately wedding on a nonexistent schedule with the stoical grace of an old general.

In truth, Callan couldn't care less about the food and the flowers, or the lack thereof. The wedding was nothing more than a sham, and a pesky waste of time that kept him from his task. With Leandre's help, he'd used all the spare hours he had to make sure his men were ready to ride the morning after the ceremony, which was no easy feat considering the castle was already in a purposeful uproar. But now all the horses had been shod, all the tack had been mended, all the provisions had been packed. Tomorrow, at least, would see no minute of ill-advised delay.

"I can't believe I don't get to give you a proper bachelor's send-off," Leandre had said when they'd left the stables. "Kind of takes all the fun out of having a wedding, if you ask me."

Callan, who was in even less of a mood for an informal bash than for a formal wedding, had grunted noncommittally. It seemed everybody was looking forward to tonight's celebration but him. And perhaps the other groom.

"I'm afraid I wouldn't be much fun anyway," he'd said.

"You never are, these days," Leandre had said softly, and he'd pretended not to hear her.

The upper gallery around the main hall offered a good view of the tables below as they were covered in tablecloths and laden with dishes. Callan paused opposite the dais, on a spot where the musicians would be seated in the evening, overlooking the massive mosaic that depicted his family's crest on the wall, a silver wolf's head on a field of black.

Sans the flowers and the guests that were still to arrive, the sight was disconcertingly familiar. Callan gripped the banister, the memories of the same ceremony two years ago threatening to overwhelm him. He hadn't been happy then, and he was not happy now, and the loss of everything that had happened in between the two points in time was still a gaping wound he tried futilely to patch up.

"Callan?" a soft voice called from behind him.

It took him an embarrassingly long second to compose himself before he turned to face Adele.

His sister was already dressed in a formal court gown, its high collar tipped with delicate silver lace. Her long dark hair was arranged in intricate braids around her head like a crown, pinned with tiny gleaming pearls. She'd never been considered a great beauty, but at that moment, she was positively lovely, a wide smile brightening her features.

At least one of them was joyous today, and Callan forced a smile too so as to not ruin her mood.

"You look so pretty. Planning on breaking some hearts at the feast?"

Adele giggled shyly.

"And you're not anywhere near ready!" she scolded. "You'll be late, and your groom will be disappointed."

"I'm sure he'll get over it," Callan said.

"Oh, you're incorrigible. He seems nice, though. And handsome."

It would only take someone as kindhearted as Adele to describe Count Derek as "handsome." Not that he was by any means repugnant, but he was certainly not the type of person Callan was usually attracted to, both physically and emotionally, however pretty his eyes might be. Perhaps it was for the best under the circumstances.

"His brother, too," Adele continued.

Callan glanced around instinctively to make sure this sentiment wouldn't reach the duke's ears. Callan himself might be used as a bargaining chip in his father's political machinations, but he knew Bergen envisioned a much loftier fate for Adele than falling for one of Camria's unfortunate brood.

"I hope you're not talking about the sulky one," he said.

"No, the tall fair one."

"Could be worse, I suppose. Will you play for us at the feast?"

"If you want. I hope your groom won't be opposed, though."

For a talented musician and, in Callan's humble opinion, a true prodigy with the violin, despite the lack of proper training in their provincial little town, Adele was far too modest. He really should work on convincing Father to send her to a musical school in the capital, like she'd always wanted.

He offered her his hand, and they descended into the hall, where Adele gently nudged him toward the exit after standing on her toes and kissing him on the cheek.

"Go. I need to practice before tonight, and you should get dressed, or you're going to miss your own wedding."

If only it were that easy.

THE VOWS WERE to be taken in the castle chapel. It was already packed with onlookers, most of them castle dwellers, since the local gentry hadn't yet made their way to Irthorg from their country estates. There were a lot of people who were bound to be disappointed by the decision to speed up the proceedings.

Callan knelt before the altar, pretending to be fascinated with the carved details of the statues of Gwenna and Gwaithil, the gods-protectors of the coastal regions of the Great Realm of Ivicia. At some point, the ancient gods must have lost interest in Mulberny, because Callan was anything but impressed with the extent of their protection. At least their serene faces, forever frozen in marble, provided a distraction from the man beside him.

The duke and Adele stood to the right, surrounded by the few nobles who were lucky to have been at the castle at the right time. Bergen's expression was as stony as ever, but Adele beamed at him with such undiluted happiness Callan had no choice but to smile reluctantly in return.

The Camrians stood to the left, the two boys and a few of their guards behind them. The older one, the one Adele found agreeable but who had a penchant for spreading gossip—Ivo, Callan thought his name was—was listening to the priestess chant the opening blessings, while the younger was watching Derek and him with a scowl he didn't bother to conceal. All of them were pointedly wearing mourning gray, despite the ostensibly joyous occasion. Even Derek, though dressed in a rich white ensemble befitting a groom of his stature, was sporting a gray ribbon tied around his right forearm. The ends of it pooled onto the flagstone floor as he knelt, hand on his thigh, his eyes downcast. A large signet ring set with a green stone sparkled on his finger. It appeared too robust for his slender hand.

Priestess Nehewia concluded the blessings, and at her sign, blue-robed attendants brought two silver goblets, filled to the brim with red wine, and placed them in Derek and Callan's hands as they turned to face each other, still kneeling.

"Derek of Camria." The priestess's deep voice rolled through the chapel as the crowd grew quiet. The dusky color of her robes accentuated the deep sepia tone of her skin, typical for those hailing from the far south, from beyond the Inner Sea. "Do you swear to honor this man as your husband with your body, mind, and soul, to bestow upon him your love and devotion, to grant him of your wisdom and truth, to share in his happiness and his sorrows, until death parts you?"

The silence in the chapel was so complete Callan imagined he could hear the wind blowing high above the chapel's domed rooftop.

"I do," Derek said. His lashes tipped downward as he dropped his gaze.

The corner of Callan's mouth curved in a sneer. The man was sickeningly meek. He had been right not to ask Derek to join him on his mission to the north despite the explicit command from his father (whose displeasure he'd have to deal with later). Perhaps he should have lied about being the one to have killed his father, just to see how Derek would have reacted. No doubt he'd simply let it stand, though, swallow his pride as he'd done with everything else. Callan was surprised he'd had enough audacity to ask the question in the first place. That one, but not all the others undoubtedly weighing on his mind. Most likely, Derek didn't want to risk doing anything that would jeopardize the alliance he'd paid for with his dignity.

But Callan hadn't been any different, had he? He was doing the same thing, taking the same damn oaths. He couldn't fault Derek for actively upholding the interests of his fiefdom, when Callan was simply doing what he was told, without having much say in the matter.

Nehewia turned to him, asking him the same question. He stared at her familiar features, her kind eyes lined with age and knowledge, and for a moment felt as though he was suffocating, as though there wasn't enough air in the world to help him utter the words that were expected of him. The priestesses cocked her head in concern.

"I do," Callan said thickly. He felt Derek's eyes on him but refused to meet his gaze.

"A word spoken cannot be undone," Nehewia intoned. Derek's brothers shifted, exchanging a glance, but said nothing.

The priestess stepped in front of them, placing a hand on each of their heads.

"By the grace of the gods, you are now joined. May the cup of your blessing always be full."

On this cue, Callan and Derek turned to face each other, and in turn, brought their goblet to the other man's lips. The wine tasted bitter, even though it was the finest vintage from the duke's cellars. Then they leaned toward one another, their lips touching in the most perfunctory of kisses.

The crowd erupted in cheers and applause as they rose to their feet. But they'd been kneeling for a long time, and the stiffness must have affected Derek. With one of his hands in a sling and the other occupied, he lost his balance for a second, and the wine sloshed over the rim of his goblet, splashing on the white floor.

There were gasps and murmurs among the guests at this sign of bad luck, an ill portent for the start of a marriage. The priestess's attendants made discreet gestures to ward off evil behind Derek's back.

The young count stared at the stain slowly spreading on the floor like a blood-spill. His cheeks burned with a matching shade of crimson.

Callan took the goblet out of his hand and thrust it at the attendant, who hurried to take away the wine in order to pass it to the guests. Out of the corner of his eye, he could see that many refused to touch Derek's cup.

"Come on," Callan said gruffly, offering his arm to his husband. Like him or not, he hated to see him humiliated for a simple slipup. If their marriage were to be a disaster, it certainly wouldn't be because of some spilled wine.

"Thanks," Derek said, his voice barely audible above the general din. He leaned on Callan's arm, and the crowd parted before them as they exited the chapel, heading to the feast prepared in the main hall.

ADELE'S VIOLIN PERFORMANCE of *Ballad of the Lovers* was lovely, but other than that, Callan couldn't precisely recall what dishes were served and what music was playing. He ate little, despite the lavishness of the feast Medwin had managed to put together. All around them people were laughing, talking, drinking, and the revelry was undoubtedly echoed all through the city in celebration of the duke heir's nuptials. The members of Callan's personal guard, those who were set to leave with him in the morning, were doing their damnedest to have a good time. Callan raised an incredulous eyebrow when he caught sight of Leandre dancing with a woman from Derek's retinue, both laughing as they whirled.

Even Ivo was dancing, though Derek's younger brother, Macon, didn't move from his place at the table, drinking himself into a wretched state. A part of Callan dearly wished he could follow his suit, but another part wondered why neither Derek nor someone of his entourage did anything to keep the boy in check. It rather figured the young Count of Camria was so poor a leader he couldn't control his own siblings enough to demand they behave with any semblance of civility.

But as Callan intermittently sought distraction in others' joy and in his own annoyance, his attention and his thoughts kept circling back to his groom. Derek seemed to share Callan's mood because he barely touched the food on his plate and kept mostly quiet. Callan noted the tiny dots of purple on his white clothes where the wine drops had spattered. Had Derek taken the faux pas at the chapel so close to heart? The sadness in his eyes was unbecoming to their loveliness. Callan had to suppress the urge to comfort Derek by telling him it was nothing but silly superstition. He might have vowed to grant wisdom and truth to his new husband, but they were still barely more than strangers.

The dissonance between their gloom and the all-round merriment was so jarring that Callan was relieved when it was finally time for them to depart, followed by another round of cheers and well-wishing of varying degrees of bawdiness. He offered his arm once again to Derek, who accepted graciously, but when they were far enough from the main hall, and the noise of the party had dwindled to the barest of echoes, Derek let go of Callan and stepped away.

Well. That certainly sent a clear message. Which was just as well, since Callan was feeling anything but excited at the prospect of them sharing a bed on their wedding night. It had nothing to do with Derek himself; under different circumstances, in another life, Callan could well find himself attracted to the Camrian. His angry thoughts during the ceremony notwithstanding, he couldn't shake the persistent suspicion that underneath the soft-spoken demeanor and quiet manner lay some hidden strength he was yet to discover. He saw glimpses of it—in the touch of gray that marred the wedding attire, in the way Derek didn't avert his gaze when conversing with the duke during the feast, despite the intentional bluntness of his father's questions.

But he had no business thinking about Derek at all. Tomorrow, Callan would be gone, and Derek would most likely return to his regular life in Camria, his precious treaty in hand, the sparrow flying safely back to his cozy nest away from any real peril.

He wasn't planning on them staying together through the night, but some appearances had to be upheld, so he led Derek to his rooms and opened the door, gesturing for him to go in.

The sitting room, which Callan had turned into a study, was illuminated only by a fire already burning in the hearth, but in the adjacent bedroom, an assortment of lit candles gave off a sickeningly sweet scent of honey and amber. The servants must have prepared the room during the ceremony because the large bed was immaculately made, covered in pristine white sheets strewn with pale pink and yellow rose petals. A suggestive tableau of glass oil bottles and artfully folded washcloths sat on the side table. Somebody, it would seem, was optimistic regarding the progression of their wedding night.

Derek's eyes were immediately drawn to the bed, and he paused in the doorway, an uncertain look in his eyes. Did he really think Callan would force him into intimacy? He'd only brought him there to stop the servants from gossiping.

Before he could voice his motives, though, Derek stepped into the room, surveying it with a sort of apprehensive interest. He ignored the opulent setting of the bed, and ran his hand over the black marble slab of the mantelpiece, bare save for a silver candlestick and a small jewelry box, which he casually picked up to inspect.

Callan's hands curled into fists, but he forced himself to remain calm. It was just a knickknack, nothing more. Derek could admire it as much as he wanted.

The box was admittedly exquisite, its lid embossed with the silhouette of a mermaid, perching on a rock and lifting her face to the sun while dipping her tail into the foamy waves. When Derek opened it, a single lock of long golden hair, tied with a piece of string, lay within, resting on the red velvet padding.

Derek raised his eyes to him in surprise, probably wondering at the incongruence of Callan's severe persona with the ornate dainty thing and its contents.

"That was Idona's," Callan felt compelled to supply by way of explanation, and seeing Derek's blank expression, he added through his teeth, "My wife."

"I'm sorry." Derek closed the box and put it back in its place. "I haven't heard much about her, I'm afraid."

Callan suspected Derek had heard enough. Obviously not her name, but without a doubt all the sinister rumors that people, even those who liked Callan as their future ruler well enough, were wont to spread to add excitement to their lives. Usually, he didn't care about them, but the wary look in Derek's eyes stung him in a way he couldn't quite comprehend.

"Listen," he said, and Derek started, his tension evident despite the mask of nonchalance. "Neither of us wanted this." Callan showed no sign he had noticed Derek startle. "We're in private. There's no need to pretend here."

"I'm not—" Derek started carefully.

"My father insisted on this marriage," Callan said, ignoring the interruption, "but it doesn't mean he can expect me to bed you against either of our wills."

Derek's eyes flashed, but his voice, when he answered, was still mild.

"Bed me? How very romantic of you. Nonetheless, I must remind you that if the marriage isn't consummated, it might not be legal."

"We kissed at the ceremony," Callan said with a hint of challenge, crossing his arms over his chest. "As far as I'm concerned, it's consummated."

Derek's eyebrows shot up. Callan wasn't terribly well versed in matrimonial law, but even he knew this take was shaky at best. But he certainly wasn't about to have sex with this man for the sake of legitimacy. His name and signature were splayed all over the marriage contract; it was enough.

"We're bound to each other on paper only," Callan continued. Perhaps this came out a little harsh, but he wanted to make his stance on the matter perfectly clear. "After tonight, you'll be free to return to Camria. We're not required to spend time together save for occasional ceremonies and court functions."

"All right," Derek said slowly, staring at him as if trying to decipher whether he was being tricked somehow.

For a brief, treacherous moment Callan wondered what the man's doe eyes would look like dark and cloudy with lust, his lips swollen with kisses. Real kisses, not like the polite peck they'd exchanged at the chapel. But it was a dangerous thought, one he wasn't prepared to examine too closely—let alone act upon.

He nodded to the door tucked in the corner of the room, almost abashedly out of sight.

"Your new rooms are there. They mirror my own."

He knew it was the kind of thorough dismissal that could be perceived as insulting. But he stood behind his previous statement. This wedding night was something neither of them wanted. And if he was quick enough to get ready in the morning, chance was he wouldn't see Derek again for a very long time.

He was expecting relief, but instead, something like hurt fleeted across Derek's features. He bowed stiffly and went through the door, closing it firmly behind him.

It should have felt like a victory, and yet the only emotion Callan could readily identify from the jumbled tangle constricting his chest was disappointment.

Chapter Five

DEREK WAS WOKEN by the sound of voices and footsteps in the adjoining room.

At first, he buried his face deeper in the pillow, refusing to be bothered by the notion of his husband entertaining people in his bedroom in the middle of the night—or early dawn, if the gray light streaming from the high windows was anything to go by. Really, if Callan wished to find more amiable company elsewhere, it was hardly Derek's business, especially after the outright refusal to share a bed on their wedding night. He should be glad Callan was leaving him alone because Derek certainly didn't want to be forced into physical proximity with a man who so clearly didn't like him.

However, the urgency of the voices, the raised tones, and the shuffling of feet soon made it apparent this wasn't any sort of romantic dalliance. Derek sat up and pushed the covers off, shivering a little. The bedroom still bore the traces of having been a lady's chamber with its soft furnishings and patterned draperies, but it was just as damp and chilly as the rest of the keep. The fire he'd started in the fireplace before going to sleep had been reduced to glowing embers, and the residual heat failed to warm the large, drafty room.

The noise got only louder. What the hell was going on? If it was some sort of assassination attempt on Callan (the possibility of which, considering the nonexistent charm of the man's personality, wouldn't surprise Derek one bit), the assailants could at least have the decency to not do it on their so-called honeymoon.

Trying to make as little noise as possible, Derek slid a dagger from the sheath he'd left on a chair along with his belt and pants, and very carefully turned the doorknob, nudging the door open enough to peer inside the room.

The bedroom was empty, yesterday's rose petals and oil assortments gone without a trace. Feeling distinctly uncomfortable venturing there alone, Derek nonetheless refused to be deterred, and crossed the room, heading for the study.

He found Callan completely dressed in what appeared to be his riding leathers, standing beside a table that bore a napkin-covered breakfast tray. Whoever his visitors had been, they were just closing the door after them as Derek cast his gaze around the room. But as discreet as he thought himself, apparently he hadn't been quiet enough, because Callan turned sharply in his direction before Derek could beat a hasty retreat.

"What are you doing here?"

His gaze bore into Derek with a strange intensity, making Derek acutely aware he was wearing nothing but a flimsy linen undershirt, which fell rather high on his hips. Callan was definitely *looking*, but whether he liked what he was seeing or was repulsed by it was unclear.

Derek blushed and lowered the dagger he was still holding in his hand. Callan had an uncanny knack for making him feel like an utter fool even when Derek was acting on the best of intentions.

"I heard voices. I thought you might be in some sort of trouble."

"In my own bedroom?" Callan raised an eyebrow, apparently unimpressed by Derek's concern.

"Should I expect people coming in and out of your bedroom at all hours?" Derek asked, and immediately tried not to wince at the note of testiness in his voice.

There was a pause as Callan appeared to consider him, and Derek braced himself for a scathing retort (which, frankly, wouldn't have been entirely unjustified).

But all Callan said was, "I told you already. There are reports about pirates raiding the coastal settlements near the northern border. We'd have to send out a troop to meet with the Bryluen garrison to counter the threat."

Derek frowned. "I thought the Agiennan raiders were all but eradicated during the war."

Callan shook his head. "Hardly. The Outer Isles are populated by many different clans that lack a strong central leadership. Not all fought in the war, and not all who survived consider themselves bound by the treaties. The beginning of autumn is a prime season for raiding, and even with the manned outposts, we cannot control the entire coast. The raiders only used to attack the smaller, more isolated villages and farms, but now they're getting bolder. And more vicious."

Derek didn't imagine the hard lines creasing Callan's forehead nor the steely glint in his eyes, gleaming in the low light of the early morning. Callan was clearly angered by the news—as Derek himself would be, had he received word his subjects were being harassed. He'd never witnessed the aftermath of a seafarer raid, but he'd seen the havoc organized bandits could wreak on remote homesteads in the eastern regions of Camria, where forests stretched for hundreds of miles with no human settlements large enough to offer help or protection to the farmers. Derek could well understand the rage and the feeling of helplessness in the face of failure to protect those who needed it.

He shouldn't have been moved by the fact that Callan actually cared about what happened to these people rather than being annoyed at having to abandon his own wedding festivities for the prospect of another bloody battle. From what he'd heard about Callan, Derek would have guessed he'd rejoice at any excuse for warmongering. But looking now at the hard line of his mouth, the rigid set of his shoulders, Derek couldn't help but feel he was genuinely worried.

Derek had a feeling Callan wasn't a man to shirk his duties, their pitiful excuse of a marriage notwithstanding. Then again, they'd both gone into it out of a similar sense of obligation. Not for the first time since meeting his husband, Derek felt stirrings of something suspiciously resembling sympathy.

He recalled the silver box on the mantelpiece in the adjoining room. Ivo had told him all about the rumors that suggested Callan had done away with his wife, but would a murderer keep sentimental mementos of his victim in his bedroom, which was otherwise pitifully bare of all personal effects? Perhaps a deranged one would, but Callan didn't strike Derek as either unhinged or particularly bloodthirsty. Undoubtedly, there was a streak of ruthlessness in his manner, but not outward cruelty.

There had to be a simple explanation for Callan keeping the box in his possession. He had loved his wife. The way Callan had gazed at the ornate memento yesterday, the wistfulness in his eyes, Derek wondered if he wasn't still in love with her.

He was uncomfortably aware that his presence was wholly foreign to this space, as if he was intruding on something deeply private, a trespasser on forbidden ground.

"Are you going to lead the patrol, then?" Derek asked, putting the thought firmly out of his mind and nodding to Callan's attire. He wasn't dressed for battle, exactly, more like for a long journey—which, Derek suspected, was only par for the course if it meant traveling along the coast as far as the northern border.

"Yes."

"I'll go with you."

He didn't know what he was intending to do until the words were out of his mouth. But now that they were, it felt right.

Derek's birth placed him in a position of great privilege, which came with only one requirement—to protect the people entrusted to his care. Marrying Callan and removing himself to Mulberny, however temporarily, did not diminish his responsibility, but rather expanded it to include his new subjects. He couldn't stand by idly, doing nothing, while they were in danger. Perhaps it was a kind of arrogance on his part to assume as much, but Callan wasn't the only one to know the meaning of duty.

"No," Callan said flatly.

Derek drew himself up for an indignant response, but Callan forestalled him.

"You're injured. It'd do you no good. You're convalescing."

His gaze slid pointedly to Derek's left arm, still in a sling. Derek's lips curved into a derisive smile, which was probably more of a rictus.

"My comfort was hardly a consideration when your father insisted on holding a wedding with such immediacy as to deny me time to either heal or mourn," he pointed out.

Callan's expression flickered at the bluntness, but Derek was not about to endure such infuriating hypocrisy to spare the man's feelings.

"I want to help," he continued firmly. "Whatever you may think of me, I'm not the sort to let my spouse shoulder all the responsibilities while I idle away my days at the keep or return home without sparing a thought for their hardships. That's not what marriage is for, and that's not what I was brought up to do. If you don't like it, you should have asked your father to set you up with a different groom."

There was another pause as Callan seemed to size him up. Derek couldn't tell if it was his fortitude Callan was assessing, or the sincerity of his declaration.

"Has my father spoken to you about this?"

"What? No."

"Were you really worried I was being murdered in my sleep?" Callan asked with something close to genuine interest.

"Well, I didn't come here to stake a claim on your virtue," Derek said.

Callan snorted.

"I wish it to be clear that I can't guarantee your safety," he said finally.

"You don't have to. I'm perfectly capable of taking care of myself."

For a moment, Derek was sure Callan was still going to refuse him, but finally, he gave Derek a short nod.

"Fine. You can come."

"Thank you," Derek said, matching the curtness of his tone. A less stubborn part of him wondered why he was thanking Callan for giving him a chance to endanger his life.

"Unless you intend to come as you are, I suggest you ready yourself," Callan said dryly. "We leave in two hours, and we have scarcely any time to lose."

"I'll be there," Derek said, turning to go back to his room.

"Bring something warm. And don't forget your pants," Callan called after him as Derek closed the door behind him.

BY THE TIME they'd reached the long, winding stretch of the coastal road leading away from the town, Derek was starting to suspect his insistence on tagging along was a mistake.

He'd barely had any rest since arriving at Irthorg, after the long journey that had left him sore and exhausted, despite his claims to the contrary. His back ached, his thighs ached, and his wounded shoulder was a constant source of agony that dwarfed all the other aches into nonexistence. He gripped the reins so tightly his knuckles were white, and only his mare's docile nature and lifelong familiarity with his quirks kept the poor animal from railing against such poor horsemanship.

To distract himself from the pain and the inevitable reflection on the stupidity of his choices, Derek tried to focus on his surroundings. This region of Mulberny was beautiful in a wild sort of way, with the sea meeting the rocky shore in a flurry of wind and white foam. The road cut through wide expanses of grass and heather, running past villages, hamlets, and farms, which became sparser the farther they got from town. Tiny islands, most of them nothing more than tall, sharp rocks, protruded from the sea all the way to the horizon.

The sky was overcast, and there was a definite nip in the air. Callan hadn't been jesting, admonishing him to bring warm clothes. With nothing to stave the wind, sharp gales blew across the plains, carrying salt and occasional raindrops.

The incessant wind didn't seem to bother the lord and his companions. Callan rode at the head of the troop, which only numbered about a dozen people. Derek wasn't sure what sort of reinforcement they would be for the harried folks up north, but he was still too unaccustomed to the ways of the place to offer insight. He rode behind his husband, a bit too acutely aware of being surrounded by unfamiliar armed men whose personal allegiance to him was questionable at best. For all he knew, they'd all fought against him at Laurel Falls, and judging by the side-looks he'd been getting, his marrying their liege lord was not enough to endear him to them.

He wished he could have taken Hamlin with him. The Captain of the Guard's quiet presence and understated competence had always been there to carry him through difficult times ever since he was a child. More often than not, Hamlin would take Derek's side when he argued with his father—though never to great avail. But as soon as Derek had learned of Callan's plans for departure, he'd charged Hamlin with keeping an eye on his brothers, leaving his entire entourage with them. He was hesitant about leaving them in Irthorg while he was away—not least because he didn't trust Macon to behave himself, and the duke not to take offense at his brother's antics—but late guests were still arriving for the wedding, and someone had to represent Camria during his absence. Derek knew Ivo would rise to the challenge, but the knowledge did little to dissuade his worry.

In the end, he had no other support to fall back on during this impromptu trip but his own determination, which was, unfortunately, rapidly dwindling. Callan barely paid him any heed save issuing him terse directions as they rode out of the castle that morning, and had kept brooding silence ever since. Perhaps calling it "brooding" was somewhat of an exaggeration, but even Derek could tell he was not best pleased.

The town of Bryluen was only a two-day ride from Irthorg, but it was already proving to be a rough one. Spurred on by the same urgency that had forced them to cut short the festivities, the Mulbernians set a hard pace, falling just short of exhausting their horses. They'd only stopped twice for food and a brief rest, and Derek almost wished they wouldn't, because getting back into the saddle was harder and harder each time.

At Callan's sign, the troop came to a halt when the sun had almost sunk into the sea, tingeing the sky and water deep purple. The road ran along the edge of a sparse pine forest, with the distant mountains silhouetted in black against the inky starry sky. They hadn't encountered any villages larger than a hamlet for the last dozen miles, with most of the coastal settlements gathered around Irthorg or the port towns farther to the north.

By now, Derek's hands were practically shaking with fatigue, and it was nothing short of a miracle he didn't fall flat on his face while dismounting. But somehow he managed to stand on his own two feet, even if the ground lurched beneath him and he had to grip the pommel of his saddle to stay upright. He wasn't much help with setting up camp either, but he did what he could, gathering kindling for the fire while others erected tents and tended to the horses. It still nettled him to some degree—he wasn't used to other people, especially fellow warriors, performing the mundane tasks he was perfectly capable of doing himself. But after a long day in the saddle, he had to concede he wasn't in the best of shape to pitch in.

At first, Derek was uncomfortable about sharing a tent with Callan, whose manner toward him was as curt as ever, but it turned out the thing was spacious enough to allow them both some privacy. Inside were two sleeping pallets, separated by a burning brazier. Derek was grateful for the warmth—they were close enough to the sea to hear the monotonous crash of the waves against the cliffs, and the night promised to be chilly.

After a quick meal of bread and dried meat, shared with the soldiers around the campfire, they both retreated inside. Derek lowered himself onto his pallet with a suppressed groan, wishing for nothing more than to stretch over the soft furs and close his eyes for as long as the darkness allowed. Callan, on the other hand, lingered at the entrance, holding the flap aside as he watched the sky turn a deeper shade of black. Finally, he turned to Derek.

"I'll go have a look around. You should rest."

"Would you like me to—" Derek began, but he was already gone.

Too tired to do anything but follow his husband's advice, Derek took off his coat, cursing under his breath as he struggled to do it one-handed, and went right to sleep.

HE WOKE IN the dead of night, staring blearily at the tent's wall billowing gently in the breeze. The coals in the brazier still gave off a pleasant warmth, but their glow was all but spent. He turned to look at the other pallet, finding it empty. Had Callan not returned at all? Where was he?

Driven by some half-formed uneasiness, Derek sat up and put his coat back on, fumbling with the sleeves. As he left the tent, the night greeted him with bitter cold and the distant light of the stars, strewn across the clear night sky like a handful of diamonds thrown carelessly onto a swath of black velvet.

Two soldiers and Callan's lieutenant, Leandre, were keeping watch by the fire while the rest of the troop slept on the ground, wrapped in their cloaks and thick blankets. Derek exchanged nods with them as he walked past and continued on to the edge of the camp, the woman's intent gaze heavy on the back of his neck. He glanced at the sleeping men, but Callan was not among them.

When he reached the edge of the copse, he stopped to relieve himself. Even so simple an act was now made difficult by his injury, and the thought further soured his mood.

A soft sound, like a shuffle, came to him somewhere off to the side, and he turned toward it, his heart hammering. Darkness lurked between the trees even though the forest wasn't particularly thick.

"Is someone there?" he called. "Callan?"

His only answer was the distant hoot of an owl. Feeling silly but urging himself not to be spooked by shadows, he stepped farther into the forest, feeling his way along the tree trunks more than relying on the feeble moonlight that barely penetrated the canopy.

Something moved a few paces ahead, and he stopped in his tracks. Perhaps coming alone wasn't such a good idea after all. What was he doing anyway, chasing after a man who was clearly doing whatever he could to stay away from him?

Trying to convince himself that the noise probably was made by something completely innocuous, like a hare or a fox going about their business, he steadied his rapid breathing.

"Callan?"

Two eyes stared at him from the darkness, glowing bright like two mirrored lanterns. Derek swallowed hard and took an involuntary step back.

A large wolf emerged from between the trees, stopping just a few yards away from Derek. His fur was white, almost snowy, tinged with gray at the tips of his ears and muzzle. His golden eyes, intent and unblinking, locked on Derek as if appraising his worth.

Derek's mouth went so dry that sucking in a breath proved difficult. He had his dagger with him, but it probably wouldn't be much use against an animal so exceptionally large, almost twice as big as the wolves he'd seen roaming the woods of his native Camria. It could probably smell his fear. He could only hope the wolf was familiar enough with humans to be wary of them and their sharp biting weapons.

He forced himself to calm down. It was a false calm, of course, with panic coursing under the thin veneer of control, but Derek held on to it instead of running away screaming.

"Easy now," he murmured, addressing the wolf. "I'm going to leave right away, see? Here's a good boy."

The wolf flattened his ears and bared his teeth, emitting a low growl, but otherwise stayed put. Derek vaguely remembered being told once that wolves didn't growl at their prey. Did that mean the animal didn't consider him a snack, but rather an opponent or a trespasser? Either way, it wasn't reassuring. He risked another step backward, wondering if the soldiers would hear him if he had to resort to screaming after all. There was hardly any point in keeping quiet if the wolf decided to attack him.

"Not here to bother you," he said, struggling to keep his voice steady. "So you can go back to whatever it was you were doing. Hunt a rabbit or something."

A twig snapped behind him with a loud crack, and Derek wheeled around to see Callan standing a few paces behind him. He drew a shaky breath, but Callan didn't look his way, his intent gaze focused on the wolf, his teeth slightly bared in a scowl.

The tense moment seemed to stretch on for eons. Derek held his breath, bracing himself for whatever came next, but then the wolf simply turned and slunk away into the trees.

Derek resisted the urge to sink to his knees in relief—not the least because he knew how difficult it would be for him to haul himself up again. Instead, he turned to Callan.

"How did you do that? Did you tell him to go away?"

"It's a wolf, not a dog," Callan said.

Perhaps it was the darkness that pushed the boundaries of his awareness, or maybe it was the near complete silence. Either way, Derek could feel the evasiveness in Callan's voice in a way he hadn't been able to before. Callan's face was shrouded in shadow, with only the moon reflecting in his eyes when he moved.

"You did," Derek said, a statement rather than a question this time.

Callan lifted a shoulder. "Maybe he just sensed a kindred spirit."

This was clearly everything Derek was going to get in way of an answer. Derek could well understand Callan's apprehension. The High Queen's laws were unforgiving toward any manifestation of witchcraft, however small, and conversing with wild animals (or whatever it was that had transpired between Callan and the wolf) would definitely fall under the category.

Was this the curse whispered about in Irthorg, laid on Callan by an Outer Isles witch for murdering his Agiennan wife? If it was, Derek couldn't find it in himself to be appalled by it.

"Well, I'm glad this was the case," he said earnestly. "I don't know if that beast was about to pounce on me, but it's you I have to thank that he didn't."

"You're welcome," Callan said after a heartbeat. "I'm glad that he didn't too."

Without another word they started back toward the camp together, the silence between them a fraction more companionable than it'd been before.

Chapter Six

THE TOWN OF Bryluen stood at the mouth of a narrow natural harbor. Newer timbered tenements, some several stories high, surrounded the older fortifications. Ships floated majestically farther out in the bay, and rows upon rows of boats were moored all along the quay. Even from this distance, looking down on the city from the higher vantage point the road offered, it was easy to see it was bustling with activity. Bryluen thrived on trade, as it was the merging point for many travel routes, both by sea and land.

But as their troop neared the outer stockade, it became clear the entire city was on high alert. The gates, which usually closed at sundown, swung open only at their approach when the duke's banners had come within sight of the guards. A much greater number of them patrolled the outer walls, Callan noted, as they cheered their troop on their way into the city streets.

He saw the same anxiety etched into the faces of the citizens, replaced with cautious hope as people stopped to gawk and wave at them riding through the muddy streets. The knowledge that the sight of the black-and-silver banners was enough to instill hope in the hearts of frightened townsfolk was both uplifting and disconcerting at the same time, leaving Callan with no choice but to meet their expectations.

They headed straight for the fort, which overlooked the harbor. The high stone walls of the Bryluen stronghold, built over two centuries ago, were interspersed with arrow slits and robust buttresses. Rays of late-afternoon sun gilded the fortifications, softening the otherwise daunting facade. The large square courtyard, decorated with the twin statues of Gwenna and Gwaithil at its center, teemed with soldiers and horses. The sight jolted Callan's half-faded childhood memories of the days just before the break of war.

Derek rode up from behind him, watching the activity. Hard lines creased the pale skin of his forehead. The ride had taken a toll on him, but to his credit, he never complained about his obvious discomfort, and Callan couldn't help but grudgingly (albeit silently) admire his forbearance.

By some kind of a silent agreement, neither of them mentioned the incident in the woods on the first night of their journey, for which he was grateful. He could well do without his new husband accusing him of witchcraft. Not that it would realistically get Callan into too much trouble, considering who he was, but there were quite enough ugly rumors circulating around him already.

It wasn't as if he could explain it to Derek, even if he wanted to. Callan had never talked about it to anyone, including Idona. He hardly knew what "it" actually was. The very notion of him possessing magical powers was ludicrous. He couldn't heal the wounded, or move rocks, or call schools of fish into the nets, in the way of Agiennan witches. He could only hear and feel things that he knew other people couldn't. Like sensing the white wolf's consciousness, a touch away from his own, and asking him to retreat because Callan didn't want to see Derek threatened.

There was nothing sinister about this ability, nothing that could be wholeheartedly called "witchcraft," if he was careful not to indulge in it. There had been tales about his remote ancestors, stories about how the first Dukes of Mulberny could summon wild animals to fight their battles and command wind and earth to do their bidding—with some of them eventually driven mad by their lust for the power the magic supplied them with. But those were nothing but stories told around the fire on long winter evenings and obscure mentions in dusty books. They had nothing to do with him.

Whatever had passed last night, it seemed Derek was ready to overlook quite a number of Callan's sins, whether real or purported. But now Callan wasn't so sure it was out of cowardice.

"It appears the garrison is well manned," Derek said quietly, steering his horse closer to him. "There are only fourteen of us. If the situation is that grave, what could we possibly do to make any sort of difference?"

"We're not here to wage another war," Callan said, reminding himself to be patient. As an outsider, Derek had only a vague idea of what they were up against. He did note Derek used "us," including himself in their number. "This isn't a military campaign that can be won with sheer numbers. They've asked for our expertise in dealing with small-scale attacks that happen seemingly at random, and we're here to find a way to stop them."

Derek still looked dubious, but he nodded without offering further commentary.

Callan didn't bother with going to his room or changing clothes. He exchanged words with the fort's elderly castellan and headed to the war room with Leandre as soon as his troop had been seen to. After a moment, Derek joined them—most likely out of stubbornness than a real sense of urgency. Callan wanted to tell him to go rest but thought better of it. Derek was a grown man, capable of making his own decisions. If he wanted to inconvenience himself for the sake of feeling like he was doing something, Callan wouldn't be the one to stop him.

The Commander of the Bryluen garrison, Lord Morgan, was waiting for them in the war room with his lieutenants, all of whom bowed deeply before Callan as he strode inside. The long, low table in the middle was covered in maps held in place with heavy candlesticks. An array of narrow windows faced the bay, the sound of the waves, the noise of the harbor, and the crying of the gulls blending into a distant din, a mundane backdrop for the palpable restlessness inside the room.

"My lord," Morgan said dryly. "Thank you for coming so quickly."

Without wasting time on further obeisance, he gestured toward the maps. Callan walked to the table, nodding to the other people gathered around it. Several silver pins marked the locations of the pirate ship landings along the coast, all the way from Bryluen to the Egret Forest that effectively marked the northern border of Mulberny.

"There have been twenty-two attacks in the last three weeks," said Lady Elsie, Morgan's daughter as well as second-in-command and in charge of the garrison's field intelligence. As always, she sat in her specially made wheeled chair that was high enough for her to easily survey all the maps laid out on the table. Her sharp eyes, when she looked at Callan, betrayed an intellect as deadly as any sword.

"So many?" Callan frowned, turning his attention to the map. The targets all seemed small and insignificant—a fishing village, a trading post, a temple. None of these would have put up the resistance that might spark the sort of viciousness he'd read about in the reports.

"Yes. They've escalated not only in number, but in malice as well," said Lady Elsie. "The Agiennans were always wont to cause mayhem, but the raids were usually swift and purposeful—they'd pillage the place and leave. Now, they burn everything in sight—houses, fields, temples, killing indiscriminately, leaving very few survivors. They even kill the livestock they can't take with them. There seems to be no rhyme or reason for these attacks or for this senseless destruction, at least not any we can discern."

"The people are frightened, and rightly so," Morgan said. "Many are abandoning their homes, flocking to Bryluen and other larger towns for safety. The city is filled with refugees, and a lot more are headed farther inland. At this rate, the northern shoreline will soon become completely deserted."

"This is highly unusual. The raiders haven't been as bold as that since before the war," Leandre said. Of course, both she and Callan had been little more than children when the Seven-Year War with Agienna had started, but Morgan, who had fought alongside Duke Bergen in past campaigns, nodded in agreement.

"Do you think someone else might be behind this escalation?" Callan asked, recalling his father's insistence on the Danulf clan's involvement.

Morgan and Elsie exchanged a look that told Callan the duke hadn't been the first to entertain that suspicion.

"It's not out of the realm of possibility," Elsie said, somewhat reluctantly. "But so far, no evidence suggests deliberate warmongering by a third party, aside from the suddenness and the brutality of this onslaught."

"I'd be loath to cast blame until we have some solid insights into this matter," Morgan said.

What he hadn't said was that no one wanted to rush into another bloody war with the clans of the Outer Isles, but the thought was clearly on everyone's mind—Callan's included.

"What have you been doing so far to prevent new attacks?" Derek asked.

Callan, who had almost forgotten about his presence, turned to him in surprise—as did everyone else in the room. Derek shifted uncomfortably under the scrutiny.

"This is my husband, Count Derek of Camria," Callan said in response to Lord Morgan's questioning gaze. He should have probably introduced him right away, but his mind was too intent on the current problem to stand on ceremony.

"Indeed," Morgan said, giving Derek a once-over. "Wasn't there some altercation with Camria not long ago? I remember Count Johan—the late count, I suppose he is now—being displeased with the position of our dam, or something to that effect."

Derek flushed, his cheeks turning crimson. Strangely, Callan realized he was annoyed, if not outwardly angry, on Derek's behalf. Whatever bad blood there'd been between Mulberny and Camria in the past, Derek was far too decent to deserve any kind of derision.

"As you see, the issue has been sorted," Callan said mildly but firmly, staving off further unpleasantness. "As a matter of fact, I'd like to hear the answer to that particular question myself."

Lord Morgan gave him the briefest nod to indicate he deferred to his wishes.

"Our troops are patrolling the coast," he said. "But they are spread thin, and we cannot afford to allocate any more soldiers toward that purpose. My duty is to protect the city and its inhabitants should the raiders decide to attack the harbor."

"Waging such an organized offensive doesn't fit their current modus operandi," Callan said. "It seems they prefer wreaking havoc on unprotected settlements rather than engaging our main forces."

"That has been true so far, but I cannot take the risk of leaving Bryluen in a vulnerable position," Morgan said. "Drawing our contingent farther north might well be precisely what they are counting on, so they could go for the bigger prize and loot the city."

There was no faulting Morgan's reasoning, considering Bryluen and its populace had had the misfortune of carrying the brunt of the assault during the war. Morgan's husband, Lord Nesten, who was a healer, had almost died while organizing makeshift field hospitals for the sick and injured, which had been far more numerous than anyone had expected. Now, the city was still in the stages of rebuilding, and Callan could well understand Morgan's misgivings. His instincts told him there was something else brewing under the surface and that the raiders' purpose had nothing to do with attacking a well-defended harbor, but he couldn't argue with Morgan based on his hunches. He was here to find out more about what was going on, after all, and that was precisely what he was going to do.

"I DON'T THINK he likes me very much," Derek said in a tone that was probably meant to be light when they left the war room, on the way to their assigned quarters. "But to be fair, none of you Mulbernians seem to."

"I think you're all right," said Leandre, who was following them down the hallway. She shrugged when Callan shot her a warning look. "What?"

"Lord Morgan can be a difficult man to handle," Callan said, choosing his words carefully. "Especially when challenged by somebody so...uhm..."

"Inept?"

"Young," Callan said with a touch of exasperation.

"I'll meet you in the courtyard in an hour," Leandre said as they entered the guest wing, and strode off, heading to the barracks.

"Wait, we're leaving?" Derek asked, turning to him in confusion.

"We didn't come here to sit at the fort and look to the sky for answers. If we want to hunt those raiders, we must take to the coast—and every minute of delay might cost someone their life."

"But the attacks have been so random," Derek said as they entered their room. "Lord Morgan said he sent patrols. What makes you think you'll have better luck stopping the pirates?"

"Nothing about these attacks is random. They are deliberate. Despite the stories the idle folks at the royal court like to tell to scare one another, Agiennans aren't mindless savages—not even the rogue clan raiders. They always scout their potential targets in advance. Lady Elsie informed me of the locations of the most recent pirate-ship sightings, which is where we are headed. This is our best bet at guessing where their next attack will take place."

Derek didn't appear convinced, but he nodded. Lines of pain and fatigue marred his face, and his clothes were still covered with road dust. Callan took a deep breath, considering how to broach the next subject as delicately as possible.

"It's just a short scouting mission. Most likely we'd be back early tomorrow. Why don't you stay here, get a good night's sleep, and—"

"No." Derek made a move to cross his arms over his chest but then seemed to remember the sling and thought better of it.

"There'll be plenty of other opportunities to prove your worth. You're driving yourself too hard. You need rest."

"I'm not here to 'prove my worth.' Certainly not to the likes of you and Lord Morgan. I'm here for the same reason you are, as hard as it may be to believe."

"I can order you to stay," Callan said, struggling to keep his grip on patience.

"You can't *order* me," Derek said, an edge to his voice Callan hadn't heard before. "I'm a count. Until you come into your inheritance, I have the privilege of seniority over you. And even if I didn't, don't ever presume you have the right to tell me what I can or cannot do."

"Fine." Callan threw up his hands, giving up on trying to reason with him. If Derek passed out during the ride, Callan would tie him to his own horse.

They took turns washing their hands and faces in the water basin, and ate the meal that had already been waiting for them on a little side table in pointed silence. Callan could see Derek had difficulty managing the tasks one-handed, but he didn't ask for help, and Callan didn't offer it. He had no desire to have his head chewed off again.

In an hour, they were both ready and descended into the main courtyard where the rest of their troop was already waiting. It hadn't been much of a rest for the horses, but Callan was loath to switch his Arrow for an animal of an unknown quality.

The sky over the fields that lay farther to the east was already turning deep purple-blue when they rode out of the northern gate, going in the opposite direction from which they'd come earlier. Callan planned to reach their first destination—a small cluster of farms and homesteads off the shore of Moss Rocks where a faraway sighting of a longship had been reported two days ago—shortly after nightfall. The darkness would provide good cover for them to lie in wait for the raiders if they indeed intended to hit that particular spot.

Lord Morgan's grim account proved to be correct. Despite the late hour, the northern road was busy with mule-driven carts and people walking on foot—families taking to the safety of the city walls, peasants and fishermen who were frightened enough to forsake their crops and their boats. The villages they rode past, built either by the side of the main road or directly on the seashore, looked half-abandoned, some surrounded by hastily erected fences and stockades. As they got farther from Bryluen, they began to see the evidence of destruction. Huts and sometimes entire villages burned down, sheep carcasses lying rotting on the ground, their bones exposed by scavengers and the elements.

The mood was definitely somber as their little troop followed the winding ribbon of the road. Dusk settled around them, smoothing the harsh landscape, turning hills and copses into ominous shapes made of shadow and silence.

By the time they reached Moss Rocks, night had completely fallen. The jagged rocks that gave the place its name loomed like the ruins of an ancient fortress in the middle of a sandy beach. The tiny lights in the windows of the nearest fishing village dotted the shoreline, mirroring the stars above.

Despite the cold and wind, the night was clear. The moon shone brightly overhead, leaving a long trail on the inky water and clearly limning the shoreline around the massive rocks. They dismounted and left the horses in a nearby thicket with one of the soldiers. This time, Callan didn't even try suggesting Derek stay with the animals. If his hunch proved right and tonight they'd cross swords with the Agiennans, he'd just have to make sure the man didn't get himself killed for his stubbornness. He most emphatically did not want another dead spouse on his conscience.

Directed by Leandre, the men took positions behind a stone outcrop overlooking the stretch of beach between the rocks and the village, their dark clothing melting into the night, their breathing and the rustling of their cloaks the only sounds to give them away. Someone was playing the flute in one of the huts, snatches of song carried on the wind.

Minutes stretched into hours, the monotonous music of the waves threatening to lull them to sleep after a long, tense day. The distant flute had fallen silent as their vigil wore on. Callan glanced at Derek, who crouched in the tall grass behind him, but his face was almost indistinct in the darkness.

"There," one of the soldiers, Rema, whispered.

Callan turned in the direction they were pointing. A long shadow drifted on the sea across the moonlit path.

For a moment, the silhouette of the bow figurehead was outlined against the glow, enough for Callan to see in his mind's eye the maniacal grin of Dagorn, the trickster sea-god of Agienna, the patron of pirates and explorers.

"Rema, take Jorn, Mathis, and Gella, and move to cut them off after they disembark. We move when they reach the grassland."

Rema nodded and slunk away, keeping low, followed by the other three soldiers. The rest kept tense silence as the ship finally reached the shore. Soft splashes gave the Agiennans away as they leapt into the water and advanced toward the beach. There couldn't have been more than twenty people aboard a ship that size, so the odds weren't terrible—provided they didn't have a witch with them.

Callan gripped the hilt of his sword, looking for the subtle changes in the quality of darkness around them. The drum of his heart was loud in his ears, drowning the sound of waves, and the bitter ghost-taste of copper filled his mouth.

He caught the glint of moonlight reflected off drawn blades, and it was time.

"Now!" he whispered, and then they were running, the wind tearing through their hair, their weapons eager for blood. The jolt of the first hit of steel on steel reverberated through his body, but instead of banishing all thought, it brought the kind of serene calm he always reached for in battle.

Callan danced among the raging, snarling shadows, the touch of his sword turning them into vulnerable flesh as if by magic. Every grunt, every clash, every curse, every thump of a falling body on wet grass, his senses were temporarily heightened to an almost supernatural degree. Maybe some kind of magic did linger in that lethal hyperawareness, that anticipation of impact, but at the moment, he didn't care.

He drove his sword under the arm of a man who swung a heavy battle-ax at Leandre's head, and spun around, straining to find Derek. An irrational panic surged through him when he didn't spot him right away, threatening to shatter his focused calm.

Shouts came from the direction of the ship, indicating that Rema and the others had reached their goal. Fire blazed, engulfing the rectangular sail, casting the scene unfolding on the shore in stark relief. The raiders, clad in furs, their faces streaked with blue and green paint and their long hair braided and adorned with carved teeth and bones, clearly hadn't expected an ambush on what they must have considered an easy hit. Despite being outnumbered, Callan's men drove them back, to the wide stretch of sand between the rocks where Rema's squad rammed into them from behind, sowing further confusion in their ranks. Several bodies were already strewn on the ground, blood pooling beneath them and seeping into the sand.

Callan finally caught sight of Derek, pressed with his back to a mossy rock, fending off two attackers. His left arm was cradled uselessly in the sling, but he wielded his sword with his right with a skill that defied Callan's expectations. As he watched, Derek ducked under one pirate's raised ax and slashed at the other's knees, sending the man sprawling with a cry of pain, and then sprang in time to parry a blow aimed at his back.

As he continued to watch, with something close to wonder, Callan's perception rearranged itself into a new understanding. He was far from considering the ability to fight as the defining merit of a person, but he'd been brought up to appreciate capability and skill of any sort, and, right now, he was witnessing Derek exhibit a surprising level of proficiency. Callan realized that despite knowing Derek had fought against Mulberny in the recent conflict, he'd never actually believed him to be a warrior, focusing instead on the softness of his manner. In Callan's mind, Derek's injury only went to prove his supposition.

But Derek wasn't soft at all. He doggedly accompanied Callan, placing himself in harm's way when he had every opportunity to withdraw. And for what? Standing by a man who'd offered him nothing but scorn, risking his life for the sake of people he had considered his enemies only a few short months ago?

Duty had been Callan's axis of existence his entire life. Perhaps Derek wasn't so different from him in that regard.

Mud and spatters of blood dirtied the white linen of Derek's sling and his face, illuminated by the glare of the fire. His second attacker slumped to the ground, and Derek's eyes met Callan's above the carnage. Derek grinned at him, saluting him with his bloodied sword.

Callan returned the salute automatically, but he couldn't tear his gaze away. He tried not to examine why he was so disproportionately glad to see Derek unharmed, or why his heart sped up at the sight of him in a way that had nothing to do with the heat of battle.

Leandre's triumphant cry, picked up by the other troopers, roused Callan from his stupor. He wheeled around, leaving Derek to permanently dispose of his opponents, and joined his men in driving the last of the pirates toward the burning ship.

Chapter Seven

DAWN WAS ALREADY breaking when they finished piling the bodies into the ship and pushing it into the open sea, still burning. A burial at sea was the way of the Outer Isles, Callan had said, and he wouldn't deny it even for the worst kind of scum he considered pirates to be. Not to mention that a blazing ship, set adrift, would send a warning sign to any other raiders who might be watching the coast at a safer distance.

They were all utterly exhausted, but the spirits among the troop were high. All the raiders were dead, and their party had only paid with minor injuries.

Derek couldn't help but notice the attitude toward him had changed as well. Instead of talking around him, as before, the soldiers now addressed him directly, asking for his help or opinion. And all he'd had to do to ingratiate himself to them was prove he could kill people just as well as the rest of them.

He couldn't deny, however, that this tentative camaraderie felt good. To his surprise, he liked most of them well enough—Leandre, with her often blunt humor and no-nonsense style of command; Rema, with their quiet efficiency; Mathis, with his quick smile and childlike eagerness to prove himself to his older companions. And even Callan seemed to change his mind about him somewhat, judging by the lingering looks he gave Derek when he thought he wasn't paying attention, and the slightly more civil tone he used when addressing him.

Derek should have sneered at that kind of condescension. He didn't want (or need) Callan's approval—certainly not for the dubious task of taking the lives of other people, no matter how despicable their actions had been. But for some reason, he was ridiculously pleased when he caught his blue-eyed gaze, tinged by some new emotion Derek was hard-pressed to identify. Respect? Appreciation? Either way, he couldn't bring himself to turn up his nose at this implied offering of rapprochement.

Seeing as the troop was in good enough shape and raring to fight, Callan had decided to push on north instead of turning back to Bryluen. He purchased the supplies needed for their extended journey at the nearby village, paying perhaps too generously for the simple fare the locals had to offer. For once, it was a decision Derek couldn't fault him for.

In truth, he'd be glad to return to the city, if only for the prospect of sleeping in a proper bed. Derek would rather die than admit it to any of the Mulbernians, but his shoulder was bothering him a fair bit, and he longed for a hot bath and some uninterrupted sleep. But he clamped down on his disappointment. There was work yet to be done, and his personal comfort didn't factor into that equation.

By noon they were on the road again. The fields and the pastures were replaced with steep hills and pine forests, and the coastal settlements grew even smaller and more scattered. Every once in a while, they came upon signs of the same kind of carnage they'd witnessed closer to Bryluen—a grim reminder of the insignificance of one small victory. It certainly couldn't bring back the dead.

Thankfully, that evening Callan called for an early halt, intending to let the men rest after a sleepless night. All Derek wanted was to crawl into their newly erected tent and pass out, but it soon became apparent he was too hungry and too wired to sleep.

Drawn by the alluring smell of cooking and the laughter, he emerged from the tent to be hailed by Leandre, who sat by a campfire next to Callan and a few soldiers. The rest were busy tending to the horses and hauling water, taking turns with various chores before the watch duty.

"Derek! Come join us."

Wrapping his cloak more tightly around his shoulders, Derek sat where the soldiers made room for him, mindful not to bang his injured arm. He felt Callan's eyes on him again but pretended not to notice as he accepted his portion of fish stew, setting it carefully on the ground in front of him.

"Things are bit more exciting here than in Camria, I bet," Leandre said, passing him a jug of wine.

A few days ago, he would have bristled at the comment. But by now he knew her well enough to realize she wasn't being derisive.

"They are, in a way," he said after taking a swig of the wine. "I must admit this is the first time I've fought actual sea pirates. And I'm afraid I don't know much about Agienna and its people in general, aside from what little I've learned during my school years. Perhaps you could fill in some gaps for me. I'd like to know, at least, what we're up against?"

"How much time you got?" Rema asked, deadpan, and the other soldiers snickered.

"Ask away," Leandre said, shooting the others a quelling look.

"Well, it seems these pirates strike where they know they'll meet little to no resistance. Could they have another advantage? Could they be using witchcraft as well?"

Callan raised his head sharply, but it was Rema who answered.

"It's true the Islanders practice magic, but even among them, real witches are rare, and there are fewer of them left after the war. Once, almost every Agiennan longship would have a witch on board to ensure safe sailing and give them an edge over their adversaries. But after the peace treaty, with the new restrictions on their sailing routes, their witches rarely leave the islands. Even the rogue clans wouldn't risk bringing one on a raid to the mainland these days."

"I'd be nervous to be locked with a witch on a ship, days on end," Mathis piped in. "You never know when they're gonna snap and go berserk on you."

"That's a bit dramatic," Jord said, taking the wine jug Derek passed over to him.

"Well, they would. Everybody knows magic eventually drives them mad. That's why the law says—"

"Enough," Callan said, cutting through Mathis's explanation.

His voice was level, but it effectively silenced them. An uncomfortable hush fell over their little circle, and Derek recalled yet again that strange encounter in the woods their first night on the road. What was Callan afraid of?

"I don't know about witches," he said in an attempt to change the subject. "But we've had a similar problem with marauders plaguing the northern regions of Camria in the recent years, though not quite to the same scale. My father and I led several forays to drive them out of our forests."

That earned him a few approving murmurs. There was no question Mulberny had had a lot to deal with, but it all served the misguided notion that whoever hadn't grown up within sight of the sea was a pampered malingerer. Perhaps now they'd understand that peace and quiet were just as fragile inland as they were along the coast.

This sparked a slew of questions about his homeland, and he was all too happy to answer, telling them about the castle that overlooked a serene lake, surrounded by a thick forest; of the granaries his grandmother had established farther to the south; of the new breed of horses they were beginning to export to much interest from the High Court.

Somewhere along the way he realized, with a start, that he was homesick. Surely, not enough time had passed for him to long to see the forests, the fields, and the lakes he was so fond of, or to miss his mother and sister. And yet, there he was, contemplating whether he should take Callan's advice and return to Camria once the campaign was over. It wasn't as if anything—or anyone—was keeping him in Mulberny.

By some intuitive understanding, the conversation steered clear of the more sensitive topics of Count Johan's death and the imposed peace treaty. Callan stayed out of it, eating his evening meal in silence, but Derek could tell he was listening.

Darkness descended around them, bringing with it a sharp bite of chill. This far north, the nights were already distinctly cold, despite it being only the very beginning of autumn. The other soldiers gradually wandered off, either to take the watch or to settle into their sleeping pallets. Eventually, Leandre, too, bid them good night, leaving Derek and Callan alone beside the fire.

He should go to sleep, Derek thought, watching the flames dance against the backdrop of tall pines and the vast sky, utterly black now when juxtaposed with the bright oranges and reds of the fire. But he didn't rise, letting himself enjoy the relative tranquility of the evening.

"Do you wish you could have stayed in Camria?" Callan asked, making him start.

Immersed as he was in his own thoughts, Derek had almost forgotten Callan was still there.

"I'd rather be there for my family," Derek said truthfully. "When I left home, it was...in turmoil. But I don't regret coming here. I've learned a great many things that I wouldn't have known otherwise. I've changed my mind about a lot of things."

Callan nodded thoughtfully.

"I suppose that's true for me as well."

Derek wanted to ask what it was that Callan had had a change of heart about. His husband was still a mystery to him. Being in each other's company for only a few days hadn't been enough to get to know one another—and Callan was, by nature, reticent. But they were alone now, sharing a rare companionable moment, so Derek let the rein slip on his curiosity.

"Did your wife ever join you on patrols?" he asked, keeping his tone casual.

Even though the question was innocuous enough, Callan's expression instantly went blank.

"There weren't as many reasons to keep a close watch on the coast while she was alive," he said. "She did love outings, though. Hunting, sailing, riding."

Derek recalled Ivo telling him that Callan's wife had died in some sort of accident—which hadn't been entirely random, if rumors were to be believed.

He didn't buy into the rumors. Perhaps it was naive of him, since Callan was little more than a stranger, and looks could be deceiving. But Derek didn't sense in him a violent or abusive streak such as he'd come to recognize a little too well living with his father, trying to navigate his moods and uncontrollable rages with various degrees of success. He couldn't fathom Callan flying into a murderous fury because he was forced to marry a former enemy. Though he'd made it all too clear he didn't want to marry Derek, not once did Derek feel threatened in his presence, even on an instinctual level. A man who took time to read books on the customs of his enemies and who respected their rituals wouldn't be blinded with hatred. And whatever other secrets Callan was hiding, iniquity wasn't one of them.

There was something else at the bottom of the murky story, and Derek knew he had to find out what it was.

"What happened to her?"

There was a pause as Callan stared at the fire. The flames reflected in his eyes, turning their color from icy blue to almost golden. Derek held his breath, but then Callan rose to his feet abruptly.

"Didn't you hear? I killed her," he said and strode off in the direction of the pines that grew down to the shoreline, his fur-lined black cloak blending instantly into the deep shadows.

Derek sighed and rubbed his forehead. It seemed his intelligence-gathering skills (as well as his tact) were sorely lacking, but he'd asked the man some difficult questions before, and his answers had always been direct. This time, he'd managed to hit a sore spot, however; perhaps even a wound that was yet unhealed. He was contemplating going after Callan to apologize when a hand touched his right shoulder.

He jumped, embarrassed to have been so preoccupied to be caught unawares. There were people keeping watch, but it was no excuse for carelessness.

"I couldn't help but overhear," Leandre said, apparently unfazed by admitting to eavesdropping, and came to sit next to him, though the fire was already burning out. "Don't take it hard. He doesn't like talking about Idona."

"Did you know her?" Derek asked.

Leandre nodded, the sharpness of her gaze softening at the memory. Her features were a bit too strong to be considered classically beautiful, but she was one of those people whose appeal had nothing to do with prettiness.

"It's strange to think about an arranged union in these terms, but they were a perfect match. Callan was too reserved to be widely liked by his subjects, or by anyone who didn't interact with him day by day, really. Respected, admired, even, but not genuinely loved. Idona changed that. People resisted her at first, unwilling to accept an enemy princess as their future duchess, but she was kind and outgoing. She'd taken to rebuilding everything her kin had fought to destroy. Her death was a great loss to everyone in Irthorg."

"I've heard the stories about him murdering her," Derek admitted. Perhaps it was the wrong thing to say, but he owed it to Leandre to be honest in return for her openness. "But that's not what really happened, is it?"

He thought back on the lock of hair placed inside a dainty silver box, on the way Callan's lips had flattened into a hard line and his eyes had gone cold when Derek had touched it. Such sentimentality couldn't be feigned— not that Derek suspected Callan would feign any sort of emotion for his sake.

Leandre shook her head.

"They were out for a swim at night. Being romantic, I suppose. It was late spring, still not the best time for swimming around these parts, but they'd both grown up on the water."

"So she drowned?"

"The current was too strong. It drew her under. Callan nearly drowned himself trying to save her, but she was gone too quickly. Her body washed ashore the next morning, so battered against the rocks she was barely recognizable. He never forgave himself for her death."

A heavy silence settled between them. Derek tried to imagine Callan giddy with infatuation, sneaking away from the castle with his ladylove for a dip, as if they were common youths out for a bit of forbidden fun instead of a married couple bound by titles, propriety, and obligations. He couldn't quite picture it. It was as if Leandre were talking about a different man altogether.

But love—real love—changed people, didn't it? At least, that was what Derek had heard from others, having never experienced it himself. Perhaps all it did was make them act the fools. It made them blame themselves for things that weren't their fault.

"Thank you for telling me this," he said quietly, watching the flames lick the velvety darkness of the sky. "I may have a better understanding of him now."

"He deserves far more consideration than people are willing to give him," Leandre said, giving him a sidelong glance. "And from what I've seen, I think you do too."

Derek sat there watching the fire slowly die long after Leandre had left to take her watch.

WHEN DEREK ENTERED the tent, Callan was already in his shirtsleeves, getting ready to sleep. He looked up from where he sat on his pallet, caught in the middle of taking off his boots.

The lit brazier cast a pleasant warmth that spread through Derek's chilled limbs. Inside this little cocoon of comfort, it would be easy to forget for a while the horrors they'd witnessed and the danger still lurking out there.

"I'm sorry," Derek said, lowering himself onto the soft furs. "I shouldn't have pried."

Callan shook his head. His shoulders slumped, as if in defeat, and he tugged off his other boot angrily. "And I shouldn't have snapped. You're my husband. You have a right to know these things."

"You loved Idona very much, didn't you?" Derek asked quietly.

For a moment, only the crackling of the embers in the brazier filled the silence.

"Idona was the daughter of the Danulf chieftain," Callan said finally. He wasn't looking at Derek, his fingers tugging at the straps of his leather boots.

"Danulf is the largest, most powerful clan in the Outer Isles. The Agiennans lack a centralized leadership, but they have a Council of the Chieftains to sort things out when needed, and Danulf has a lot of influence. When the war ended, most of Agienna was devastated. Mulberny suffered great losses, without question, but Agienna lost most of its fleet and was depleted of its resources. They had no choice but to capitulate, but it wasn't easy. The Agiennans are a proud people, and many would rather fight to the very last man than to admit defeat, especially on the sort of terms Ivicia required. Aegir, the Danulf chieftain, was the one to rally the council and broker a peace treaty with Mulberny. To secure it, I was wedded to his daughter, and she removed to Irthorg, a sort of a hostage of good will in the eyes of her people. By all accounts, neither of us should have fallen in love with the other, but we did. We thought we'd be together forever. We talked about what we were going to name our children."

He paused, his expression becoming wistful. Watching him, Derek felt stirrings of sympathy for Callan and this woman he'd never met, whose situation had been so similar to his own. But it wasn't entirely the same because she'd obviously found love with the man she'd been forced to marry, while Derek could never hope for more than them tolerating each other's company for the duration of their forced proximity.

"She sounds like an exceptional sort of person," he said, remembering what Leandre had said about her.

"She was," Callan agreed, still avoiding his gaze.

"I know it must be meaningless to you," Derek said hesitantly. "But if I believed I could do something to make the gods return her to you, I would."

Callan raised his head, looking at Derek for the first time during their conversation with a sort of mild surprise.

"It's not meaningless," he said. "Thank you."

There was a long pause while they regarded each other with a new sort of understanding. Derek would be hard-pressed to say what it was, exactly, but something had shifted in the gap between them, making it seem less of a chasm.

"The Agiennans must have been upset over her passing," Derek said, changing the subject to a slightly safer topic, though perhaps "safer" wasn't the right word to describe the aftermath of a tragedy.

Callan grimaced, but his posture relaxed infinitesimally.

"That's an understatement. Upon hearing of his daughter's death, Aegir pulled out of the treaty, swearing vengeance upon me and my house. For a while, we thought war was going to break all over again, but it seemed the rest of the clans were tired of fighting. The peace held, and even the Danulf didn't resume their attacks against us."

"But you think they might be behind this new wave of raids on your coast?" Derek asked, recalling Callan's debate with Lord Morgan.

Something like approval flickered in Callan's eyes, as if he was surprised that Derek had made the connection.

"It's too soon to tell," he said. "Not all the clans have signed the treaty with Mulberny. Those raiders we encountered yesterday were Vanir. They're a small rogue clan, living almost entirely off piracy and theft. But yes, both my father and I fear the Danulf might be spurring them on. Agiennans don't let go of blood feuds so easily."

Derek sighed and rubbed his shoulder absently, trying to ease the ache.

"All this seems so...senseless. So much death and destruction simply because some men refuse to see reason."

"That's how wars are usually started," Callan said, but his tone was gentle rather than mocking. He leaned sideways on his elbow, as if he and Derek were having a friendly chat. Maybe they were, in a sense, if one disregarded the gruesome subject matter.

Derek laughed bitterly. "Tell me about it. If it weren't for my father's pigheadedness, we wouldn't be sitting here right now, and he'd still be alive."

"I take it you weren't in support of his feud with Mulberny?"

"To put it mildly. To be fair, I don't think the duke, your father, had been in the right in the matter of the Sevia River dam. It stemmed the flow needed to irrigate the fields of our northern regions, and the crops were suffering from the shortage during the summer months. But it could all have been resolved with an amended agreement. There was no need to declare war, for gods' sake."

"And you couldn't persuade your father to take a different course of action?" Callan asked.

"My father didn't take well to people challenging his decisions." Derek tried to keep the pain out of his voice, but apparently, he wasn't doing a good enough job, because Callan was now looking at him with something closer to concern. "Least of all me. I could never do enough to please him."

"Then he was a fool," Callan said firmly. "Forgive my lack of respect. But you're the only member of your family I've seen exhibit any sort of common sense."

Derek snorted in disbelief. "Don't tell me you didn't think I was posturing by insisting on accompanying you on this foray."

"I was wrong. You know what you're about. I'm sorry I doubted your motives and abilities, and I won't make the same mistake again."

Derek stared at him. He'd suspect Callan was having him on, but there was no hint of mockery in the way he steadily regarded him. Did he really just admit he was wrong about Derek? Did he *apologize* for underestimating him?

Callan stretched out on the pallet, his eyes half-lidded. Derek's gaze traveled the languid lines of his limbs, lingering where the fall of his shirt exposed lightly tanned skin over hard muscles. In repose, as his considerable strength lay dormant and his expression wasn't as tightly guarded, glimpses of vulnerability shone through. He was beautiful—not with the cold kind of beauty befitting a statue or a god, but with that of a man made of flesh and blood. Derek couldn't help but wonder how Callan would look exposed further, having shed a few more layers of his mental armor. Suddenly, he wanted to meet the man who could be madly in love with his spouse, who could smile and say kind things and be generous with his affection, because, somehow, he knew beyond a doubt Callan was capable of all these things.

If he wasn't careful, Derek would be in danger of finding himself developing the exact sort of feelings he'd so readily scorned before. And that, he knew with even more certainty, could lead to nothing but heartbreak.

Chapter Eight

THE NEXT TIME they faced the raiders, they weren't so lucky.

It was Mathis who spotted the approaching longship as they hid in the tall grasses surrounding an isolated hamlet. The forest encroached on the tiny settlement from all sides save the sea, so there were plenty of places to safely hide the horses.

There was no music this time. The hamlet was half-abandoned as it was, with some of the houses boarded up, their yards empty of fowl and livestock. The remaining villagers kept their doors tightly shut and their windows darkened, but it was a poor disguise against reconnaissance from the sea.

The narrow beach afforded no room to maneuver between the thickets of trees, so their troop went on the offensive as soon as the ship touched shore and the first raider jumped into shallow water. Screams and battle cries erupted into the crisp night air, mixed with the clashing of steel against steel.

Callan kept Derek in his sights—not because he didn't trust him to hold his own, but because his gaze kept slipping, drawn to him as if by some sort of homing spell, like the ones the Agiennan witches used to find their way back to a familiar place when sailing uncharted waters.

This inexplicable urge to see Derek close by, to make sure he was unharmed, was a dangerous one. He was a tangle of contradictions, the mildness of his manner (which Callan had so sorely mistaken for weakness of character) hiding a sharp mind and a prickly sense of honor. Callan had no business wanting to pick on all those different strands, to be fascinated with all the distinct facets of Derek's personality. Worst of all, he shouldn't wonder what his lips would feel like against his own, or whether his body was as lean and perfect underneath all those clothes as he imagined it to be.

They were mere strangers, thrust together for a short while by some whim of circumstance, and would drift apart just as quickly, returning each to his own life. Derek had said he wished to be home for his family, after all. Callan hadn't allowed himself to be close to anyone since Idona's death, not even to take simple physical pleasure in anyone's company. That was all there was to it—his loneliness and the stirrings of his flesh playing tricks on his mind.

Callan ducked as Leandre, coming from the right, swung her blade at the raider who charged at him with a heavy ax, slicing his arm at the elbow. His bellow of anguish was cut short as Callan plunged his sword into his chest. He wheeled around in time to see Mathis go down, blood spattering in a wide arc from a deep gash in his flank.

"No!" Callan started toward the young man, while the others chased the retreating Vanir pirates to their ship, but Derek and Gella got to Mathis first, kneeling on the sand now wet with blood.

"We got him," Derek said when he saw Callan, his face a pale smear in the moonlight. Gella's cheek was scraped raw and her hands were shaking, but she was already cutting away Mathis's leather jerkin and pressing his ruined shirt to the wound to stop the blood. "Go!"

Callan gave him a curt nod and ran after his men.

THE SMELL OF blood and salt hung heavy in the air as they huddled around Mathis's prostrate body, shivering when the cold wind got under their soaked clothes. The ship was slowly drifting away on the currents, its sail blazing against the starry sky, but no one paid it any heed.

Aside from Mathis, no one was severely hurt, but Callan noted the collection of injuries—the scratches, the cuts, the bruised faces. This was a harder victory, the final price for which was yet to be determined.

"There's only so much I can do," Gella said, wiping her brow. "We've bandaged the wound, but it's too extensive. He needs a doctor. A good one."

"There's no surgeon to be found in this wilderness," Rema said. Their brow was covered in tiny droplets of sweat, glistening in the glare of the distant fire against their dark brown skin. "Only village healers. And Bryluen is a two-day ride away."

"Then we ride harder," Callan said.

There was a murmur of assent around him. No one would see the boy die while a chance still remained, however small, to save him.

They made short work of the preparations, and then they were back in the saddle, climbing the rocky slope to the main road. The villagers watched them from half-opened doors and windows, but fear kept them from approaching an armed company.

They took turns with Mathis, who was too weak and in too much pain to ride his own horse even during his brief bouts of consciousness. They were all tired and strung out, men and animals, but didn't stop to rest, eat, and tend to their own wounds. No one spoke as they rode through the rest of the night and morning, coming to a halt only at noon for a short break before pushing on.

They'd only had a few brief hours of sleep after sunset. That time no one bothered with tents and a proper camp, and even Derek slept on the ground, wrapped in his cloak. Callan hated seeing him putting so much strain on his already injured arm, but there simply was no time for the luxury of comfort.

They rode all through the next day and reached Bryluen in the late afternoon, the city's towers gilded with the rays of the slowly setting sun. Wasting no time, they headed straight to the fort.

Lord Morgan and Lady Elsie would no doubt want to question Callan about the encounters with the Vanir, but first things first. After leaving the horses in the hands of the servants, Callan and Leandre led the way to the infirmary while Jorn and Gella carried the unconscious Mathis on a stretcher between them. Rema stayed behind to make sure everyone else was taken care of.

Callan wanted to stay by Mathis's bedside, but the elderly gray-haired physician ushered Leandre and him outside, politely but firmly.

"The boy's condition is grave enough without you tracking dirt all over the sickroom," he said, and Callan had no choice but to defer to his authority.

"Come," Leandre said, putting her hand on Callan's arm. "There's nothing we can do to help him now. He's in good hands."

"I should've been more mindful of him." Callan shook his head. "It's my fault."

"You're always so eager to castigate yourself." Leandre let go of his arm and rounded on him. The warm light coming from the hallway windows softened her skin and crowned her fair hair with a glowing halo, but it couldn't erase the signs of tension and weariness from her face, still smeared with splashes of mud from the road. "Mathis is young, but he's a soldier. He was picked to be a member of your personal guard for a reason. Soldiers face risks every day. You know that. No one's to blame but shitty luck."

"I know. But it doesn't make it any easier." Callan turned away and strode down the corridor away from the infirmary.

"Your husband appears to be of like mind," Leandre said, falling in beside him. "The way you spoke about him before his arrival, I was expecting a pampered courtier. But he pulled his weight along with the rest of us. Even Rema was impressed."

"I regret saying those things about him." Callan rubbed his neck wearily. "He's...not at all what I was expecting."

Leandre stopped right before they reached the stairs, turning to him and forcing him to halt as well.

"Would it be so bad to give him a chance, Callan?" she asked quietly, her eyes searching his intently. "Forgive me if I speak out of place, but I'm asking as a friend. Derek seems like a decent fellow. He cares what happens to the people around him, and for those who can't protect themselves—and he's not afraid to do something about it. He could make a good companion for you."

"Perhaps," Callan said after a short pause. "But I don't think I'd make a good companion for him."

AFTER PARTING WITH Leandre, there was suddenly nothing more for Callan to do, and the exhaustion he'd successfully fought off the last few days came back with a vengeance. He briefly contemplated making his way to his guest room and falling asleep, but the doctor had been right about the dirt. His clothes were covered in a thick layer of dust, and his hair was matted with sweat and salt residue. So, he dragged himself to the baths.

The steam and the hot water threatened to lull him to sleep right there in the washtub. The baths offered some privacy, as they were divided by wooden partitions into individual stalls, each with its own tub and a low bench for dressing and grooming. Callan took advantage of the relative quiet, taking the rare few moments of idleness to clear his mind of all thoughts and soak in the water, letting his stiff muscles gradually relax and his mind drift away from the worry that gnawed at him.

There was a shuffle, and Callan's eyes flew open. Derek stood at the entrance to the stall, holding a bundle of clothes. His face was flushed, either from the heat or from embarrassment, but his eyes were riveted to Callan's bare chest where his upper body rose from the water.

Half-forgotten awareness coursed through Callan, settling in his groin. Startled by his own reaction, he sat up, and Derek tore his gaze away, meeting his eyes instead.

"I'm sorry. The servant pointed me here; they must have been mistaken. I'll leave."

"No," Callan said. "Don't go. I'm done."

He stepped out of the washtub as Derek hastily turned away toward the wall. Callan was grateful for that, because the intensity of the man's earlier scrutiny had made certain parts of his body take undue interest. He wrapped a towel around his waist and drained the tub, the water flowing down a grate that ran the length of the wall. Instead of calling a servant, he filled the tub again himself with clean water from the heated metal buckets outside while Derek placed his clean clothing on the bench and slowly began to undress.

Callan couldn't help but notice how stiff and awkward his movements were. His shoulder was clearly encumbering him, and after days in the saddle, his back was probably aching.

"Would you like me to help you with that?" Callan asked before he could think better of it.

Derek turned to him. The steam made his short auburn hair curl at the ends and stand out, framing his pale face like a halo. For a moment, Callan thought he was going to refuse, but to his surprise, after a long pause, Derek nodded and took the sling off his neck, stretching his left arm with a wince.

It had been a long time since he'd helped anyone undress. Callan's heart thudded wildly in his chest, but he did his best to keep his touches impersonal, helping Derek out of his dirty shirt. His skin was smooth and flawless, marred only with an angry red scar where the arrow had gone clean through his shoulder. It still appeared tender, but nothing suggested inflammation, and, despite the recent exertions, it was healing nicely. The unknown Camrian surgeon had done a fine job.

Callan moved to help him untie his pants, but Derek shook his head.

"I got this," he said, but didn't move away, still looking up at Callan. Light hair dusted his chest, a narrow streak of it running down below his navel. Callan followed its path with his eyes, over the taut abdomen, lingering where Derek was holding the ties. With his coat and shirt gone, there was no hiding his arousal in the tight pants, as if Derek's fast breathing and flushed cheeks weren't enough to betray it. Callan absently wondered if that part of the man's anatomy was as shapely as the rest of him appeared to be. The undershirt Derek had worn when he barged into Callan's bedroom intending to scare off potential assassins hadn't been short enough to offer Callan an insight into that particular question.

By now, Callan's own cock was tenting the towel in a rather unequivocal manner. He couldn't remember the last time he'd been so hard—and so mortified by his response to the sight of another person's body. He had no right to experience this kind of feeling toward Derek, to desire him, to wonder how he might look completely naked. But, gazing into his doe eyes, framed with dark lashes as if outlined in kohl, he couldn't quite remember why.

Without thinking about what he was doing, he leaned in. Derek's lashes dipped, and his lips parted slightly in silent invitation, his breath ghosting over Callan's heated skin. Callan closed his eyes.

"My lord," someone said, and Derek jumped, hurriedly stepping away from him.

Callan straightened. His frustration must have been evident on his face, because the servant bowed hastily and darted to put a stack of fresh clothes on the bench.

"Forgive me, Lord Callan, but Lord Morgan requires your presence," he said with another bow and was gone before Callan could protest.

Derek took another step toward the tub, avoiding his gaze.

"You should probably go, then," he said, and Callan couldn't tell if he sounded disappointed or relieved.

Callan turned away from him, dressed in silence, and left.

EVENING HAD ALREADY set by the time he emerged from Morgan's war room. They'd been debating for what seemed like hours, but, finally, Morgan had agreed to send a contingent up the northern coast under Callan's command, as well as triple the number of scouts.

He didn't know what had incited the Vanir to ravage the Mulberny shores with such unmitigated brutality, but they were largely opportunists, opting for the easy prey. Despite Morgan's misgivings on the matter, he doubted they'd risk making a landing in such a heavily guarded harbor as Bryluen when there were so many unprotected, if less lucrative, spots to pillage. If, with the help of Elsie's spies, they countered the attacks with a show of strength, the Vanir would be forced to set their sights elsewhere. Those little villages were not enticing enough a prize to risk getting slaughtered over.

Callan went down to the infirmary to check on Mathis, but the doctor he'd met earlier was still busy. The care nurse he managed to speak to, however, wasn't too optimistic.

"I'm sorry to say it, my lord, but it's unclear whether your man will last the night. With the damage to his liver and kidney, it's a miracle he's survived for as long as he has."

Callan returned to his room in much heavier spirits than before the exchange. He knew as well as anyone that casualties were an integral part of war, and yet he couldn't help but wonder if he'd done enough. Mathis was barely out of boyhood, too young to die. If only Callan had paid more attention to him during the skirmish, if only they'd been a tad faster getting back to the city... But he couldn't change what had already happened. It seemed his list of regrets was doomed to grow longer and longer with each passing day until he was crushed under the weight of all the guilt.

A fire burned in the hearth, staving off the darkness and chill. Somehow, he'd forgotten he was sharing the room with Derek and was startled to find evidence of the other man's presence—his saddlebags by the bed, a half-eaten meal on the side table by the window. But Derek wasn't there, despite the late hour. His sword and cloak were also nowhere to be seen.

Truth be told, after what had happened (or almost happened) earlier, Callan was dreading facing his husband. These new...feelings were entirely too confusing. They'd be easy enough to dismiss if it all boiled down to simple lust, but deep down, Callan knew that wasn't the case. His fascination with his husband had started long before the awkward faux pas at the baths. It began when Derek rode alongside him, facing the same hardships as everybody else despite the acute discomfort of hard travel, when he was risking his life to defend this land though it wasn't his home. No, it was this stubborn determination coupled with wit and a sharp mind that Callan had found so appealing, even before he took into consideration the man's physique. He was edging closer to the path he'd forbidden himself to take again after

Idona; the one he believed himself incapable of following with anyone else but her.

Wouldn't it be funny if he only fell in love with people he was forced to marry against his will? Hilarious.

To distract himself from these thoughts, he rang for an evening meal and wine, and settled to wait for Derek. As much as he wanted to sleep, they probably needed to talk if they wished to avoid further mutual chagrin.

Minutes stretched into hours, and Derek still hadn't returned. Callan rose from his seat at the table and went to the window to look down at the courtyard, illuminated by a multitude of torches. Had he made Derek so uncomfortable by his advances that he'd felt like he had to avoid Callan altogether? Had he somehow made him feel imposed upon?

Callan bit his lip, considering the possibility. It hadn't been his intention; his action had been quite spontaneous, and Derek hadn't seemed averse to the idea of Callan kissing him. But perhaps he'd misread the situation entirely. What if he'd been so caught up in the surge of yearning he'd made an unwelcome move?

He needed to find him and resolve the matter—apologize and make clear it wouldn't happen again. He'd just have to keep a tighter rein on his misplaced desires and jumbled emotions. Derek shouldn't be driven from their quarters by fear. Callan would be perfectly fine sleeping in the barracks with the rest of his troop.

"Do you know where Lord Derek went?" he asked a servant who came in to take away the empty dishes and Derek's uneaten portion.

"No, my lord. He did receive a letter, though, just before your lordship arrived. He then left straightaway."

"What letter? From whom?"

"I'm sure I don't know, my lord."

Vague unease stirred in the pit of his stomach. What could possibly be so important that Derek felt he had to address personally at this late hour? He thanked the servant and grabbed his own sword belt before going out.

Questioning the staff he met on the way, he managed to track Derek down to the stables. His mare was in her stall, resting, but the stable hand informed him that Lord Derek had taken another horse.

"He said something about his brother being detained at the southern gate," the stable boy supplied helpfully, eying Callan's wolf-emblazoned jerkin with something close to awe.

"Really? His brother?" Callan frowned. He assumed this had to be Ivo, the older one, although, frankly, he considered either of Derek's brothers to be bad news, for different reasons. The city guard kept a tight watch these days, but Callan had a hard time believing they'd deny entry to a member of Derek's family, and by extension, his own. Something didn't add up about this story, especially considering Derek's retinue was supposed to be residing at Irthorg at the moment, ostensibly still celebrating the young count's nuptials.

He paused in indecision. His instincts screamed something was wrong, but on the other hand, rushing to Derek's aid without clear indication anything was amiss was silly. These days, however, Callan preferred to err on the side of caution.

The main hall of the barracks was noisy and well lit, the off-duty soldiers relaxing after their communal meal. He spotted Leandre immediately, sitting at a table off to the side with half their troop, chatting over tankards of ale. When she saw him, she raised an eyebrow and got up to meet him.

"You think something happened to him?" she asked after Callan had told her why he was there. She sounded dubious, but she didn't outright dismiss his concerns, which was part of the reason he meshed so well with her. They took each other's hunches seriously, after years of fighting together side by side, trusting each other with their lives.

"I'm not sure, but I'd like to check on him, just in case," he said.

He was almost embarrassed to admit he was worried. For all he knew, Derek might have gone off to town to seek whatever nighttime entertainment Bryluen had to offer. But by now he also knew Derek well enough to know that was highly unlikely.

"I'll join you," Leandre said.

In five minutes, they were on their way to the south gate through the busy streets of the city, having taken Derek's lead and borrowing fresh horses from the keep stable. The gate, when they reached it, was shut, and they had to rouse sleepy soldiers from the guardhouse to answer their questions.

"No one asked to be admitted, my lord," the bewildered guard said. "The gate has been closed all evening."

"And no one left?" Callan asked, exchanging a troubled glance with Leandre.

"Only one farmer's cart, all loaded, my lord, not half an hour ago."

"A cart?" Callan repeated. His hands tightened on the reins instinctively. Earlier unease grew into a full-blown panic, his heart threatening to burst out of his chest. Leandre threw him a dark look, which meant she was thinking exactly the same thing. "Which direction did it take?"

Chapter Nine

THE CART JOLTED as it rolled over another bump in the road, and Derek gritted his teeth in frustration.

How could he have been so stupid as to fall for such an unsophisticated ploy? He must have been too addled with fatigue—and then too distracted by the sight of Callan's bare chest to think clearly.

Derek groaned around the rag that was stuffed in his mouth. What a fool he'd made of himself. What was he thinking? Clearly, not an ounce of rational thought had been involved when he'd given in to the temptation to feel Callan's touch against his skin. He'd made it clear enough that he wanted nothing of Derek. Their union was established for convenience, not passion. Callan was still mourning the love of his life, for gods' sake. The least Derek could do was respect his wishes and leave him well enough alone instead of pouncing on him the moment he saw Callan naked.

In any case, the point was now somewhat moot, and he was most definitely paying the price for his lack of skepticism at receiving a note from an unknown source. But at the time, he'd been too worried about the possibility of Ivo showing up with more bad news from Camria, or in some sort of trouble, maybe even fleeing persecution by Duke Bergen for some ridiculous offense. And then, of course, came the humiliation of having been jumped in a dark alley by four masked assailants.

What had been the point of surviving a battle with the Mulbernians and then two skirmishes with Agiennan pirates if he couldn't even defend himself from getting clocked on the head and hauled away like a sack of potatoes? In an actual burlap sack, no less.

With his mouth gagged and his hands tied behind his back, there wasn't much Derek could do. The coarse fabric obstructed his vision, but he could tell it was pitch dark. They must be well away from the city. If he strained hard enough, he thought he could hear the distant sound of the sea lapping against the rocky shore, but the pain in his roughly twisted shoulder and the aching bump on his head were making it difficult to focus.

Breathe through it and pull yourself together.

If he didn't gather his wits about him, he'd be in much worse pain, he was certain. He hadn't gotten a clear glimpse of the men who'd kidnapped him, but he could hear them talking amongst themselves in hushed voices. They weren't speaking the common tongue of the realm, and he didn't recognize the language until one of them mentioned *egondar*, which was the Agiennan pejorative for "mainlander"—one of the few Agiennan words Callan's soldiers had taught him.

Shit. What could the Agiennans possibly want with him? Derek wasn't important enough to warrant the risk of infiltrating a large city teeming with armed guards—unless, of course, their goal was to retaliate against Mulberny by kidnapping the new husband of the fiefdom's heir apparent. And if they were counting on a rich ransom, they were bound to be disappointed. No one in Mulberny cared enough about him to pay for his safe return, and it would take a long time to gather whatever funds were needed in Camria.

Derek closed his eyes, his frightened thoughts circling back to Callan, to the dry, no-nonsense tone in which he'd dispelled Derek's self-deprecation, the unexpected gentleness with which he'd helped him disrobe for his bath. Perhaps Derek's earlier assertion wasn't entirely true, a treacherous voice whispered in his ear. Perhaps there was someone who cared—just as Derek had grown to care for the man he'd wanted so badly to despise.

Derek mentally shook his head. No. He couldn't hope his muddled, hatchling feelings were in any way reciprocated. He had no one to count on but himself, nothing to fall back on but his own endurance, the way it had always been.

The rickety cart came to a sudden halt. Derek suppressed a groan as the jolt echoed beneath his shoulder blade, and lay still, listening for any sign of what was coming.

There were more voices, louder this time. They were definitely close to the sea now, its monotonous drum clear behind the shouts and laughter. Then somebody hoisted him off the cart and threw him on the ground, none too gently. At least the gag suppressed his grunt as his chest hit the hard earth and pain radiated from his shoulder to every inch of his body.

A thin blade sliced through the burlap, nearly missing his cheek, and somebody tore away the sack. Harsh light blinded his eyes for a second, and he blinked, adjusting his vision.

Several men stood above him, a few of them holding blazing torches. Behind them, the shape of a ship's bow stood out against the backdrop of the oily black water, its fanciful carved face with a lolling tongue illuminated by the reddish glare. The face seemed to wink at Derek, mocking his predicament.

They were definitely Agiennan. Callan could have told him what clan they were by the cut of their clothes and the weave of their braids, but Derek was ignorant of these things. He shrank instinctively as the man with the knife stepped closer, but he only bent to cut the ties that bound Derek's feet and, grabbing him by the right arm, hauled him upright.

"Walk," he said, his accent so thick Derek struggled to understand him—but this man, at least, was no Islander. His clothes and speech marked him a native of Sansia, a northern kingdom that kept its own language and customs, unlike most of the fiefdoms of Ivicia.

Derek stumbled to his feet. With so many men surrounding him, attempting an escape was out of the question, even if his legs hadn't been cramped from lying so long in an uncomfortable position. The four men who'd ambushed him in Bryluen, dressed in the somber, nondescript clothes of Mulbernian townsfolk, were now joined by at least a dozen others in full Agiennan garb.

"Move," the Sansian said, gesturing toward the ship with his knife.

Derek balked. If he set foot on that ship, he was as good as dead. Not that he deluded himself as to his overall chances of survival, but out there on the sea, they'd be practically nonexistent.

Another man shoved him from behind, and he took an involuntary step forward to keep from falling. Surely there was something he could do to stall. The men who'd taken him off the street, at least, spoke the common tongue well, and he turned to them, making assertive mooing noises around his gag, intending to make them take it out so he could try to deal with them.

But he didn't have a chance to see if they'd oblige him. At the sound of hooves thudding on hard ground, the men around him turned in alarm and jumped out of the way as a long blade sliced through the air.

"Leandre, grab him!" Callan shouted, as a second rider emerged from the shadows from the opposite direction, galloping toward Derek.

His heart leapt. Even presented with undeniable evidence, he could scarcely believe his eyes. That Callan was here, that he'd come to Derek's rescue—it hardly seemed real. Spurred by renewed hope, Derek turned toward Leandre.

But the Agiennans' initial confusion only lasted for a few seconds. Seeing they were only up against two people, even armed and on horseback, they rallied instead of scattering. One of the Agiennans, little more than a youth, stepped forward and closed his eyes, making a weird gesture with his hands. Both Leandre and Callan's horses reared, whinnying, as if spooked by some unseen apparition. Seizing the opportunity in the momentary confusion, one of Derek's kidnappers clutched at the saddle behind Leandre, ducking under her raised sword, and she wheeled around, trying to fight him off and regain control of her mount. Struggling to keep his balance, Callan hacked at the men coming at him with axes and short swords, aimed at him and at the legs of his horse. Wounded, the animal stumbled, and several attackers rushed to tug at Callan from behind, pulling at his cloak. Losing his balance, he tumbled backward, right into the arms of his foes.

With his hands tied behind his back, Derek wasn't sure what he was trying to accomplish when he lunged toward him. But he didn't have the chance to find out, as the Sansian man who'd commanded him to walk earlier grabbed him by the hair from behind. Derek twisted, trying to kick him in the knee, but the man slashed at his thigh, cutting deep. New pain blossomed, and Derek grunted when his assailant shoved him down to his knees, holding a knife to his throat.

Derek gulped at the cold bite of steel against his exposed skin. He stilled, watching in helpless horror as Callan was dragged on the ground, kicking at his assailants; as Leandre let out a cry of anguish when a short spear struck her side, and she fell heavily, slumping into an unmoving heap. Riderless and spooked, the horses bolted across the dark grassy plain, away from the glare of the torches and the Agiennans' cries of triumph. The cart horse shifted nervously but stayed in place as the young Agiennan placed a soothing hand on her neck, stepping back from the calamity caused by whatever witchcraft he'd employed.

No. This can't be happening.

Leandre couldn't be dead—she couldn't, not for something so pointless as trying to save Derek's life.

His vision blurred by angry tears, Derek saw Callan stagger to his feet, having managed to fend off his attackers. He'd lost his cloak, and his clothes were bloody, but there was a dangerous gleam to his eyes, and he bared his teeth at the men that surrounded him, like a cornered wolf. Several bodies lay around him, unmoving.

The man holding Derek tightened his grip and shouted something in broken Agiennan. Callan whipped his head, taking in the picture of Derek on his knees, gagged and bound. The knife pressed into his skin, a hairsbreadth away from breaking it, and Derek stopped breathing.

Time slowed to a standstill. Callan paused, his blue gaze piercing him to the core. *No*, Derek wanted say, having guessed his captor's meaning. *Don't do it. They'll kill you. Not for me.* But he could only stare, his eyes no doubt wide with terror, his body rigid.

With a jerky motion, Callan threw his sword aside. Slowly, so slowly, he went to his knees, and in the next moment toppled to the ground as one of the Agiennans hit his head with the butt of a spear.

Derek was yanked by the hair and pushed back, into the black water. Strong hands hauled him over the railing onto the flat shallow deck. Dazed, he made no move to resist. He was thankful for the gag. It was the only thing that kept him from giving his kidnappers the satisfaction of hearing him weep.

DEREK HAD NEVER been on a ship before, and this was not how he'd envisioned his first sail. Huddled together with Callan in a wooden cage that only permitted them to either sit or lie down, he could barely see the water from where they were situated by the mainmast. Perhaps it was for the best—the motion made him queasy, but at least he couldn't watch the waves rise and fall around them as the ship sped on its way, carried by the strong winds in the swiftly rising dawn.

He was dirty, thirsty, and battered. His head hurt. Blood had finally stopped seeping from the gash on his thigh, but the cut smarted, throbbing in unison with his badly abused shoulder. He hoped the scabs around the arrow wound wouldn't open again because he suspected he couldn't count on medical treatment anytime in the near future.

But he wasn't the one who needed it most. Callan lay next to him, his head resting in Derek's lap. He was in much worse shape, dried blood crusting the roots of his hair. Whoever had hit him hadn't held back. Earlier, Derek had removed Callan's leather jerkin to ease his breathing, but he'd only moaned and remained unconscious, his chest rising and falling in a broken rhythm.

Derek had never felt so helpless. Once they were on board, the Agiennans had removed his gag and untied his hands, but they either didn't understand or simply ignored his questions and pleas for water. They also took everything of value they found, including his father's signet ring.

He was beginning to fear Callan might not reach the end of their journey, wherever their kidnappers might be taking them. And it was Derek's fault because, when push came to shove, it turned out he couldn't uphold his cavalier assurance about being able to take care of himself. He'd let himself be overpowered, and Leandre and Callan, having been compelled by some silly noble impulse to come to his rescue, had paid the price. The Agiennans might have played a dirty trick on them using magic, but Derek's arrogance and incompetence was really to blame here.

He ran his hand over Callan's matted hair, even though he suspected he wouldn't have welcomed the intimacy had he been awake. But Derek also knew from experience that being held through pain was comforting, and it was all he could do to alleviate some of Callan's suffering at the moment. And his breaths did seem to become a little less raspy at the touch, unless Derek was so dazed with thirst he was imagining things.

Maybe Callan dreamed it was Idona soothing him. Gods knew being lost in such a dream was better than facing their current reality.

"Hey," Derek ventured again when one of the sailors approached the cage. "Where are you taking us?"

The man said something, a string of words Derek couldn't understand. Seeing Derek's confusion, he added with heavy accent:

"Leader. To see you."

Encouraged that this man seemed to at least understand him, Derek tried again:

"Water. Please?"

The sailor scowled at him. Like most of the other Agiennan warriors, he was tall, clad in deerskins and mismatched bits of armor. Lanky blond hair hung to his shoulders, some of it plaited and interwoven with different-colored leather strands. Derek was sure the colors and the intricate ties had some significance, but he had no idea what it was. The men who'd accosted him at Bryluen, including the Sansian thug, were nowhere to be seen.

"Please."

Perhaps resorting to begging wasn't the best idea when it came to dealing with people who seemed to value warrior prowess above all else, but Derek was past caring what his kidnappers thought of him. Awe, respect, pride— none of it really mattered as long as what had to be done got done, and his language skills were too limited for any sort of bargaining with people who didn't speak the common tongue of Ivicia.

Whether it was out of compassion or a desire to keep his prisoners alive till they reached their destination, the Agiennan walked away and returned after a minute with a waterskin, which he shoved between the cage bars.

The water was cold and stale, but Derek had never tasted anything sweeter. He gulped it down, shaking with need, but was careful not to finish it all at once. He couldn't count on repeated kindness from his captors, and he didn't know how long the trip would last. Instead, he pressed the waterskin to Callan's slack lips while holding his head up, urging him to take a sip. Some of the water sloshed onto his chin, but Derek managed to get Callan to swallow a mouthful. Afterward, he closed his eyes and leaned against the cage bars, tasked even by this small effort. Callan's head rested on his good arm, making it go numb, but he didn't dare move him.

Derek wracked his brain trying to recall anything he could about the Outer Isles, but, unfortunately, living so much farther inland, where the threat of the sea pirates and witches was nothing more than a peddler's tale or a passage in a book, he'd not been particularly interested in learning more about the region. He had no idea who'd want to kidnap him, but he suspected Callan's arrival had disrupted his captors' plans, whatever they were. The duke's heir was a much more valuable prisoner than his unlucky son-in-law—and a much more dangerous one in the current shaky political climate.

The sailors otherwise paid them little heed, and Derek relaxed a fraction. He'd face whatever was in store for them when it came, but for now, he succumbed to exhaustion, lulled by the sound of the waves crashing against the hull.

HE WOKE WITH a start. He must have been asleep much longer than he intended, or had passed out completely, because it was dark again, the deck illuminated only by a single lantern that swung on its peg on the mast along with the sway of the ship. His mouth was dry, salt crusting his lips, and his body felt battered beyond the ability to function.

"Hey," Callan whispered by his side, and Derek turned to him sharply, wincing as pain flared in his head at the movement.

Callan half sat, leaning—or more accurately, slumping—against the frame of the cage, regarding him with hooded eyes. His clothes were damp with sweat and what appeared to be traces of vomit, but Derek's heart fluttered at the sight of him, like a butterfly mesmerized by the brightness of a flame.

"Hey," Derek said, sitting up and licking his lips. He wouldn't ask whether Callan was all right, since all the evidence pointed to the contrary. "Do you know where they're taking us?"

"I've only overheard snippets." Callan's voice was soft, either from weakness or as an attempt at discretion. "These men are Undin. They're barely a clan, and hold no land of their own. But there are more witches born among them, and their magic allows them to fare far and wide over the sea, far beyond the reach of the other clans, so it keeps them from being total outcasts. They worship no other gods but Dagorn, the Trickster, and break deals as easily as they make them. I don't know what they wanted with you, but my bet is they're going to sell us to the Danulf."

"Idona's kin?" The chill that ran down Derek's spine was not entirely due to the cold night wind. He recalled Callan telling him that Idona's father had sworn vengeance against him. It would curry no small favor to deliver Callan to the man who believed him responsible for his daughter's death.

Callan nodded. The snoring of the sailors sleeping on the open deck and the muted voices of those manning the oars punctuated the heavy silence.

"How did you find me?" Derek asked. He dreaded thinking about the future, but the past was equally troubling.

"I heard you'd received an urgent missive. When I tracked you down to the south gate and was told that only a single cart had gone through, I knew you must have been on it. Then it was about overtaking it in time."

"I'm sorry. I should've known it was a trick. And now you're here, and Leandre... It's all my fault."

Callan shook his head. "Blaming yourself will get you nowhere."

Derek reached out for Callan's hand, cold and clammy where it rested on the damp wooden deck. After a moment, Callan's fingers entwined with his own.

"Thank you for coming for me," Derek whispered. "Even though I was never the husband you wanted."

"Maybe," Callan said, his eyes glinting, infinite dark pools beneath swollen red eyelids. "But I think you are the one I needed."

Chapter Ten

DAWN GREETED CALLAN with the sight of a jagged shoreline. The Outer Isles were a massive archipelago, consisting of hundreds of closely situated islands, but the three larger ones, occupied by the more numerous clans, were the heart of its territory.

Callan had been there before, first on a reconnaissance mission and military forays, then as part of the delegation for the peace treaty. His guess regarding their destination was right—they were being taken to Cirda, the land of the Danulf. The discontent among the clans must have reached a critical level if they were willing to risk a high-profile kidnapping, even if the original target had been Callan's spouse rather than Callan himself.

He glanced at Derek, who was sleeping again, his head resting against Callan's shoulder. It'd gone numb sometime during the night, but he hadn't moved so as not to disturb Derek. He needed whatever rest he could get.

Callan's head throbbed, and nausea made bile rise to his throat with each sway of the ship, though he was hardly a stranger to sea voyages. Sometimes his vision blurred and went dark around the edges, and he purposefully didn't let himself fall asleep for fear of slipping into deeper unconsciousness. That blow to the head had come just short of splitting his skull, but otherwise, he'd been lucky. He was still alive, which was more than he could say for his best friend and sister-in-arms.

I'm sorry, Leandre. Sorrow washed over him, threatening to leave him a quivering, teary-eyed mess. Death always followed in his footsteps, so close he could feel her ghostly breath, the cold almost-touch of her bony fingers. The Unnamed Goddess favored him with her attention, but she was a jealous one, taking away those he loved so he could court none but her until the day he'd succumb to her eternal embrace.

But not yet. The steady rise and fall of Derek's chest, pressed against him, was both a comfort and reminder the fight wasn't over. *I won't let you have him. You'll have to take me first this time.*

The keel of the ship hit the sand, and he blinked. He was talking to gods in his head instead of watching his surroundings. They really had knocked his brain out.

The deserted shoreline was marked with piles of smooth rounded stones, spaced on the edge of the grassland at regular intervals—holding markings, a sign for other Agiennan seafarers. In the distance, the tops of conical thatched roofs peeked from behind a line of low pines, and smoke rose from the chimneys even at this early hour.

Derek groaned beside him, stirring into wakefulness. He sat upright, rubbing his forehead.

"Where are we?"

"Cirda Island. The Danulf holding."

One of the sailors came up to the cage and shoved a bowl of dried fish and a waterskin through the bars, preventing Derek from asking more questions. The pungent smell of food made Callan's stomach turn, but he forced himself to drink his fill, watching as several of the

Undin men jumped into the shallow water and made their way to the shore, undoubtedly to bargain. When they reached the stony outcrops, three or four Danulf watchmen stepped out from the line of trees, stopping them. After a short exchange, two of the watchmen escorted the Undin sailors toward the houses.

The clansmen would be here any minute. Callan looked around but saw no way they could take advantage of the short intermission. Plenty of crewmen milled around the deck, keeping an eye on them. With Derek and Callan both too weak to break out of the cage even if no one was paying them any heed, they'd have to take their chances when they were off the ship.

"We could try to reason with them," Derek whispered. "They must understand that by harming you they'd be starting another war."

It was undoubtedly true. But seeing the recent organized raids, the spike in violence, Callan wasn't at all sure war wasn't exactly what the Danulf (if not the rest of Agienna) wanted.

Long minutes passed before a group of people emerged from behind the trees. Callan recognized the tall, broad-shouldered figure of Aegir, the Danulf chieftain, even before he could discern his face. His mouth dry, he watched as the Danulf approached one of the stone piles and halted. At the sign of one of their compatriots coming back with the Danulf, the Undin crewmen hauled Callan and Derek out of the cage, tied their hands behind their backs, and shoved them over the railing.

Their muscles cramped after sitting for so long, they crashed awkwardly, splashing into the water. Callan heard Derek gasp and curse, but then the Undin took hold of them and dragged them onto the sand, right at the feet of the waiting chieftain and his envoy.

Callan tried to rise, but a strong hand clamped on his shoulder, forcing him back down on his knees. He gritted his teeth and raised his head in the only act of defiance he could manage.

Aegir had aged since he last saw him, though barely three years had passed. Deep crow's-feet lined the gray eyes under bushy eyebrows, and his long hair, braided with carved metal and bone beads, had gone almost completely white, as had his long beard. But his heavy gaze, as it settled on Callan, was no less sharp and unsettling than he remembered.

"I see you, Callan son of Bergen," Aegir said gravely in Agiennan, greeting him for all the world as if Callan were an official guest rather than a prisoner.

"I see you, Aegir son of Ainar," Callan said with the same inflection.

"And this—" Aegir turned to Derek. "—is your new husband?"

Derek shifted uncomfortably on his knees under the chieftain's scrutiny, but wisely said nothing.

"Yes, unfortunately," Callan said, keeping his tone neutral. His only chance of keeping Derek out of harm's way was to feign disinterest, even dislike toward him. Otherwise, he was sure, the Agiennans would have no qualms about making sport of Derek just to elicit a reaction out of him.

At least Derek couldn't understand what he was saying.

"It's him. Pay them," Aegir said to a man on his right, indicating the Undin.

"Shall we call for the assembly of the Council of the Chieftains?" the man asked, his voice so low Callan barely heard him.

Aegir paused, considering. "No," he said finally. "This is Danulf business. Bring the mainlanders inside." Without a second look, he turned and strode off.

This was not a good sign.

"Whatever happens to me, say nothing," Callan murmured to Derek, keeping his eyes averted and his voice level. "Let them think you're harmless, or they'll torture us both."

Derek's expression grew grimmer, but he nodded before they were hauled up and pushed toward a narrow path that wound through the trees toward the homestead.

News of their arrival must have spread like wildfire, because people gathered outside of the houses to watch their escort through the village with unmistakable hostility. The wounds of the war ran too deep, even before Idona's death had shattered the tentative peace. There was too much Danulf blood on Callan's hands to be forgiven, to have earned anything but their lasting hatred. The words followed them, murmurs and shouts. *Oathbreaker. Murderer.*

Callan paid them little heed, used as he was to the sort of infamy that carried dark looks and hushed whispers, but he could tell Derek was nervous. His posture was tense, and he kept casting wary glances at the crowd, as if expecting them to start throwing stones at them at any moment.

Callan's head was spinning so hard he was afraid he'd slip and fall flat on his face. The village sprawled amid the pine forest, much larger than he remembered it, the thatched-roof houses built haphazardly with no outward sense of order, surrounded by sheep pens and pigsties. The main hall, a large wooden structure surrounded by a spiky stockade, stood a little to the side on a gentle elevation. It served as the residence of the chieftain, a place of gathering, and a point of muster during times of war.

He remembered the heavy oak doors, carved with the shapes of entwined serpents. Here, he'd taken Idona's hand in marriage before the stony faces of her kin and her gods. Here, they'd made love for the first time—not that awkward fumble they'd had on their wedding night, but the next day, when Idona had taken him up the forest path to a clearing where the cliffs dropped abruptly into the sea. She'd laid him down in the grass and rode him, wild and free like a creature of starlight and seafoam, until they were both falling into dawn.

Callan's breath hitched in something close to a sob, which earned him a hard shove from the man who was leading him. He shook his head, grasping for clarity. Now was not the time to lose himself in old memories, not while he had to fight to save the life of the man walking beside him.

The dim interior of the hall was illuminated only by a fire, which burned low in an open hearth in the middle of the long space. Aegir sat on a high chair at the far end, surrounded by the clan elders. Several guards, armed with spears and axes, lined the walls.

The air was stuffy, stale. Callan swallowed hard, fighting another bout of nausea, and focused on the way the feeble light reflected off the scales of the serpent that decorated the heavy fibula holding Aegir's fur-collared cloak closed.

They were shoved down on their knees again. This time, Callan didn't try to resist.

"Finally, the murderer is brought before us," Aegir said, speaking in the common tongue. It was no doubt done for Derek's sake, although why the chieftain would bother was a mystery to Callan. "Do you deny your guilt?"

Callan shook his head. He always knew this day would come, the day he'd pay in full for his failure.

"This is bullshit," Derek said angrily beside him, in complete disregard to his earlier promise.

"Be quiet," Callan hissed at him. Of all the opportunities to exhibit assertiveness, Derek picked the worst time to start.

"I will not! Your daughter's death, as tragic as it was, was an accident," Derek said, addressing Aegir, his head held high, his eyebrows knitted together in consternation. "Callan didn't murder her. He tried to save her."

"Were you there?" asked an old woman who sat on Aegir's left. Her graying hair hung in thick braids past her shoulders, her robes covered with blue and scarlet embroidery. Her pale eyes traveled from Derek to Callan, and back again.

Callan knew her. Logitt, a clan elder and Aegir's maternal aunt. A healer. *A witch.*

"Well, no," Derek said. "But I know Callan, and he would never—"

"Derek. Shut. Up," Callan managed to grit out. All he wanted was for Derek to stop talking and for the room to stop spinning.

Derek fell silent, his brown eyes smoldering with an emotion Callan would've found touching under other circumstances. But Derek's indignation was counterproductive to the goal Callan was desperately trying to achieve.

"This is a sign from the gods," another elder said. Some nodded, but the rest seemed dubious.

"I've waited a long time for this moment," Aegir continued as if no one else had spoken, his voice echoing in the cavernous hall. "The moment I will make the proud Mulbernian scream his pain."

"If I could trade my life to have Idona safely returned to your side, I'd do so gladly," Callan said, locking his eyes with Aegir's. "But I cannot. All I want is to spare both our people the hardships of another war. Let him"—he nodded to Derek—"carry a message back to my father stating that I've submitted to your judgment willingly, and that he's not to retaliate against Agienna. Then do to me what you will."

His heart was pounding too loudly in his ears, drowning the sound of his own words. He could only hope he'd made his point. The elders exchanged glances but stayed silent. Logitt pursed her lips, her eyes boring into his soul.

"War," the Danulf chieftain scoffed. "There will always be war. It's just another turn in the Great Cycle. It only makes us stronger, makes us harder. Maybe the next time it will be the Duke of Mulberny to offer *his* daughter as expiation, to be married to one of our children to secure yet another treaty—and we'll be the ones dictating the terms."

Callan knew Aegir only mentioned Adele to get a rise out of him, but the thought of her having to carry his burden was more than he could bear. His heart sped up, his vision blurring dangerously around the edges. He should say something, anything, to steer the conversation back to whatever they'd been discussing before going so far off topic, but he couldn't remember what it was.

Your groom will be disappointed, Adele said in his head. And then he was falling, the worn wooden floor rushing to meet him out of unfathomable depths.

FOR ONE TERRIFYING moment after opening his eyes, Callan couldn't remember where he was.

Then the pain kicked in. He was lying on something soft but prickly. Straw. His head throbbed, and he felt weak as a newborn kitten, but he made himself open his eyes. Above him, long metal hooks were affixed to smoke-charred beams on a low ceiling. When he tried to move, he discovered his leg was chained to the wall, his boots gone.

Someone shifted on the straw beside him.

"How are you feeling?" Derek asked, his voice laced with concern.

"Like crap," Callan said. He rolled onto his side, wincing as colorful spots danced before his eyes. Gods, how he hated being so fucking helpless. He wasn't even wounded, really, yet he could barely stay conscious, let alone move. "How's your shoulder?"

Derek sat a few paces away, leaning on the wall, chained in much the same manner. Pale and dirty, he looked only marginally better than Callan felt.

"As well as can be expected," he said, which probably meant it hurt like hell.

Their prison was small and cramped, only a few feet wide. Judging by the smell of the rotten straw, it hadn't been used in a while. A bucket of water had been left in the corner between them, just within range of their chains. But at least they were together—for the time being.

"Listen," Callan began, his voice scratchy as dry sand.

But he didn't have the chance to tell Derek everything he wanted, for at that moment, the door opened and Logitt came inside, the hem of her fur-lined wool cloak trailing behind her in the mud. Callan caught a glimpse of armed guards just outside, but the door shut behind the clan elder almost instantly.

"You're awake. Good," she said, raking him with her watery blue eyes.

Anxiety spiked and his pulse quickened. Callan hated to admit it even to himself, but Logitt terrified him far more than Aegir ever could.

His own obscure connection to magic notwithstanding, Callan knew why witchcraft had been forbidden throughout the realm for generations. It was dangerous, unpredictable, corrupting. These were the reasons why he'd fought so hard to quell every trace of it in his own blood. An unwanted legacy of darker times, it threatened to overwhelm him if he wasn't careful, yet it eluded him the only time he'd called upon it willingly.

Not the only time. That time when Derek had come upon the wolf in the forest, Callan had drawn upon the dormant magic. But it wasn't really witchcraft, was it? He hadn't actually talked to the wolf, or commanded it, like the young Undin witch had done with his horse. The wolf had simply...understood.

He recoiled—or at least tried to—when the old woman knelt by his side, but she pressed a warm, dry palm against his forehead, easily overpowering him. Pain exploded behind his eyes, as if a spike had been driven right through his brain, and he couldn't hold back a gasp.

"What are you doing to him?" Derek demanded. His chain rattled as he pushed himself upright.

"Hush, child," Logitt said, her thick accent making the words sound almost foreign, even though she answered him in the common tongue. She brought her face closer to Callan's, watching him carefully, as if measuring every infinitesimal reaction, the depth of every breath. "I'm healing him. He was hit too hard on the head. It will wear off soon enough on its own, but magic speeds things up."

It was more than he could take. Callan thrashed, clawing futilely at the straw, but then the pain receded as quickly as it had sprung. He slumped on his back, gulping air—but his headache was gone, as was the nausea. He could focus on minute details once more, and all the little sounds around him were crisp and clear, instead of reaching him as if from underwater.

"Callan?" Derek said tentatively. The chains were too short for them to actually touch each other, and in any case, displays of affection, even simple concern, under the Agiennan woman's intent gaze would be dangerous. Despite his best intentions, Derek was making it increasingly difficult for Callan to convince the Agiennans there was nothing between them but mutual antipathy. It was hard enough to fake as it was, and he pushed the thought firmly down.

"I'm all right," he rasped. "I'm all right."

A shiver went through his body at the notion of her using witchcraft on him, as if he could feel its tainted residue on his skin. But there was no denying it had worked, even if he was still too feeble to move.

"Why would you heal him?" Derek asked Logitt suspiciously. "He's your enemy. Your chieftain hates him."

"Yes, he does," the woman said as she rose. "He wants to see if the wolf can fly like an eagle."

"What does that mean?" Derek demanded, but the healer didn't answer.

Callan shut his eyes briefly, suppressing a shudder. He could have told him exactly what it meant but didn't. Executions, even those of spies and prisoners of war, were rare in Agienna, but they were always brutal—and the "blood eagle" death, wherein the victim's ribs were cut from the spine and pulled apart in a mockery of wings, was perhaps the most gruesome of all.

Logitt knelt beside Derek next. He flinched at her touch, but she hushed him again and put her hand on his left shoulder, murmuring some sort of a spell. Derek arched, convulsing with what had to be agony, and then sagged against the wall, wheezing.

"Rest," Logitt threw behind her shoulder as she headed for the exit.

"My shoulder," Derek said wonderingly as the door closed and they were alone once again. He raised his left arm and flexed his fingers, looking at it as if he'd grown a new limb. "She really did heal it. I didn't...believe it was possible."

"Don't trust her," Callan pushed out. "Don't trust her magic. I don't know why she did that or what they have in store for you, but you have to try and get away."

"I'm not leaving without you," Derek said stubbornly, tearing his eyes away from inspecting his newly healed arm.

"Yes, you are," Callan bit out. "You've heard her. Aegir won't listen to anyone. He wants my blood, and frankly, I can't blame him."

"She might have said it just to scare you," Derek said firmly, with a conviction as false as the intention behind it was heartfelt. "I saw the faces of all those other people who were sitting there with Aegir. They are as disinclined to engage in another conflict with Mulberny as we are with them. He's the only one who's pushing for it. The others aren't as blinded by anger as he is; they wouldn't let him execute you on a whim."

Callan shook his head. He didn't fail to notice Derek had said "we," and that small word pierced his heart with the simplicity of its meaning. But there could be no "we" for them now, and the realization cut as deep as any sword. He'd been too proud, too self-absorbed to see what a precious gift he'd been given the day the priestess joined his and Derek's hands together, and now it was too late to beg the gods for another pass. He'd squandered all his chances, save this last one.

Whatever the reason behind Logitt's benevolence in healing his concussion, now he was able to think clearly once again, his mind unclouded by the fog of pain and disorientation—at least until the torture started. It was a narrow window of opportunity, but he had to take advantage of it to make sure Derek didn't share in his fate.

"Promise me," he said, dropping his voice, "that you won't show them we care for each other. The only way for you to survive this is if they think this marriage is nothing more to us than a seal on paper."

There was a pause as Derek seemed to consider his words.

"Do we?" he asked finally. His voice was low as well, almost intimate. "Care for each other?"

Callan realized, with a pang of regret, that he'd never hear him use this tone of voice under different circumstances, in another sort of darkness.

"I do," Callan said.

Only two little words. Saying them aloud was like tearing a protective layer off his soul, leaving it raw and exposed, yet they'd never felt more right than at this moment.

"I do too," Derek said softly, a heartbeat later, and for the first time since their capture, Callan found himself fighting back tears.

Chapter Eleven

THEY'D TAKEN CALLAN away just as evening was setting in. Panicked, Derek had tried to object, to demand the guards tell him what was going on, but they ignored him as they would a yapping dog. Callan had thrown him a quelling look, and Derek clamped down on his outrage, if not his worry.

He fidgeted, wide-awake despite the late hour, his heart racing. He strained to hear what was going on outside his small prison but could hear no roar of an incensed crowd clamoring for blood. Either the execution was taking place somewhere farther away, or it had not happened yet.

With every ounce of his being, he prayed for the latter. But prayers were not enough. The gods never answered prayers that weren't backed by actions, and as usual, he only had his own acumen to count on to get Callan out of this mess.

He knew Callan was certain this was the end for him. He'd seen the bleakness in his eyes, born not of despair, but of acceptance. Callan had steeled himself for the punishment he believed was his due, for the death he'd been courting his entire life.

Well, fuck that. Derek wasn't going to take the solution Callan had proposed, serving as a harbinger of tragedy to be sent back to Duke Bergen. For Derek, their earlier whispered "I do's" hadn't been a goodbye; they'd been a promise, and he was damned if he'd break it while he still breathed.

The dull pain, his constant companion since the arrow had gone through his shoulder at Laurel Falls, was gone. Derek tried not to dwell on the reason why the witch had bothered to heal it; for now, it was enough that his arm was as strong as it'd ever been. The cut on his thigh still smarted when he moved, but the pain was bearable.

The chain attached to the metal cuff around his left ankle was bolted to the wall. Made of sturdy metal links, it was rusty with age and disuse, as were the bolts that held it in place. He could try to yank it off the wall, but there'd be no hiding the racket. The guard stationed outside the door would be on him in moments, and he wasn't deluded enough to think he could overpower him bare-handed—or, indeed, at all.

Perhaps he could try talking to the clan elders, appeal to their common sense, make them see Callan was not the man they thought he was. He could promise to broker some sort of renewed understanding between the Danulf and Mulberny, one that wouldn't be fraught with prejudice and distrust. But he had to do it as fast as possible and be clever enough not to let his desperation show.

After a few minutes, the guard unlocked the door in response to Derek's insistent shouting.

"I want to speak with somebody," Derek said quickly, before the burly Agiennan could shut him up with a well-aimed slap. "Somebody from the council. I have important things I want to discuss with them."

He didn't know whether the man understood him, but he shut the door again, plunging the space into complete darkness. The hut had no windows, and the only source of illumination was the thin crack under the door.

He shouted some more, to emphasize his point, but for long minutes nothing happened. Maybe simply trying to pull the chain wouldn't be such a bad idea after all since he was being ignored anyway. He was seriously considering it when the door opened again, snapping his attention.

Logitt stepped inside, carrying a clay oil lamp. The tiny flame cast harsh shadows into the recesses of her wrinkled face, giving it a sinister appearance, though Derek suspected some of the effect was generated by his own imagination. With the practice of magic forbidden throughout Ivicia, these had been his first direct encounters with it, and he couldn't quite hide the deeply ingrained fear they inspired.

"You're a fussy one," the woman observed, regarding him dispassionately as Derek cowered before her on the straw-covered floor. "What do you want?"

She wasn't the one he'd hoped to speak with, but he had a feeling no one else was coming.

He recalled Mathis's words, about witches going mad, succumbing to their magic. But Logitt didn't seem in any way unsound. If anything, her gaze was only too sharp and cunning for his comfort.

"First of all, I want to know where your people had taken my husband," he said, sitting upright with as much dignity as he could muster. "Is he dead?"

"Not yet," Logitt said.

It wasn't a very satisfactory answer, but Derek was willing to take what he could if it meant Callan was still alive.

"I know you don't like him," Derek said. "Believe me, I can understand the sentiment. But you have to ask yourself, is the death of one man worth the lives of so many people who are going to carry the brunt of another war? You have the perfect chance to change the tide for all of Agienna. If you release us and prove your good faith both to the Duke of Mulberny and the High Queen of Ivicia, you have my word that the terms of the peace treaty will be amended. There shouldn't have to be any more bloodshed for Agienna to prosper again."

"Your word?" Logitt repeated. She knelt before Derek with much less effort than he would've expected for someone her age, and brought the flame closer to his face, making him blink and squint against the light. "The elders of the clan will not respect your word. To them, you're nothing but a child hiding behind a meaningless title, a sparrow caught up in a murder of ravens. Now, your husband... We've taken *his* word. Do you know why?"

Derek shook his head, mesmerized by the fire's reflection in Logitt's pale eyes.

"Because he's our kin. The Dukes of Mulberny, as they call themselves now, came from these Isles centuries ago, before your great unified realm ever existed. They were witches, mindbenders, sorcerers. Oh, they want so badly to forget it. They call it a curse and try to deny the magic that flows in their veins, to erase the time when they ran with the wolves and called upon winds and rain, but it still sings in their blood, even if it takes different forms now."

Logitt's words resonated weirdly with what Callan had done what seemed like eons ago, on the night when Derek had come upon the lone wolf in the woods. But he said nothing to Logitt about it. It felt much too private to be shared with anyone.

"We believed Duke Bergen when he forced us to sign that miserable treaty, promising us prosperity. But in reality, it cut us off from all trade and fishery by forbidding us to come near the shores of Mulberny. We believed his son when he vowed to build a new future with one of our daughters. But yet again, they've shown how little they care for those who were once their people. The war might be over, but we are still starving because of Bergen's decrees, and Idona of the Danulf is dead. No words can change that. The hope we had for a new future is gone."

Derek licked his lips nervously. He could try arguing with her, but he sensed it would be futile. He was painfully used to his arguments being ignored.

"If I'm so insignificant to you, why did Aegir have the Undin kidnap me?" he asked.

"Aegir doesn't command the Undin. No doubt they realized the Danulf would pay a pretty price for Callan and seized the opportunity. You were merely collateral."

That left Derek puzzled. Whatever the Undin wanted with him, they'd targeted him specifically. Callan and Leandre coming to his aid with such disastrous consequences had not factored into their plans, as far as he could tell. No doubt, Callan was a much bigger prize, and that had made them change their course for promise of a larger profit. But their original intent regarding Derek remained a mystery since it was clear either the Danulf had no hand in it, or Logitt was badly misinformed. Whatever had transpired, Derek refused to be the cause of Callan's downfall.

"You can't just kill him," he said, putting every ounce of his conviction into the plea. "Please."

There was a pause as the old witch studied his face by the flickering light of the homemade lamp.

"Blood begets blood," she said finally. "There's no breaking that cycle—not until the Mulbernians look back to their past and honor it, until they see us as kin and do right by us, accepting their 'curse' as their birthright. Only then can our trust be rebuilt and the course of the future set on a different path."

"But Callan can't do any of those things if he's dead!"

"As I said, he's not dead yet, and neither are you, little lordling." Logitt rose to her feet and headed for the door without so much as a backward glance. "Remember, I didn't waste my magic on you for nothing."

LONG HOURS PASSED, and the world outside grew quiet, with only the distant hooting of an owl somewhere in the forest that surrounded the village breaking the silence. A tiny flame still flickered in the oil lamp Logitt had forgotten on the floor beside him.

He knew he should get some sleep, but he was too anxious to relax, despite the exhaustion. Every time he closed his eyes, he pictured his mother crying, his siblings (yes, even Macon) holding a funeral vigil with an empty casket. He imagined Callan kneeling before Aegir as the chieftain raised his battle-ax, and opened his eyes quickly so as to not see the rest.

Somehow, over the course of the last few chaotic days, his feelings toward his arranged husband had changed. He'd gotten to know something of the man beneath the cold, sometimes menacing exterior. Certainly not everything, but enough to want to find out more about him. To want *him*, and not just in a sensual way—though there was no denying the physical attraction. Lust, Derek could deal with, but these tentative feelings he was afraid to put a name to were entirely new to him. He couldn't have denied them even had they been one-sided—which, by Callan's own admission, they weren't. Callan had come to his rescue when Derek needed him and was now about to pay the ultimate price for his unfortunate attachment.

The thought of losing him was far more terrifying than the fear of his own uncertain future. Derek's failure at diplomacy didn't mean he could give up. He wouldn't sit here and bemoan his own helplessness.

He sat up and cast about his empty cell with renewed determination, making use of the feeble light from the lamp. But there was nothing he could use to pry the shackle open without drawing the guard's attention. The locked door was the only way out. His clothes were filthy and torn, he was barefoot and shackled, and all he had at his immediate disposal were straw and a bucket of stale water.

None of it was particularly helpful. Pushing down on growing despair, he forced himself to calm down and think, until his gaze fell again on the oil lamp. The thick wick, sticking out of a hole in the clay dish, burned steadily.

Derek stared at orange flame, his thoughts racing. Maybe the witch hadn't forgotten the lamp. Maybe she'd left it on purpose—and he could use it to his advantage. Stealth wasn't the way to go about it at all; what he needed was a distraction, and the larger, the better.

Not giving himself the chance to consider how risky the idea was, he kicked the lamp hard with his left foot. The lamp landed on the pile of straw that'd served as Callan's pallet, the oil splashing. Fire caught on to it immediately, but for a moment, it seemed as if the straw might be too damp to support it.

Don't die out, don't die out. Derek pushed himself to his feet and upended the water bucket onto his own pile of straw. Then he crouched and blew on the tiny flames until they took hold.

Blood pounding in his ears, he waited, watching the fire build until the waves of heat rolled over his face. Finally, judging the situation to appear dire enough (which it undoubtedly was, considering he was trapped and practically tied to one spot), he took a deep breath and screamed.

"Fire! Help! Anybody!"

A few seconds later the door opened, and the guard poked his head inside. All traces of sleepiness and irritation evaporated from his bearded face as he caught sight of the flames licking the ceiling beams.

"Please, undo me! I'm going to burn!" Derek pleaded, wide-eyed, injecting as much panic as he could into his voice. To emphasize his words, he yanked at the chain as he backed away from the fire, clutching at the bucket he pretended to have used to douse it, and whimpering with fear that was only half-feigned.

The guard glanced at the bucket, but it was decidedly empty, and there'd hardly be any time to fetch another one.

With what Derek assumed to be profuse swearing, the man crossed the cell and bent beside him to undo the leg cuff with a pin key.

Derek raised the bucket and brought it down hard on the guard's head. The man toppled into the wet straw by Derek's feet, the pin flying out of his slackened hand.

Derek hissed in frustration and dropped to his knees, sifting through the straw. Acrid smoke burned his eyes and nostrils, making him cough violently. His hands were shaking with the surge of genuine fear, but finally, he managed to fish out the long rusty pin and hurriedly unlock the cuff. He gripped the unconscious guard under his arms and dragged him outside, leaving him well away from the little prison that was nothing more than an outbuilding of the chieftain's main hall. Enemy or not, the man had tried to help him, and Derek wasn't about to let him be burned alive.

Shutting the door behind him to contain the fire for a few more minutes, Derek glanced around furtively, shivering with the sudden chill. The backyard of the large house was deserted save for a few stray rats and empty carts. No one had spotted him yet, but the hardest part would be finding where Callan was being kept before someone caught a whiff of the smoke or discovered the fire. Guided by the moon and the faint glare from the burning structure, he circled the yard, keeping to the deeper shadows.

Could Callan be inside the hall? No doubt, there'd be people sleeping inside it at this hour, and Derek was afraid to try to find his way in an unfamiliar space, full of potentially hostile and pissed-off people. There were no windows, only skylights that were too high on the wall for him to peek through, so he crept around the long house until he reached the wide-open yard around the front steps.

A low fire, barely more than glowing embers, was burning in a deep pit at the center of the yard. Behind it, under the shallow stairs that led inside the hall, stood a high pillory with a man slumped against it, his neck and wrists trapped in round holes formed by two heavy boards. It was positioned so he could only stand, leaning on the supporting pole that was rooted deep in the ground. The man was stripped to his waist, his dark matted hair obscuring his face, but Derek had no doubt who the unlucky prisoner was.

He bit his lips to stop from calling out Callan's name, and hunkered further in the shadow of the wall. But there was no one around, not even a single guard. Callan was alive, his chest rising and falling steadily. It wasn't too late to save him.

After assessing the path was clear, Derek hurried toward the pillory, keeping low. The boards were held together by a metal pin through two metal loops—not an intricate lock, but one the prisoner had no hopes of reaching with his hands sticking out alongside his head. When Derek tried to pull it out, however, it wouldn't budge. It had probably been hammered in place with a mallet rather than pushed in by hand.

Callan lifted his head slowly, roused by the noise.

"Derek?" he whispered. His eyes widened in alarm, but the corners of his mouth tugged in a smile, so incongruous in his dirt-smeared face. "How?"

"I'll tell you later." Derek wrinkled his nose. "What's that smell?"

"Piss," Callan said succinctly.

A wave of anger rose in Derek as he guessed not all of it was likely Callan's. Irrational, seeing as the main point of a pillory was public humiliation. But he couldn't reconcile himself to the thought that Callan, always so poised and dignified, had been forced to endure it.

"They tortured you?"

"Not really."

He had been beaten, though; ugly bruises were starting to form on his face and arms. Considering Callan's state, Derek dearly hoped he'd never have to see what the aftermath of "real torture" looked like. At least he didn't appear to have been flogged.

"Damn it, it's too tight." Derek huffed in frustration as his nails scraped against the rusty metal when he tried pulling on the pinhead.

Raised voices came from behind the main hall, the fire having no doubt been discovered. Derek had to do something fast, before someone came running through the yard and caught them in the act. "Damn it!"

"What's happening?"

"There's a fire in the prison."

Giving up on attempting to pull the pin out, Derek grabbed a stone from around the fire pit and hit the underside of the pin, forcing it upward through the loop.

"You set the prison on fire?" Callan asked incredulously.

Derek risked a quick look at the strange expression on Callan's face, suspended between bewilderment and admiration. It made something hidden and repressed in Derek's soul unfurl.

He averted his eyes, concentrating on the task at hand before he was driven to distraction. In any case, it wasn't as if he could take full credit for Logitt's unexpected assistance or the guard's lack of vigilance.

The commotion was growing larger, and with it the danger of discovery. And still the damn pin was stuck in the loops. Derek hit it with everything he had, giving up on keeping it quiet. With all the racket coming from the backyard, it hardly mattered.

Callan's hands flexed in the pillory holes, curling into fists.

"Leave it. They'll be here any second. You have to get away."

Derek didn't deign to respond. Instead, he dropped the stone and pulled at the now protruding top end of the pin, grunting with the effort and scratching his fingertips raw against the rough metal. He staggered backward when it came loose and hurried to fling back the upper board that pressed down on Callan's neck.

Finally free, Callan stepped back with a moan, raising his head and flexing his back. Derek could practically hear his cramped muscles unlocking, but he had no time to ogle his husband's powerful frame. He took Callan's hand, and they ran together past the stockade into the dark woods.

Chapter Twelve

CIRDA WAS AN island. There was nowhere to go save for the thick forest that covered the higher northern area, in the opposite direction from where the longships and boats were moored. At some point they'd have to double back, most likely running into the search party hot on their heels, but it wasn't as if they'd had a chance to think their plan through.

They were running hard, hands still clasped, stones and twigs biting into their bare feet. Derek's labored breathing, interrupted with curses as he stumbled and nearly fell, filled the air. Callan's vision adjusted easily to the darkness, always had. He didn't want to dwell on the reason, but at the moment, it was a blessing rather than a cause for concern. He pulled Derek along, choosing the easiest path in the undergrowth over mossy stones and wet earth as the ground gradually sloped upward. Every muscle in his body screamed in protest, but he didn't let himself slow down until they were far enough from any signs of habitation. By now, the Danulf must have found both their prisoners gone. They would see that no boats were missing from the harbor, and the next step would be hunting them down. As big as the island was, Callan doubted he and Derek could outrun the hounds.

"Stop," Derek panted, and Callan halted. Tall pines loomed around them like the pillars of some mysterious chamber, silent and ominous. Somewhere in the distance, a wolf howled, a lonely, desolate sound in near complete silence. It was so quiet Callan was sure the frantic beating of their hearts must echo through the woods, betraying their whereabouts as surely as their scent.

Without saying another word, Derek tugged on his hand, drawing him closer into an unexpected embrace. Callan hesitated for only a heartbeat before closing his arms around him, squeezing so hard it was bound to hurt, but Derek didn't pull away. Instead, he buried his face against Callan's shoulder and shuddered as a sob tore out of him.

Callan closed his eyes, reveling in the feel of Derek's hair against his cheek, the sensation of stubble rubbing against the skin of his neck in time with Derek's ragged breathing. They were both filthy, stinking like something dragged out of a refuse pit, but neither of them cared.

He didn't know how long they stood there, holding on to each other on the boundary between shade and moonlight. Finally Derek stepped back, looking up at him, his eyes slightly puffy, but didn't let go entirely, his hands lingering on Callan's upper arms.

"What now?" he whispered.

Callan took a deep breath. Derek had done his part, and now it was up to him to come through if they had any hope of getting off this island alive. He had to put aside the unpleasant memories of being pilloried and the guilt and grief over the death of his dearest friend, and focus on what lay ahead. Derek was with him, unharmed and well, and that was all that mattered. Callan had been perfectly willing to accept whatever punishment Aegir would mete out, but Derek's determination to rescue him fueled his own resistance to this fate.

"We can't hole up and wait for the storm to pass," he said. "They'll tear Cirda apart searching for us. We must leave, and the harbor is the only way out."

"Wouldn't they be guarding the boats, though?" Derek frowned. "Even the fishing sloops. It'll be nigh impossible to steal one if they'd be expecting us to do so."

"We must get to one, but not to steal it," Callan said. "If we cut it loose, it'll create a distraction that'd shift their attention elsewhere while we get onto one of the larger ships and hide in the cargo hold."

"Like stowaways?"

Callan nodded. "These ships are not exactly spacious, and we'd be at a high risk of exposure. But I don't see any other way. We'd stand a much better chance of slipping by unnoticed at any other port but here."

"All right." Derek finally released him, and then looked around, as if taking in their surroundings for the first time. "How do we get back from here?"

He seemed to have taken Callan's plan in a stride, despite how shaky it was. Callan wasn't sure he deserved the vote of confidence, but he was grateful for Derek's willingness to go along with his proposal.

Had Callan really thought him timid and spiritless? He should fall on his knees, thanking every deity he could think of for bringing Derek into his life. He'd believed no one could compare to Idona, and Derek was so different than her. But they shared all the truly important things—courage, intelligence, kindness. Callan had never wanted to marry Derek, but as it turned out, he couldn't have wished for a finer man as his husband.

Maybe, just maybe, he could hope to get to know him even better, both as his friend and his proper spouse. And all he had to do was keep him alive. Keep them both alive.

Callan knew Cirda Island well enough, but the majority of that knowledge was theoretical. He hadn't spent nearly enough time in these woods to be certain they wouldn't end up lost. But there was no other choice but to pick a direction that would take them to the harbor while keeping them safely away from the main village and the surrounding homesteads, closer to the island's eastern shore.

"Gods, I'm so thirsty," Derek muttered when they started out at a much slower pace than before. "Should've drunk some of that water before spilling it."

Callan smiled despite himself, ducking under a branch. This was the first time Derek had complained about anything in his hearing, and he was unexpectedly touched by the small show of trust.

"I'm thirsty too," he confessed. "And I'd kill for a bath."

"No kidding," Derek said, following closely on his heels. He was groping blindly in the thicket, struggling to keep up. "Next time we're captured by formidable clansmen with a personal grudge against you, could you at least choose the ones who might not take you for a chamber pot?"

"I'll be sure to do that," Callan said, matching the mock gravity of his tone and swatting low hanging branches out of his way.

Soon, however, the terrain became too rugged for divided attention, and they fell silent as they trudged through the blanket of fallen pine needles. The trees grew sparser as they climbed steadily uphill, and the stars peeked from behind the branches, dispassionately following their path.

After about an hour they stopped to rest and assess their progress at a stony outcrop. The island was spread before them, the thick forest a slightly different shade of black than the sea that surrounded it, most of its vast expanse lying behind them to the north. To the southwest lay the main village where fires had sprung up despite the late (or rather early) hour. The curved line of the natural harbor was invisible from this vantage point. The more distant farms and smaller hamlets, connected to the larger settlement by a network of narrow roads that cut through the woodland and whatever pastures the island had to offer, were still asleep, oblivious to the prisoners' arrival and their unlikely escape. To the east, far beyond the calm sea, the edge of the sky was suffused with the pale gray light of predawn.

They'd have to climb down again, but at least now Callan had a clear idea of the direction—going by the side of the eastern cliffs would take them to the harbor without risking coming too close to the village, even though it would be quite a detour. Considering the state they were in, it'd take them much longer to cover the stretch of ground, and the danger of discovery was growing by the minute, but there was hardly any choice.

After a short while, they came upon a tiny stream, half-hidden amid tree roots and foliage. The water was a little muddy, but they drank anyway before continuing on.

"Cirda is actually one of the isles closest to the coast of Mulberny. Most of Agienna lies farther north and to the west," Callan said, mainly to distract himself from his bleeding feet.

"I've never traveled by sea before," Derek said. "The farthest I've been from home was when my father took me to Oifel for the High Queen's vicennial reign celebration."

He hesitated a fraction before adding: "That's where I first saw you, actually. I remember you arriving at the welcome banquet with the duke."

"Really?" Callan frowned. "The celebration was five years ago."

"I don't know if anyone has ever told you, but you're somewhat hard to forget."

Callan snorted, but he was weirdly pleased by the compliment. There were quite a number of people who've had a hard time forgetting him and letting go of their grudges, but he knew that wasn't what Derek meant.

He wracked his brain trying to think back on that long-ago visit to Oifel. Adele had been too young to go and be introduced to the court properly, so it'd been only him and his father at the Queen's celebration. Derek couldn't have been much older than she was now. But Callan couldn't remember him at all. He didn't even recall seeing the late Count Johan there—not that he'd been socializing much with the other courtiers. It'd been a fraught time, with the war with Agienna still raging, and their stay at the capital barely extended beyond paying their respects to the Queen.

If he'd only been paying attention then, his life could've been different. If he'd met Derek then—but no. Back then he would've been too dismissive of the shy youth Derek must have been, just like he'd been dismissive of the man when he'd first met him. They both would've been too young to see beyond the superficial, and now...now it might be too late for them to explore the opportunity. Perhaps it'd been too late for them even before they'd been brought to this gods-forsaken island.

"What's that?" Derek said, stopping.

Callan shook off the extraneous regrets and halted as well, listening to the rustles of the forest around them. Now he could hear it too—the far-off sound of barking.

"Fuck," he muttered. They were being hunted, and if they could hear the dogs, that meant pursuit was already too close on their heels. "Run!"

"Running" was probably too grand a name for their renewed mad dash through the trees, stumbling and falling and pulling each other up again. They were tired, bruised, and desperate, and there was no place to hide. The barking was getting closer, enough for Callan to discern shouts and raised voices behind the dogs.

Just half a step behind him, Derek stumbled over a thick root and fell, sprawling awkwardly. He grunted and rolled onto his back, drawing his leg up.

"Damn it!"

"Come on, get up," Callan said, grabbing his hand, but Derek shook his head, his face shrouded in deep shadow.

"No, don't. I think I sprained my ankle. I'll slow you down."

Callan would've been offended at the suggestion if they'd any time at all to spend on hurt feelings, but as things stood, he could only bodily lift Derek up and drag him along, supporting his weight as much as he could without actually carrying him. Cursing under his breath, the other man limped beside him, slinging his arm around Callan's naked shoulders as they struggled to keep going. Derek's heart hammered against his straining rib cage like a frightened bird, echoing Callan's own.

A wolf howled somewhere close by, in either a warning or a taunt to the hounds. Derek stopped so abruptly Callan missed his step, sending them both nearly tumbling again.

"Did you hear that?"

"I think the wolves are the least of our problems right now."

"No, listen." Derek gripped his hand, as if afraid Callan might recoil. "The elder, Logitt. She told me about your ancestors, that they were witches, mindbenders, whatever that meant. She said they used to run with the wolves, and the bond was still there. Maybe you could...reach out to them."

For a second, Callan thought someone must have struck him without him noticing, because all the air seemed to have been knocked out of his lungs, leaving him unable to breathe.

"There's no bond," he somehow managed to push out. "That's an old wives' tale, nothing more."

"You've done it before!" Derek said. "There's a wolf's head on your coat of arms, for gods' sake!"

"Lots of nobles have animals as their sigils! It doesn't signify anything! Yours is a sparrow—does it mean you can fly away?"

"You were with me that night when I came upon the white wolf in the woods. You talked to it!"

"I did not 'talk' to it!"

"Well, you did *something*! And if you could ask it to stand down, or whatever it was you did, you could ask the wolves to help us throw off the hunters," Derek said, his voice stern and pleading at the same time. "You could—"

"No."

Couldn't Derek bloody see what it was he was asking of him? Consorting with wild animals, using the dark magic of his feral ancestors that not even his father and his grandmother, the previous duchess, had openly acknowledged to him—it was a sure path to the madness of witchcraft. Every book he'd ever read on the subject warned against its inevitability. Even now he could feel the dark magic's tantalizing pull, the allure he'd resisted, consciously or not, his entire life. If he gave in to it, would he emerge as himself again, or would he succumb to the frenzy completely, becoming no more than a beast in human form?

Derek's grip on his hand tightened. There wasn't enough light yet to clearly distinguish the expression in his eyes, but the smell of his fear and frustration was palpable. The sounds of pursuit drew closer, the excitement of the hounds and the crash of human bodies through the thicket ripping through the night.

"If you *are* a witch, so what? I know you, Callan. You're far too decent to abuse your power. Whatever...potential, ability—call it what you will—that you have, it's a blessing, not a curse. What matters is how you use it."

Callan drew a shaky breath. Derek's eyes were nothing more than gleams in the darkness, but there was no guile in his voice.

"I trust you," Derek said, and those three little words, more precious and meaningful than any others, hit Callan like a battering ram, shattering all his carefully erected defenses.

His skin burned where Derek touched him, the awareness of his warmth seeping into muscle and sinew. It coursed through his blood, filling him with such buoyancy he felt like he could fly, while rooting him to the ground, anchoring him in the here and now rather than letting him roam the darkest recesses of his mind untethered. He closed his eyes, surrendering, welcoming the state of utter calm that had always been his companion in battle.

The world shifted. His pulse thrummed along with that of every living creature around him, the scent of their passage through the underbrush sharp in his nostrils. The eagerness of the dogs and the anger of the humans who ran behind them rippled through him, his heart speeding with the urge to flee, to hide from the coldness of their steel weapons, deadly and utterly foreign in these woods that teemed with life.

Derek's hand was like a brand, searing into his flesh. Callan's nostrils flared as his scent threatened to overpower him, sweet and tantalizing to the point of distraction. Heat pooled at the base of his spine, urging him to pounce, to claim, to sink into his body. Without thinking, he moved closer, crowding Derek.

Derek's smell changed subtly, but it wasn't with fear. It became ever sweeter, muskier, as if Callan's unconcealed arousal triggered his own, but instead of moving, either closer or away, he shook Callan's arm.

"Focus. There's no time for that now. They're almost upon us. Please, focus."

The words sounded foreign, and Callan struggled to decipher their meaning. But the human part of his brain that was still there understood, even if the rest of him didn't. He took a step back, tearing himself away from Derek with supreme effort, and reached out farther, seeking those who could hear his silent cry in the wilderness.

Help. I'm hunted. Help me.

And they answered. The wolves had roamed these hills since before Cirda was an island, since before humans had come with their ships and their axes, and they recognized one of their own. They turned, and they listened, and they came.

A howl went up somewhere to the south, much closer than anyone would wish to hear while traipsing through unknown woods, followed closely by another, and then another. The dogs' barking became frantic as shadows made of fur and bone surged between the trees, driven by Callan's plea. He bared his teeth, snarling along with them, tasting the blood in his mouth, the screams and shouts and yelps of pain and terror ringing in his ears.

Somebody was calling to him, repeating a name that sounded strange and familiar at the same time. He growled, a dangerous low sound reverberating in his throat—a warning. But the human ignored it, stepping in front of him, his eyes bright and beautiful like the stars that were gradually fading from the sky.

"Callan," he repeated, "Callan!"

Something snapped, and suddenly he was back, as if someone had reeled him into his own body. Callan gulped, sucking in air, cut off from his heightened senses. He clutched at Derek's shoulders, heaving and disoriented, his head spinning with the abrupt loss. This was worse than when he'd taken a hit to the head because now he couldn't take refuge in unconsciousness. Folding, he turned away and retched, coughing up water and acid.

"You're all right," Derek said, running his hands over Callan's hair and bare back. He was shaking as hard as his voice, but Callan couldn't sense why. "You're all right. Come on."

Callan nodded and pushed himself upright. Clutching at each other, they stumbled onward, upward, the receding darkness behind them ringing with wails.

The rising sun touched the horizon as the forest opened before them. They came upon a clearing at the edge of a cliff and collapsed in the high grass that rippled with a fresh morning breeze.

Callan whimpered, burying his face in the wet earth. Next to him, Derek's breaths were coming out like ragged moans.

What did I just do?

He didn't want to know the answer. He didn't want to think about it. They were both still alive, and that was everything that mattered.

No, not everything. He rolled, facing Derek, and reached out to him with a trembling hand, already bracing himself for rejection, inevitable now that he'd exposed the abomination lurking inside him.

But the rejection never came. Derek caught his hand, their fingers intertwining, and pulled him closer, so Callan was lying almost on top of him. Instead of hate or disgust, there was a strange look in his eyes, raw and needy and tender, and then he closed the distance between them and pressed his blistered lips against Callan's.

It was probably as far from an ideal romantic kiss as it could possibly be, but it was also so much more. They drank each other, their lips and tongues meeting in a dance, overwhelming in its newness and yet as familiar as if they'd done it for years, parting only when there was simply not enough air to continue.

Gazing at him from below, Derek lifted a hand to smooth Callan's hair off his forehead. His features blurred, and Callan realized with a start he was crying. He couldn't tell precisely why—for relief, release, or regret.

"I..." he began, but the tears choked him, burning his throat.

"Me too," Derek said softly, destroying that last barrier between them, and then pulled him in for another kiss.

Chapter Thirteen

CALLAN DIDN'T ASK about what had happened in the woods when he called upon the wolves, and Derek didn't tell him, figuring he'd inquire about it when he was ready. It was clear Callan had a hard time reconciling his aversion to what he considered dark magic with whatever he'd awakened within himself in his desperate attempt to save them.

Derek couldn't help but feel a little guilty. He was the one who'd insisted Callan try it despite the man's unequivocal reluctance. But it had given them another chance at survival, a chance to show how they really felt, and he could never regret that. However it was all going to end, at least they'd know they'd come to care for one another.

It sounded so surreal, with them knowing each other for such a short period of time, having been married in such haste, but it didn't make it less true. Extreme circumstances were perhaps the best measure of a person's character, and their circumstances could've hardly been more extreme. Yet Callan had met them with unwavering dignity, with a selflessness that had left Derek smitten. If he were to search the entire realm of Ivicia far and wide, he wouldn't find another man worthier of his affections.

Whether Derek was worthy of Callan's affections was a different question entirely. If they ever returned home, perhaps Callan would reexamine his attachment with a more critical eye, inevitably finding Derek lacking—in looks, political capital, and character. But right now he tried not to dwell on future heartbreak. The present left no room for either joy or pensive reflection.

They trudged through the grasslands along the edge of the cliffs this side of the island, heading north. The near miss with the search party made them temporarily forgo the plans to sneak back to the harbor. The environs of the main village were too dangerous for them now. They had to either find a solution or a new plan, and soon. Derek's sprained ankle didn't allow him to do more than hop awkwardly, leaning heavily on the other man. He didn't want to think about how he was going to steal aboard a moored ship in this condition.

To distract himself from the pain, he threw a furtive glance at his husband. Callan's perfect profile was outlined against the blue-gray sky, the dark stubble standing out against pale skin. He looked tired, almost haggard.

Derek wanted nothing more than to kiss him again.

"You're staring," Callan said. He didn't turn to him, but the corners of his mouth tugged into a smile.

"You can't fault me for admiring the most beautiful thing on this blasted island," Derek said. Callan's taut muscles moved under Derek's arm where he was leaning on his shoulder, and he was momentarily distracted by the mental image of those strong arms wrapped around him, that powerful body pinning him down.

He wanted to live long enough to see how it'd feel in reality, if only for a short while.

"You have the worst taste."

"This coming from you," Derek said derisively.

Callan stopped and faced him, cupped the side of Derek's face, and tilted it upward, so he could meet his eyes. The look he wore was serious, almost grave, but the traces of the earlier smile still lingered on his lips.

"I'll have you know I have impeccable taste," he said and kissed him.

Derek responded readily, eagerly. He still couldn't quite believe he was kissing the very same man he'd had to reconcile himself to marrying only a week ago. But it felt so good, so *right*, that he didn't pause to wonder how he'd come to change his mind so drastically.

Finally, they broke apart, compelled by the rising sun to continue their miserable journey. Derek listened for sounds of pursuit, but none came. Whatever the outcome of the wolves' attack on the hunting party had been, at the very least they'd turned away from their quarry.

The ground gradually leveled, and at length, they came upon a rivulet that cut through the grass and cascaded in a thin stream into the sea below the cliffs. The water was clear and cold, and Derek had never tasted anything more delicious than that first sip. They both drank greedily and then followed the rivulet back into the thicket, wading in the shallow water to cool their battered feet and mask their scent as much as they could.

"We have to get some rest," Callan said once the trees closed around them again.

Derek nodded. As loath as he was to stop, there was no denying they were literally falling off their feet, especially him. So, instead of pushing forward, they found a narrow ravine where the stream almost disappeared beneath the mossy rocks. The bank of the ravine, held by the gnarled roots of a large tree, provided enough cover, at least at a casual glance, and while the wet earth and pine needles weren't the most comfortable bed, they could at least settle without getting muddy.

It was just for a few minutes, Derek told himself as he sat down heavily beside Callan, wincing at the pain that lanced through his leg. Just a few minutes to catch their breath and rest their aching muscles and clear their heads.

WHEN DEREK OPENED his eyes, the rays of light between the pines all fell at wrong angles. He started, sitting up from where he was pressed against Callan's warm, solid body.

"Shh," Callan said, putting a steadying hand on his shoulder. "It's all right."

"What time is it?" Derek asked, blinking owlishly and squinting at the light. "Have you slept at all?"

"Yes, don't worry. I'm fine. And I'm guessing it's early afternoon."

"Afternoon? We've slept through the day?"

He pushed himself upright and nearly fell. His ankle was badly swollen and hot to the touch, much worse than it'd been that morning, and the cut on his thigh threatened to open with every unwary move. He could stand, but only barely. Walking would be torment, even favoring his good left leg.

Callan got up and held him, putting his arm around his waist. His touch was fast becoming familiar, a soothing comfort it would be all too easy to get accustomed to.

"We needed it. And in any case, it's better if we move in the dark."

The sleep had gone long way in restoring their strength, but it'd been far from comfortable, and now hunger was beginning to make itself known. Derek hadn't eaten since they'd been fed dry fish on the raiders' ship, and for Callan it'd been even longer. If they were going to spend any more time on the island, they'd have to somehow forage for whatever food they could scrape up.

They started off again, following a deer trail that skirted the edge of the forest. The high cliffs receded into long miles of rocky beach, and they caught glimpses of the white-frothed green expanse of the sea amid the tree trunks. The sore ankle made it a very slow process; it seemed as though they'd barely covered any ground before the sky above the sea was turning purple and blue, and the water's brilliant green darkened into murky gray.

"Look," Callan said, stopping.

Derek lifted his head. He'd been too busy scanning the ground to prevent himself from tripping to pay much attention to what was going on around him, and, frankly, too preoccupied with the pain and the gnawing hunger.

Tiny lights flickered somewhere in the distance, and wisps of smoke rose from what had to be chimneys. It was the first sign of human habitation they'd come across since escaping.

"Is that a village?"

"If it is, it's a small one," Callan said. "Stay here. I'll go take a look."

As wary as Derek was of staying alone in a strange forest teeming with wild animals and people who were out to kill him, he wanted even less to appear like a whining weakling, so he nodded and sat down to wait.

Though he was grateful for a chance to rest his leg, Derek kept jumping at every sound. The shadows lengthened, and he was seriously considering going after Callan—even if it meant crawling on his hands and knees through the foliage and grass—when he finally returned, nearly crawling himself to avoid being spotted from the shore.

"It's a fishing village," Callan said in response to his questioning gaze. "Not much activity going on there except for a few folks tending goats and mending nets. I don't think they've heard anything about us yet."

"Do you think we might be able to steal some food?" Derek asked, though he wasn't thrilled about taking anything from people who were so poor. Their presence, however unwilling, had wreaked quite enough havoc on the denizens of Cirda.

"Actually, if we wait till sundown, I think we might be able to steal a boat," Callan said slowly, his blue eyes alight with something close to tentative hope.

"Really?" Derek's heart beat faster with both hope and dismay. Stealing a boat was a much graver crime than stealing a handful of beets and carrots. "I must warn you, though, I'm not much of a mariner. I can barely swim, much less sail a boat."

"I can navigate well enough if the sky is clear," Callan said. "But we're a two-day sail from the coast, at least. It's a no small risk."

The prospect of dying at sea was hardly better than dying on land, but their options were sadly limited. Any way that would take them off this damned island was bound to be fraught with mortal peril, and trusting their fate to a dingy fishing boat was no better or worse than cowering in the belly of an enemy ship, risking exposure.

"If you say it can be done, then that's what we'll do," Derek said, and Callan squeezed his hand briefly before helping him up again.

They hid behind a dune covered in tufts of yellowed grass, watching the village. It numbered only about half a dozen huts, perched on a rocky elevation above a beautiful beach, peppered with mooring posts. The fishermen were still out at sea, and Callan and Derek waited in tense silence as the sun began to set and dusk enveloped the houses and the compact sheep pens. It was fully dark by the time the boats began to come back to the shore one by one, to be met by spouses and children who hauled heavy buckets of the day's catch to the kitchens.

Night settled as the lights inside the little houses went out one by one and their inhabitants went to bed. Watching the simple routine, Derek wistfully recalled his old life in Camria. The details that had been so clear before had started to fade, washed away by new experiences like paints in a flood. His life, even in childhood, had never been uncomplicated, especially growing up as a sort of counterpoint to his father in all matters pertaining to their family, but until recently, it had been quiet enough to perhaps be considered boring.

He glanced at the man beside him, who was intently watching the village and the edge of the forest. Nothing about Callan was boring, from his striking good looks to his tumultuous past. Even his droll and arrogant attitude had been only a mask that concealed how much Callan really cared—for his people, for his comrades-at-arms, for his late wife. For Derek, though only gods knew what he'd done to deserve such devotion.

Driven by a protective instinct, he moved closer to his husband. The cold breeze had gotten under his own tattered shirt, making him shiver. Callan, who was half-naked, must have been freezing.

Callan flashed him a distracted smile that made Derek's heart skip a beat. His beauty was still undeniable, though he stood there dirty, bruised, and ragged, but when he smiled, Derek was truly and utterly lost.

"Ready?" Callan whispered, and Derek nodded. At that moment, he'd follow Callan into the fires of hell, should he suggest it.

But Callan's intention was far more practical. Keeping low, they slunk toward the water edge where the boats were moored, rocking serenely. The remote location of the village meant no one would be watching for possible thieves; not even a dog's bark disturbed the peace.

They chose one of the boats that were moored farthest from the houses, with Callan picking the sturdiest-looking one. They took out the nets and every bit of fishing tackle they could see in the moonlight, leaving it on the sand, and then untied the boat and pushed it out into the sea.

The oars felt unexpectedly heavy in Derek's hands. This was nothing like the carefree summer sailing outings on the lake outside the castle in Camria. Sitting low in the water, these boats were much more robust, almost unwieldy for an inexperienced sailor. Thankfully, Callan seemed to be much more familiar with the vessel, and he was steering it with a confidence Derek could only envy, despite being no less physically wrung out. He couldn't quite adjust to the fact that he now had free use of his shoulder and had to consciously remind himself of it when he rowed.

The moon shone brightly, leaving an ephemeral trail that spanned the inky expanse all the way to the horizon, its thin line separating the darkness of the water from that of the star-studded sky. With every stroke of the oars, the shore drifted farther and farther away until it was barely visible.

"I can't believe we did it." Derek's voice carried on the water, and he flinched at how loud he sounded. "We got away. It was almost too easy."

"We're not out of danger yet," Callan said. The muscles of his back bunched and flexed as his oar rose and fell. "The most important thing now is to stay on course and pray they didn't send ships to patrol the coast."

"I didn't know you prayed," Derek said half-jokingly, mostly as a distraction from the ache building in his arms and the throbbing in his abused ankle.

There was a long pause, accentuated by the rhythmic splashes of water.

"I do sometimes," Callan said, sounding oddly shy. "When I'm desperate enough to forget how rarely the gods listen. Ever since I learned you'd been kidnapped, I've been praying for the gods to keep you alive. Perhaps this time they didn't turn away from me."

A pang of shared sorrow lanced through Derek at the mention of "this time." Callan must have prayed for Idona's life as well, to no avail. It was small wonder he was mistrustful of the gods' providence. But they were here, alive, together, be it for the grace of a deity, or by their own daring.

"I don't understand. Why kidnap me at all?" The question still weighed on Derek's mind, even if the matter was devoid of its earlier urgency.

"The Undin probably did it in hopes of ransom."

"They sure went to a lot of trouble," Derek said, frowning to himself. Even allowing for the idea that his family could afford a ransom payment or that Duke Bergen would be willing to help, the reward could hardly be worth the risk of sneaking into a Mulbernian city in disguise and bringing a witch with them. "Someone devised a pretty elaborate scheme, with the fake letter and everything. They'd have to have been very cognizant of my situation with my siblings to come up with something like that."

"We'll have to look into it more closely if we ever come back to Bryluen," Callan said. "I'm certain Lady Elsie will have dug into it already."

"*When* we come back," Derek corrected him stubbornly. There was no way they'd gone through everything just to fail when they were so close.

"When we come back," Callan agreed, the smile evident in his voice though it was too dark to see.

THE MORNING GREETED them with a rosy glow lighting up the water's edge and the white sails of a ship in the distance.

At first Derek was afraid it was an Agiennan longship, sent in pursuit. But the silhouette was entirely different, with three tall masts and an unadorned bowsprit. The rectangular sails bore the stylized shape of a seagull, marking it as a merchant ship from Hundara, a coastal fiefdom farther south of Mulberny. It was most likely back from its journey to trade for timber and furs with the nomads of the northern plains.

As tired as they were, they made as much noise as they could, shouting and waving a dirty rag until the ship turned in their direction. Then it was only a matter of Callan announcing himself and promising a large reward for their safe passage to Mulberny. A short explanation of their predicament was thankfully enough to convince the captain to make the detour, considering Irthorg wouldn't take them too far out of their way.

Derek kept looking back, waiting for Agiennan ships to spring out of the waves and block their path, but the sea around them was empty and as calm as they could wish for. So he allowed himself to be led to the hold after Callan, to be watered and fed. It was basic sailor fare—salted meat and dried fruit—but even that felt like a feast. After the meal, he fell asleep stretched out beside Callan on a makeshift pallet in the belly of a foreign ship, lulled by the gently rocking motion and the sense of safety. He wished they could stay like that, cocooned in each other's arms, for a little while longer before facing whatever the new day would bring.

Chapter Fourteen

"THIS KIND OF insult to Mulberny cannot stand," Duke Bergen said.

Callan sighed inwardly. He could well understand the rage his father felt upon hearing that both his son and son-in-law had been abducted and taken into enemy territory, and that rage could hardly be quelled by the bedraggled state in which Callan had returned home. Even though he hadn't been seriously injured, there was no hiding the scrapes and bruises, the chaffing on his neck and wrists from the long hours spent in the pillory. Every argument Callan had offered by way of justifying Aegir's actions against him only served to incense the duke further, and he'd prudently given up on that particular avenue of reasoning. But he wasn't about to concede his maltreatment as the cause for another war.

"The High Queen will not be pleased with another conflict," he said, doing his best to appeal to his father's political sense—which was as sharp as the rest of his faculties, if not sharper. "The current treaty allows trade to prosper along the northwestern routes by keeping the Agiennans at bay. A new war would mean a significant cut in income from import taxes."

Bergen made an impatient sound. His sharp profile was outlined against the clear sky as he gazed out of the window, drumming his fingers on the stone ledge.

"But they don't stay at bay, do they? Her Majesty would understand that such brazen provocation from Agienna cannot be met with restraint either by Mulberny or by the realm itself. These attacks on our shores, this abduction and attempted murder—this is all just the beginning. If the clans see us do nothing, they'll perceive it as weakness, as a concession to raze our towns and sink our ships. War is inevitable, but if we strike against the Danulf now, swiftly and with great force, there will still be a chance the rest of the clans won't support them. We should be the ones setting the rules, not reacting to other players' moves."

"This is not a game," Callan said. "People's lives—"

"Do not lecture me!" Bergen turned toward him abruptly, his blue eyes smoldering with icy fire. "I know full well this is not a game. I almost lost you, and you have the audacity to tell me they had the right to torture you, to plan to kill you in the cruelest way imaginable to appease their misplaced sense of honor! Thank gods they didn't have the chance to rid me of my son."

"Gods had nothing to do with it," Callan said, clinging to calm in the face of his father's anger. "It was Derek who saved me."

"Yes, Count Derek," the duke said with a strange expression. "How fortunate he was there. Considering he was the reason you ended up a prisoner in the first place."

"There was...something else," Callan said reluctantly.

He hadn't mentioned it before in his accounts of their captivity and ultimate escape. It was an easy detail to gloss over, but not nearly as easy to forget. Even now, Callan wasn't sure dredging this up was a good idea, but his father had to know.

"I...I called upon the wolves for help," he said. "I summoned them to go after our hunters."

Bergen went still. His eyes bore into him, and Callan squared his shoulders, bracing himself for his father's wrath.

"You did what you had to do to survive," Bergen said finally, pushing the words out as if with great difficulty. "Who knows about this?"

"Derek," Callan said. "And Logitt, I suspect."

Bergen huffed dismissively. "No one will take the word of an Agiennan witch if she were to accuse you. Now, Derek... Do you trust him to keep his mouth shut about this?"

"Yes," Callan said without thinking.

Only a week ago, he'd have thought such a level of confidence in another person, save perhaps for Adele or Leandre, impossible, but it seemed Derek had thrown all his notions about caution and discretion into a wild disarray that Callan was still struggling to make sense of. But he knew with absolute certainty he trusted Derek with more than his life. He trusted him with his soul and all its appalling secrets, because Callan's stupid heart had apparently decided it needed Derek to keep beating. And, what was more amazing, Derek looked past all the ugliness and still wanted the man behind it.

"Tell no one else of what you'd done," Bergen said. "Not even Adele or Priestess Nehewia. No one else must know."

He didn't have to explain why. An accusation of dabbling in witchcraft could spell trouble, Callan's title notwithstanding.

"Is it really a curse?" he asked quietly.

He'd never dared to speak with his father about it, not so openly. Callan had known about the curse from an early age, but the matter had always been hushed whenever he tried to bring it up, so eventually, he gave up on trying to hash it out. No one wanted to examine something so shameful, so perverse, too closely.

For a long moment, he thought Bergen wasn't going to acknowledge his question, but then the duke sighed and rubbed his temple. He suddenly looked much older than his age, as if the long years of strife and worry had finally manifested in the lines of his gaunt face.

"The witches of the Outer Isles, those gifted with magic, do not consider themselves cursed," he said. "They use this power freely, to heal, to protect their ships, to conquer their enemies. If there hadn't been so few of them born in recent years, they'd have an advantage over us. But magic, even used for what one considers good, always has a price. It'll consume your soul if you're not careful. And you have to be very, very careful, son. As your ancestors—the wise ones—had been since claiming this land as our own."

Callan nodded. It wasn't the direct answer he wanted, but he suspected it was the best one his father was willing to give.

"I will inform the High Queen about the current situation with Agienna," Bergen said, changing the subject. He was gazing out of the window again, watching the green waves roll in endless succession. "Her Majesty and I haven't always seen eye to eye, but I'm sure she will now agree we have no choice but to retaliate."

CALLAN WENT TO visit the remainder of his personal guard in the barracks. All its members had since returned from Bryluen, aside from Leandre and Mathis, who was still in critical condition and could not be moved from the city's infirmary. Now, with Leandre gone, Rema was to assume the duties of Callan's lieutenant. It was a somber promotion, with none of the usual cheer. Rema was well loved and respected by the soldiers, and Callan didn't doubt their competence and dedication. They'd make a fine lieutenant, Callan contemplated as he went up to his rooms, but in Leandre, he'd lost so much more than a brilliant officer. He'd lost a true friend, and nothing could make up for that.

He'd just unfastened his sword belt with a weary sigh when there was a soft knock on the inner door that connected to Derek's bedroom.

"Come in," he said.

Derek paused on the threshold, as if unsure of his welcome. Since their return to Irthorg, they'd barely seen each other, Callan too busy, locked in his father's study with his lieutenants and Lord Morgan's emissaries, and Derek bed-ridden, resting his sprained ankle. It was still bandaged, but at least now he was able to walk without clutching at the walls.

"I wanted to see you," Derek said shyly, his expression unexpectedly serious, solemn. He was standing in the doorway between their rooms, his hair fringed with gold, lit by the setting sun peeking through the high window. Callan's heart moved at the sight in a way he'd been sure wasn't possible anymore.

"I missed you," Callan said, because it was the simple truth.

He crossed the room to take Derek's hand. The man's eyelashes dipped, casting long shadows on his cheeks, tinged with a hint of blush. It was strange how all of a sudden they were awkwardly uncertain around each other, as if without the imminent danger, they weren't sure their closeness was appropriate.

Well, Callan was done with being appropriate. He'd do whatever it took to woo his husband.

"You look good," he said, touching the tips of Derek's hair ever so lightly. "Are you feeling better?"

Derek nodded. "I wish you'd get some rest too. You've hardly slept at all since we came back."

"I'm fine. There's a lot to be done. I plan to ride again to Bryluen as soon as possible to meet with Morgan and Elsie. I doubt the raids will stop now; if anything, they'll only intensify, especially if my father is right and the Danulf are the driving force behind them."

Derek pursed his lips, thinking it over.

"I'll go with you," he said finally.

"Are you sure?" Callan asked gently. He seemed unable to stop touching Derek's overgrown locks, and Derek didn't seem to mind at all, so he kept caressing them, luxuriating in their feathery fluffiness. "I thought perhaps you'd want to go home to Camria."

"Do you want me to go home?" Derek's dark brown gaze was steady, but Callan sensed an edge of challenge in his voice.

"No. No, I don't," Callan said.

It felt like a proclamation of sorts, no less momentous for its implicitness. And Derek seemed to take it for what it was because he turned his head, leaning into Callan's touch, and pressed his lips softly to the chafed skin on Callan's wrist. His heart hammering so hard it surely must be audible, Callan swiped a thumb over Derek's cheek where the slightly rough texture of his jaw met smoother skin.

Had he ever considered him tolerably average? What a pompous fool he'd been. Derek was positively gorgeous, from his unruly curls to the slightly sardonic turn of his lips, his dark eyes so deep Callan was sure he could drown in them if he wasn't careful.

"That night in the woods," Derek said, rousing Callan from his distracted admiration. "When you let your mind reach to the wolves. You wanted me. I could feel it."

Callan recalled the moment with embarrassing clarity—his own agitation on the cusp of madness, the heightening of senses that made the allure of Derek's proximity irresistible. He'd held the beast inside in check, but who was to say what he might have done otherwise? It was too scary to dwell on. He'd never call on his magic around Derek—or any other person—ever again.

"I'm sorry."

"Don't be sorry. I wanted you too."

Callan took a deep breath, almost expecting to be hit again with the cloying scent of his arousal, but now, without the enhancement of magic, his perception was limited and clouded with self-doubt.

"What would you have me do?" he asked. Peering into Derek's eyes, he knew the answer, but this was too important to misconstrue.

"Stop talking and kiss me," Derek whispered and tilted his head upward, bringing their mouths together.

The kiss was everything Callan wanted it to be and yet so different from what he had expected. Derek's lips were cool, yet their slide against his sent a wave of burning heat down his spine. Every nerve ending in his body tingled with the kind of raw desire he hadn't felt since—that he hadn't felt for a long time.

Perhaps it was wrong of him to succumb to it, to even want to explore this unexpected, bright attraction. He'd vowed he wouldn't let himself get attached to anyone ever again, having no right to devastate someone else's life, as he was wont to do. But this connection he'd formed with someone he'd seemed least likely to like, let alone care for with such intensity, felt so right. As he held Derek in his arms, some emaciated part of Callan's soul came rousing back to life, like a patch of dried earth sprouting fragile shoots of new grass after a much-needed rain.

He sucked in his breath as Derek slid gracefully to his knees. He knew, even when Derek stepped into his room, what was going to happen between them, yet he was almost caught unawares by Derek's intention. Something close to panic rose inside him, but it was laced heavily with desire, so he stilled himself, willing his racing heart— futilely—to slow down.

Derek ran his hands tentatively down the front of Callan's pants, resting his palm lightly over the rapidly hardening bulge, and looked up at him, wordlessly asking for permission. Callan nodded tersely and bit his lip as Derek deftly undid the fastenings and gently rubbed his cheek against Callan's half-mast erection.

"You're very...in proportion," he murmured with appreciation.

Callan huffed in embarrassed amusement. Tentatively, he threaded his fingers through the silky texture of Derek's hair and was rewarded by Derek's sigh of pleasure, his breath ghosting over the sensitive flesh. Callan's cock leapt to attention, and his grip on Derek's hair tightened instinctively when he licked his lips and took him into his mouth.

It was an exercise in willpower at first, holding himself back from thrusting, keeping his touch undemanding. But Derek clutched Callan's hips with a punishing force, urging him to forgo his restraint while working his lips and tongue with unmistakable eagerness, and Callan let his control slip, surrendering to the simple, half-forgotten pleasure.

It couldn't last. It had been too long since he'd enjoyed anything other than his own touch, and even that served nothing but the hollow need for immediate release. He wanted to bask in the exquisite torment that the drag and suction of a wicked tongue could bestow, but the heat was building too rapidly at the base of his spine, the tension cresting higher and higher, until something snapped—in his brain or in his chest, he couldn't tell—and he was swept along in the flood.

He steadied himself on Derek's shoulders, panting as his lover lapped his softening cock with leisurely attentiveness, and then looked up. Derek's lips were swollen and glistening, his cheeks flushed red, his eyes dark and glinting. His tongue flicked to swipe a trickle of moisture at the corner of his mouth, and Callan came nearly undone again at the sight.

"You're so beautiful," he said huskily.

Derek's eyes flickered. He rose to his feet unhurriedly, though his erection was visibly straining against his pants. Without another word, he took Callan's hand and pulled him over to the bed, leaving him no choice but to follow.

They took their time undressing each other, tasting lips and skin. The soft down mattress dipped as they lay on it, bathed in the failing light which was quickly fading from gold to purple.

Callan ran his hands over Derek's chest and taut abdomen, reveling in the quiet, pleased noises his touch elicited. Derek was exquisitely proportioned in his own right, the lines of his body lithe and elegant, like those of a fine tall ship, built for speed.

Up until this very moment, Callan hadn't realized just how long and how much he'd been yearning for this. Ever since the kiss they'd shared on Cirda, right after the wolves had come to their aid—no, even before the kiss. Ever since they'd set out on their mission to patrol the coast, when he witnessed firsthand what kind of man his husband really was. A brave, intelligent, capable man. And a kind, selfless one. Callan didn't know what he'd done to deserve someone like Derek in his life again, but he was sure as hell not going to question his luck. Especially not now, with Derek writhing and sighing in pleasure under him.

"What do you want?" Callan asked, tearing his eyes away from where he was stroking Derek's cock. The sight of his flushed face and parted lips was as equally rewarding as the feel of the hot, velvety flesh under his fingers.

"Do you still have all those oils from our wedding night?"

"They're here somewhere."

"Use them," Derek said, spreading his legs wide in an unmistakable invitation that did nothing for Callan's straining self-control.

Thankfully, the oils and washcloths were still there, discreetly tucked away inside a chest of drawers. Callan took out a small bottle and, returning to his place kneeling between Derek's legs, applied it liberally to his fingers.

Derek's breathing changed, coming out in throaty gasps, louder and louder, as Callan's gentle probing became deeper, more intimate in his search for the right spot to make his lover wholeheartedly welcome the intrusion. He was successful, at last, because Derek arched with a moan, bunching the sheets in his fists.

"If you continue to do that, I'll come all over you," Derek warned.

Callan smirked and twisted his fingers, making him whimper. "You're saying that as if it's a bad thing."

"It's not. But I want to come with you inside me," Derek said, watching him through half-lidded eyes with an expression that could reasonably be called leering.

"If you continue to talk like that, I'll come all over *you*."

"That would rather miss the point." Derek leaned back, bucking impatiently against Callan's hand. "Please, Callan. I'm ready for you."

He needed no further encouragement before he withdrew his fingers and covered Derek's body with his, seeking his mouth, craving to be enveloped wholly in his warmth.

The sun set slowly somewhere far to the west, shrouding the room in dusk in its wake as they moved against each other, with each other. Derek's fingernails dug into Callan's skin, and he bucked up, meeting Callan's thrusts with his own. The rest of the world fell away, leaving just the two of them, locked in a rocking rhythm as old as the crashing of the waves. In that moment, in each other's arms, they evoked a kind of magic that was no less potent for its simplicity.

"Callan, I..." Derek whispered in his ear, his voice hitching.

"I have you, love," Callan murmured without thinking. "You can let go."

Derek gasped and arched, clinging to his shoulders like a man desperate to find purchase in a storm. True to his word, Callan held him as pleasure rippled through Derek's body.

"Come to me," Derek panted, his eyes glittering in the gathering shadow like dark jewels.

The raw emotion in his voice broke the dam, releasing the heat pooling in Callan's groin like a flood, draining him of all the fear and pain that had been pent up inside for so long. He collapsed on top of Derek and heard him grunt through the daze. He wanted to apologize, but words seemed so distant. Strong arms enveloped him, and he finally let himself drift away, lulled into a deep sleep by an almost forgotten sense of contentment.

Chapter Fifteen

DEREK NEVER IMAGINED, when he'd first come to Irthorg, that he'd actually be enjoying his stay in this stark place. But the unfamiliar faces around him were starting to become friendly, and there was hardly any opportunity for solitude.

His ankle, which thankfully hadn't been broken, was slowly healing, but he couldn't bring himself to spend days on end lying in bed or sitting by the fire reading. He thrummed with a joyous, boyish energy, and it drove him outside, to explore the grounds and take in the breathtaking vistas only visible from the highest points of the keep and its ancient fortifications. Callan often joined him on his walks, despite his admonishments not to overexert himself, showing him spots that offered the most beautiful views. And sometimes those spots held no other attraction than being secluded enough for Callan to push Derek against a wall with just the right amount of roughness to turn Derek's blood to liquid fire and do things that left them both breathless and spent.

The weather grew colder every day. That morning, the wind was too strong for Derek's liking to enjoy the upper walkways, so after breakfast, Callan and he descended into the lower levels. There was an area of greenery behind the storage sheds that bordered the smaller yard the guards used for archery practice. Once a lush garden, it had been left untended, and now weeds and brambles grew wild. The few apple trees were heavy with fruit, but no one bothered to pick them, and many had fallen to the ground to rot.

"This is a pretty patch of wilderness," Derek said, stooping to run his hand over the tallest grass blades. "Seems almost out of place. Everything else is kept in such immaculate order."

"This was Mother's favorite spot," Callan said. He picked his way to the crumbling outer wall where a stone bench stood half-hidden by a briar bush. "When I was little, I used to climb the apple trees while she'd sit here with her needlework. After she died, everybody sort of forgot about the garden. It's too out of the way. Father remembers it, but he never comes here."

"Why not?"

"He loved her very much. I think the memories are a bit too vivid here."

Derek could understand that. The place where a person spent most of their time was always filled with their energy, even after their death. He'd felt it too, in his father's study after he'd been killed. The memories were etched into every floorboard, every piece of paper. Derek had had a hard time being there without him, half expecting him to turn up at any moment and inquire irritably what Derek was doing in there. It must have been more difficult for the duke, whose feelings for his late wife must have been very different from the trepidation Count Johan had instilled in most of his family.

Reconciling Duke Bergen's hard image with tender feelings and genuine grief was a challenge, but it wasn't impossible. Derek had already observed enough of the man to know he loved his children dearly, even if his love often became overbearing. But it certainly wasn't the lack of caring that made the duke act the way he did.

"But you come here," he said as they both sat on the bench.

The roar of the sea against the high cliffs was barely audible, and the tall mossy walls created the illusion of being ensconced in a bubble of lush autumn, the kind filled with the fragrance of fruit and berries and decaying leaves. Derek could see why Callan's mother had favored this corner of the castle rather than a chamber overlooking the infinite expanse of sky and deep water.

"Only recently," Callan said. "There were times I needed to be alone."

For a while, they sat quietly side by side, with only the chirping of birds interrupting the silence. Derek kept stealing glances at the man sitting next to him. After a week of recuperation, the bruises on Callan's face had faded into dirty yellow, but they still did nothing to detract from his handsomeness. His dark hair had grown just enough to get into his eyes, and he kept tossing it back impatiently. These were the kinds of details Derek would hardly have noticed before but now seemed to command most of his attention.

"I don't usually talk about it, but when Idona died, it shook me rather badly," Callan said at last. He picked up a dry twig and twirled it in his hands, focusing on it instead of looking at Derek. "I blamed myself for letting it happen. I still do."

"Is that why you let the rumors about her being killed run so rampant? Because you were feeling guilty?"

"Yes. I figured the gossip wasn't so far from the truth, and people would talk anyway."

"You're so quick to accept punishment for anything bad that happens around you. Not everything is your fault," Derek said gently.

"I can't think otherwise. If I don't control my fate, how else can I protect the people around me?"

"You can't always protect them." Derek placed his hand on Callan's arm, the muscles tense under his fingers. "Sometimes, people do awful, stupid things you can neither anticipate nor remedy. And sometimes, they're faced with forces they can't overcome. None of that is the fault of those who love them. We can only do our best and hope that it's enough."

Callan finally turned to him. His blue eyes were serious, their expression almost too intense, and Derek found himself unable to look away. Sometimes those eyes were dark whirlpools of lust he yearned to drown in, and sometimes they were chunks of ice so sharp they could cut, but now he could see something else in them, something fragile and vulnerable, like a tender flower blooming from under a thick blanket of snow.

I love you. The thought came with sudden clarity. He wasn't surprised by the emotion. He'd been lost to it, completely and irreversibly, for a long time, before they'd come back to Irthorg, before their mad dash through the hostile island, maybe even before they'd held each other aboard the pirate ship. He couldn't deny it, and he couldn't hold it back any longer.

He opened his mouth, his heart pounding in his chest with a mix of anxiety and excitement, but before he could say the words, Callan leaned in and kissed him, so thoroughly Derek's thoughts scattered, and his breath caught.

"We're to ride for Bryluen tomorrow," Callan said after releasing him. "Do you still want to come? The weather is changing, and it'll be a hard ride. Your leg—"

"Is going to be fine," Derek said firmly. "I've been walking on my own for days now. Of course I'm coming. In fact—" He leaned closer to Callan and dropped his voice to a suggestive whisper. "—if it isn't too wet outside, we could slip away into the woods at night."

"Why? Do you want to see the wolves again?" Callan asked.

A small smile spread on Callan's lips as his fingers skimmed the length of Derek's arm in a casual caress. After a week of sharing the same bed every night, Derek had become quite familiar with this smile, a private thing only reserved for those rare moments when Callan put down his guard and just let himself feel. And if that feeling was half as beautiful as Callan's smile, Derek would count himself the luckiest man in all of Ivicia.

"No wolves. Just you and me," Derek said. A shiver of elation went through him when Callan's eyes darkened with desire. It was still hard to believe that he, of all people, inspired such ardor in a man like Callan, who could surely enjoy the charms of any person he wanted simply on the merit of his looks.

But by now he knew casual liaisons of that kind weren't in Callan's nature. Even without him saying anything, Derek deduced the last person to share Callan's bed had been his late wife.

He reached over to Callan, brushing his lips against the other man's. Callan responded eagerly, hungrily, deepening their kiss so their tongues were locked in an exploratory dance, courteous and heated at the same time. Derek moaned into his mouth, melting against Callan's solid body as if he were a drop of rain clinging to his skin.

"My lord," someone called from the direction of the gate, and they both jumped, untangling themselves like a pair of boys caught groping in the hayloft.

"Beg your pardon, my lord," the guard said, addressing Callan. He had to almost shout to be heard over the expanse of the overgrown garden, but he kept a respectful distance, seeing their delicate position. "Commander Rema asks you to come to the stables to inspect the horses."

Callan stood up. "I'm sorry," he told Derek with visible regret. "I have to see what they want."

"Of course." Derek smiled up at him, hiding his disappointment. But Callan's duties came first, and they still had the entire night ahead of them to gift each other pleasure. "I'll see you later."

DEREK SAT ON the stone bench for a few minutes, waiting for the heat of arousal to subside and listening to the birds singing in the apple trees. Callan was right; it was peaceful here, the little overgrown garden lovely in its unassuming shabbiness.

Finally, he pushed himself up with some effort. He was able to walk just fine, but with his foot still a bit swollen and sore, he wasn't quite as hale as he tried to make Callan believe. But pushing through pain came naturally to him now, and he considered this nothing more than a minor inconvenience.

He took the long route back, slowly making his way around the storehouses for no better reason than idle curiosity. He was familiar with the running of the keep back in Camria, but at Irthorg—more a fortress than an estate—things were done differently, and he was glad of the opportunity to see the more prosaic side of daily life in a castle so large.

Nearing a corner of the farthest shed, he heard voices and paused. He recognized the slightly higher pitch of Medwin, the castellan, and risked a peek from behind the shed, reluctant for some reason to intrude on the conversation.

One of the men was indeed Medwin, the gilded chain of his post glinting in the morning sun against the somber black of his clothing, but he wasn't the one who drew Derek's attention. The man he was speaking with was standing with his back to Derek, but something about his stance tugged at his memory. Derek shrank farther back behind the shed, compelled by a mix of curiosity and uneasiness. It was hardly an honorable thing to do, eavesdropping on a private meeting, but he couldn't shake the feeling he'd met the other man before, and his instinct told him to stay where he was.

"You know what will happen if the duke's son is harmed again," Medwin told the man, keeping his voice low. A furrow creased his forehead, and his mouth was curved in distaste. "You're lucky His Grace didn't have you hanged after the first time."

"It won't happen," the man said. "Those Undin pricks got angry after he gave them a good beating. Wouldn't hear of just leaving him be, especially not when there was somebody willing to pay for the privilege of gouging his pretty eyes out. Greedy fuckers. I don't deal with them anymore."

Derek clutched the wooden wall of the shed to keep his head from spinning. He knew that voice, tinged heavily with Sansian accent, the same one that had issued him curt directions when his kidnappers' cart had stopped on a lonely rocky shore where their ship was waiting, right before Callan and Leandre had arrived and the night had erupted with screams and death and the clash of steel. There was no chance of him ever forgetting it.

But, for the same man to be speaking with the duke's castellan, discussing the details of the duke's son's kidnapping? It was unthinkable. Yet here he was, wearing the modest garb of a local tradesman, receiving...orders?

"Make sure it's done quick," Medwin said and then proceeded to take a small leather pouch out of the pocket of his coat. The pouch made the distinctive metal clank of heavy coins when the other man snatched it from his hand. "But make sure there would be no doubt as to the 'culprit.'"

"A Danulf arrow will do the trick," the man said. Derek didn't see his face, but he couldn't mistake the smirk in his voice. "No need to go through the entire charade, snatching him up and whatnot. Clean and simple, it is."

"I don't want to know anything about it," Medwin said sharply. He glanced around him nervously, but save for Derek, who was safely hidden from view, the place was completely deserted. "Just do it."

The man bowed with an exaggeration that tipped into mockery. Medwin pursed his lips and nodded curtly, indicating the man to follow him toward the main yard.

Derek held his breath until they were well out of sight and then sagged heavily against the wall. A thousand thoughts raced through his mind, but he could only retain one of them—Medwin had been arranging a murder. And considering his insistence on Callan's safety, Derek had a pretty good idea of whom the intended victim might be— as well as who was behind the scheme.

But he had to be sure. Perhaps his mind was playing tricks on him, and this was all some terrible mistake. Surely, a mistake would be so much more plausible than Derek accidentally stumbling upon a conspiracy to kill him?

With a renewed determination, Derek hurried in the direction the men had taken, but by the time he'd reached the main courtyard, there was no sign of the Sansian man anywhere. The open space bustled with the usual daily activity of a large keep, carts and horses and people all coming and going through the main gate. Finally Derek spotted Medwin, who was talking to a stable hand, and purposefully made his way to him.

"Who were you talking to back there just now?" Derek asked, keeping his voice low but firm. Sometimes the best tactic was a direct and blunt offense, meant to throw his opponent off guard, but it was one he rarely employed, and now his heart was hammering with something close to anxiety.

"Pardon me, Your Grace?" Medwin turned to him, visibly startled. The stable hand bowed and scampered off.

"The Sansian. Who is he?"

Something flickered in Medwin's eyes, gone too quickly to tell whether it was fear or annoyance.

"A cloth merchant. I was placing an order for new linen."

Derek frowned. The answer was so readily offered as to sound rehearsed. And new linen hardly necessitated such secrecy.

"Then why were you discussing arrows?"

This time, there was no mistaking the alarm in Medwin's eyes.

"Arrows? I'm sure I don't know what you mean, Your Grace," Medwin said, the agitation in his voice belying the polite words.

"I heard you," Derek said, pressing his advantage now that Medwin was clearly nervous. "It was no linen you were ordering. You paid him to commit murder."

"I did nothing of the sort, Your Grace. Now, if you'll forgive me, I must be away on the duke's business." Without actually waiting for Derek to excuse him, Medwin wheeled around and strode off, almost running.

Derek started after him but paused. It'd do him no good pressing the castellan. Despite his status, he was a guest at Irthorg, devoid of any real authority. But he knew someone who had it in spades.

DESPITE THE DISCOMFORT it caused his ankle, Derek couldn't stop himself from pacing. Callan's rooms, as sparse as they'd seemed to him at first, had become intimately familiar over the course of the last week, but now he barely registered the furnishings and the warmth of the fire.

He was impatient for Callan to return, yet in his heart, he wished he could delay a little while longer. It wasn't a conversation he was eager to have. There was no pleasant way of asking a man whether he knew his father was planning his groom's murder.

There'd been all those rumors about Callan. Ivo had warned Derek about them; even Macon, in his less than sympathetic way, had done so. Perhaps he should have heeded them instead of letting himself be swept away by feelings that had clouded his judgment. After all, where there was one dead spouse, there could easily be another.

But no. Callan couldn't have anything to do with it. Whatever game Bergen was playing, Callan wasn't a part of it. This Derek knew with a certainty that outweighed his outrage. Had Callan wanted him dead, he wouldn't have come to his aid, risking his own life and sacrificing that of his lifelong friend. Derek lacked experience when it came to love, but he'd met with enough dislike and indifference to realize Callan's feelings toward him were genuine.

But were they enough?

The door opened, and Derek jumped, startled out of the frantic cycle of his thoughts.

"A servant told me you were waiting for me here," Callan said, closing the door behind him and leaning against it with a lazy smile. "To be honest, I hoped you'd be much less clothed by now."

This time, Callan's teasing failed to send the familiar thrill down Derek's spine. He said nothing, and Callan's smile slipped, becoming a frown as he took in Derek's agitation.

"What happened? Are you all right?" he asked, taking a step toward him. Derek drew back, and Callan halted, a puzzled expression on his face. "Derek?"

"I heard something I wasn't supposed to." His voice sounded foreign, as if someone else was pushing the words out of his mouth.

"What is it?"

Derek took a deep breath. There was no easy way to say this to the man he'd do anything to protect. But there was no hiding something like this from Callan, even if it caused pain and confusion.

"Your father was the one who arranged for me to be taken by those pirates. Kidnapped and killed. And it'd look like the Danulf did it. And what's worse, he's still keen on having it done. I chanced upon Medwin as he was paying the intermediary. Your father wants me dead."

"What? That makes no sense. My father was the one to push for this marriage. It was I who wanted nothing to do with it at first."

Derek bit his lip. Callan's reluctance to marry him was hardly a revelation, but hearing him admit it so casually hurt almost as much as the notion of his father-in-law wanting to be rid of him.

"It's true," he said, clamping down on a flare of resentment and making an effort to sound as calm as possible. This was a much more serious matter than petty slights. "I heard it all myself."

He told Callan brusquely of the meeting he'd witnessed behind the sheds next to the little forgotten garden. The Sansian's words still rang in his ears, and though he hadn't seen his face, there was no doubt whatsoever as to who it was, what part he'd played in Derek's abduction from Bryluen, and what the duke's intention was even now.

As he spoke, Callan's hands tightened into fists and flexed again. His face was devoid of any expression after the initial shock, his blue eyes betraying no emotion. The wall between them, the one that had taken so long to disassemble, one brick of scorn and distrust at a time, was back again in full force.

A heavy silence hung in the air when Derek finished his account, so complete that the crackling of the fire in the hearth seemed as loud as thunderbolts. He'd never thought moments of quiet could be so thick and suffocating, as if the silence itself was filling his lungs like water, chilling his heart.

"You can't accuse the Duke of Mulberny of such a grave misdeed based on nothing but conjuncture," Callan said finally.

"Conjuncture?! Do you think I'm lying?"

"No, I don't." Callan raised his hands in a pacifying gesture, which, conversely, made Derek angrier, as if Callan was implying he was being hysterical or unreasonable. "But you might have misheard or misunderstood. Think about what you're saying. My father, conspiring with rogue Agiennan pirates and outlaws against you, and, by extension, Camria? That's preposterous. Even if there is some kind of plot afoot, which I doubt, you have no proof he's involved in it."

"I know what I heard!" Derek's voice rose, coming dangerously close to shouting, and he made a conscious effort to calm down, even though Callan's cold impassiveness infuriated him further. "I know what I saw. If you question Medwin, you'll understand I'm right. Or better yet, ask Bergen."

Callan shook his head. "This is absurd. I'm not going to insult my father by giving these insinuations credence."

Derek bit his lip. The small amount of pain was infinitely better than letting himself betray the depth of his hurt.

"If my word means so little to you," he pushed out, "then there is nothing more we can say to each other. There can be nothing more between us."

Callan sucked in a sharp breath, his eyes momentarily going wide.

"That's not what I meant. Derek, you...you must know how I feel about you."

"Do I?" Derek asked, dropping his voice. "If I'm right—if it comes to choosing between me and your duty to your father and fiefdom, which would you choose?"

Callan didn't answer immediately, and the pause told Derek everything he needed to know.

Ivo, Macon, even his mother—they all had been right. He shouldn't have forgotten where he belonged, and with whom. And apparently, it wasn't here in this rough land that he'd been foolish enough to believe could welcome him. He should have known better than to trust the tender emotion he'd allowed to grow inside him. He should have known better than to allow himself to fall in love with Callan—or to believe that Callan could possibly love him in return.

Callan made a step forward, reaching for him again, but Derek stepped back.

"Don't. I'm leaving," he said, surprised at how level his voice sounded despite the ache that seized his throat, making it hard to breathe. Tears welled in his eyes, distorting his husband's chiseled face.

"Leaving?" Callan repeated, as if he didn't comprehend the meaning. He looked so stricken that, for a moment, Derek's resolve wavered.

But it wasn't something he could let slide simply because he didn't want to upset Callan. Callan, who apparently cared enough for him to not want to see him leave, but not enough to actually investigate his claims. Derek was in mortal danger, and in this murky political game, his family (if not his husband) needed him alive.

"Yes," he said, blinking away the tears. "As soon as I pack my things."

"It'll take time to have all your retinue ready. At least give them time to prepare—and for yourself to reconsider," Callan said, a note of pleading entering his voice. Derek shook his head.

"I'm not staying here a minute longer than necessary. I can't. If my men aren't ready, they'll catch up to me on the way."

"You can't go alone! What if someone *is* after you? You won't be any safer on the road."

"Well, if something happens to me, it'll save Duke Bergen the trouble of trying to have me assassinated all over again."

For one awful moment, Derek was sure Callan was going to hit him, but instead, his face twisted into something Derek hadn't seen even when he had been nearly tortured by the Agiennans.

"Derek. Please."

"Goodbye, Callan," he said quietly.

He was half expecting Callan to block his way as he brushed past him, but his husband made no attempt to stop him. Without looking back, Derek crossed the threshold between their rooms and let the door swing shut behind him with a resounding bang.

Chapter Sixteen

CALLAN STARED AT the closed door, fists bunched by his sides and his thoughts churning like tidal waves at the bottom of the cliffs.

What the hell had just happened?

There was no answer to that question which would satisfy him, only a kind of furious astonishment. Where did this outrageous notion of Derek's even come from? Callan knew him to be rash at times, but to insist that Callan's father had hired assassins to kill him was simply beyond the pale. And for him to believe Callan would in any way consider the accusation was nothing short of insulting. And making Callan choose... It simply wasn't fair. How could he choose between the man he loved and family loyalty—especially when, as far as Callan was concerned, there was no need to weigh the two bonds against each other?

That was the problem, wasn't it? He loved Derek with the kind of depth and intensity of emotion he'd believed his heart incapable of anymore. He thought it'd died the night Idona had drawn her last breath. But Derek, by some incogitable magic, had awoken it again, like a fairy-tale prince rousing his lover from an enchanted sleep. Callan didn't know when exactly he'd fallen in love with his husband, but now, he was well past the point of no return on the path to another heartbreak.

He should never have let his heart take over his senses. It was both foolish and dangerous, and brought about nothing but pain. Everything in Callan's experience had taught him that, yet he'd been stupid enough to believe this time was different. That Derek was different. That what they'd shared could cross out years of ache, guilt, and disappointment.

Apparently, he'd been wrong. Callan stalked across the room into his study and slammed his palms against the desk with a thud, making the array of colorful glass inkwells atop it rattle precariously. How could Derek fall so readily for so vile a slander? Callan's throat constricted, a red haze momentarily clouding his vision.

But he needed time alone to cool off before making any sort of move. He'd fought enough battles in his life to know no good resolution had been born out of anger, and now too much was at stake to make the wrong step.

Callan made himself relax and take a deep breath, stepping away from the desk before he could make more of a mess. There was still work to be done if they were to depart tomorrow. Even if Derek wouldn't be going with him, he had to return to Bryluen as soon as possible if he wanted to find out what was behind these attacks.

As much as Callan tried to conceal his foul mood behind his usual mask of bland inscrutability, the guards and household staff apparently weren't fooled. Everyone ducked out of his way as soon as they caught a glimpse of his face as he descended into the main courtyard. Callan gritted his teeth and set out to find Rema again. Perhaps he was being a stickler to the point of disruptiveness, but minding the minutia of equipping a troop for a hard ride north was infinitely better than seething helplessly in his rooms, separated from Derek by a single door and a chasm of hurt.

But before he could head off to the stables, a large carriage, drawn by four horses and accompanied by five armed riders, came through the main gate and pulled up to a stop. A small cart, covered with a tarp, was attached to the back of it.

Callan's stomach twisted unpleasantly with premonition when he spotted Lord Morgan's crest on the side of the carriage. The guards in the yard, roused by the unusual sight, gathered round, their weapons at the ready despite the display of friendly colors on the riders' uniforms and on the banner atop the carriage roof. In the wake of Callan's capture, it was small wonder the Irthorg contingent was suspicious of everything out of the ordinary.

He flexed his hands again, tensing in anticipation despite his best efforts at tranquility, but schooled his features, waiting while the stable hands took the reins and a servant in dark clothing jumped down from the back of the carriage to pull out the folding step. There was a shuffle inside, and then the door swung open, revealing the occupants.

"Lady Elsie," Callan said, unable to keep the surprise out of his voice despite his attempt at reserve. "What are you doing here?"

Elsie, accompanied by an attendant, was seated at the back of the carriage, her delicate frame wrapped in thick wool blankets against the chill. Her shrewd dark eyes met his, and the awful sense of foreboding intensified. Whatever had driven Lady Elsie to travel all this way in person, it couldn't have been good news.

"I have something of great importance I wish to discuss with His Grace. But perhaps it'd be best to speak with you first, all things considered."

"We're heading to Bryluen tomorrow," Callan said. "But I see you've anticipated us."

A loud moan came from the direction of the cart, and everyone in the yard turned their heads in alarm.

"What's that?" Callan asked. At first, he'd thought the cart might house Elsie's wheeled chair and other baggage, but it appeared he'd been mistaken.

"An Undin prisoner," Elsie said calmly.

Callan frowned. The Undin were the ones who'd kidnapped them at Bryluen and later delivered them to the Danulf. He opened his mouth, but Elsie forestalled him with a raised hand.

"I think I'd better speak with you first. Alone," she added with emphasis.

"Of course."

Together with Elsie's servant, he unstrapped the crate with her chair from the back of the carriage and helped her sit down comfortably. He led the way up the side ramp into the keep, with Elsie and her attendant following.

He chose one of the smaller drawing rooms on the main lower level. His late mother, and to a lesser extent, Adele, used these rooms when receiving guests, but they were still kept in immaculate condition, despite the slightly outdated furnishings. Soon, a fire was burning in the hearth, and tea and refreshments were brought while Callan paused outside to instruct an urgently summoned Gella to take Elsie's prisoner into the dungeons as quietly and discreetly as possible.

"I was very glad to hear of your safe return," Elsie said once they were both seated, and her attendant had poured them tea before taking her leave. They faced each other over a dainty side table set out with confections, for all the world as if this were a casual social call and the palpable tension in the air didn't exist. "I confess, for a while, it seemed like a hopeless business."

"I must credit my husband for making our escape possible," Callan said.

There was no doubt he owed Derek his life. His heart clenched with a mix of gratitude and regret as he recalled the moment when his grim resolution in the face of a horrible death had been replaced with an impossible hope at the sight of Derek creeping determinedly around the pillory. A wave of shame rose inside him at the memory. No matter how infuriated he'd been by the accusations, he shouldn't have spoken so dismissively to Derek. He didn't deserve Callan's contempt, not after proving time and time again how deeply he cared about him. Of that, at least, there was also little doubt in Callan's mind. Derek loved Callan just as much as Callan loved him.

Elsie made a noncommittal sound.

"Why are you here, Elsie?" Callan asked, changing the subject to more pressing matters. "Who is this prisoner you're escorting?"

"Next time you're dashing off to attempt a daring rescue, do notify someone, or at least take more than one person to accompany you," Elsie said dryly. "It took a while to notice you were both gone from Bryluen, and to begin to guess what had happened. But once you and your husband's absence was discovered, my father sent men after you. Thankfully, you managed to leave enough dead bodies behind for us to realize who was responsible for your kidnapping—and by that point we were praying to all the gods it was only a kidnapping and not something more sinister—and to track them down and capture some of them."

"I'm impressed. It must have been no easy task, considering the culprits."

Elsie nodded, but she was watching Callan with a strange expression as she sipped her tea. He shifted, growing more uncomfortable in the face of her somber mood.

"What did they have to say?" he asked.

"They gave us the name of the person who arranged the abduction."

"Aegir?"

"Duke Bergen."

Callan went very still. For a moment, he thought he could hear the roar of the distant sea, but it was only the blood rushing in his ears.

"That's ludicrous," he said at last, his voice sounding foreign, detached from the whirlwind of conflicting emotions that threatened to choke him. "My father would never have arranged my kidnapping."

"Not yours," Elsie said. "But your new husband's. No one counted on you going after him and disrupting the Undin rogues' plans. And when they had you, it was a simple choice between adhering to their previous bargain with His Grace or surrendering you to Aegir for a much greater profit."

Callan stared into his untouched teacup, not really seeing it.

"The Undin must be lying," he said, but he already knew it was a hopeless attempt at denial. This new information fell in too neatly with what Derek had been trying to convince him of earlier. These were parts of the same riddle, one he didn't care to solve.

Could Derek be right? Could the duke actually be trying to rid of him? But why would Bergen do that? What purpose could Derek's death possibly serve? Callan knew for a fact his father cared nothing for Camria. Whatever his reasons were, they had nothing to do with annexing a fiefdom weakened by the death of its ruler—even if Derek feared it to be the case.

"It's a grave accusation, but I'm inclined to believe it," Elsie said. "The prisoners would gain nothing by implicating the Duke of Mulberny himself in this matter unless they knew it to be true. This is why I came here with such urgency—to find out exactly what part you and His Grace played in this scheme, and, well, to control any possible damage. But I see now you had no knowledge of it."

"No," Callan said, his voice carefully controlled. "No, I didn't."

There was a short pause.

"No one knows of this save for Lord Morgan and me," Elsie said, focusing again on her tea and avoiding his gaze. "And the interrogators, of course, but they know their job too well to let such information slip. Rest assured that our loyalty lies with His Grace."

"Yes," Callan said thickly. "I appreciate your discretion."

He stood up abruptly. There were so many things he had to do, but first and foremost, he needed answers. And there was only one person who could give them.

"Forgive me, Elsie. I must speak with my father right away."

Before he can think of a diversion tactic. Before he has the chance to silence the Undin forever.

He didn't say that aloud, but Elsie must have understood because she nodded. Sympathy flickered in her eyes, but neither of them acknowledged it.

"Of course," she said. "Good luck."

THE EARLY AUTUMN sun had already begun its descent into the sea as Callan stormed down the corridors. He knew his father's habits well, and, true to his guess, he found Duke Bergen taking a walk on the upper battlements, as was his wont at this hour, before spending the evening in his study. The weather was turning bleak, with heavy storm clouds rolling over the frothy sea—a perfect match for Callan's foul mood.

"Callan?" The duke frowned when he saw his son coming up the stairs. His fur-lined cloak was wrapped tightly around his tall frame against the gusts that blew through the embrasures. "I was just about to go down and meet with Lady Elsie. Do you know why she is come?"

"What have you done?" Callan demanded, ignoring his father's question.

"About what?" Bergen asked, unperturbed by his son's apparent turmoil.

They were alone on the walkway; the nearest guard stationed on the walls was well out of earshot, but Callan still lowered his voice.

"Lady Elsie is escorting an Undin captive who swears he was hired by you to abduct the Count of Camria out of Bryluen, luring him away from the keep by falsifying a message from his brother. According to him, you intended to have Derek murdered."

Callan had to give it to his father—there were only a handful of things that could truly ruffle him, and being accused of premeditated murder wasn't one of them.

"Well then, it seems you already have a rather good idea of what I've done," he said calmly.

"But why?" Callan demanded, failing at keeping the frustration out of his voice. "I cannot imagine you'd consider Camria's offense so dire as to—"

"This has nothing to do with Camria." Bergen cocked his head as his eyes, cold as the winter sea, bore into Callan. "And why do you care so much for this baby sparrow and his godsforsaken fiefdom? When your nuptials were announced, you looked like someone had read your death sentence."

"Things...have changed," Callan pushed out with an effort.

There was a tiny pause.

"I see," the duke said finally. "Though I must say I'm surprised, son."

"Why? You weren't surprised about Idona."

Bergen's expression softened.

"Idona was different. No one could help but love her, and I couldn't have wished for a better match for you. She was accomplished in every way, intelligent, capable, charming—as befitting a future duchess. Derek, on the other hand, is..." He cast for the right word. "...expendable."

Callan bit down on his indignation. There was no use telling his father that Derek was as much all those things as Idona had been, that he was smart and competent and brave, that he had brought spring into Callan's winter-shrouded heart. Had Callan himself not been guilty of thinking the same of Derek when he first met him, of entertaining the same low opinion? Unlike him, his father hadn't had the opportunity to get to know Derek better, to spend time with him beyond one or two cursory conversations. And it was Callan's fault, too, because up until now, he hadn't bothered to tell Bergen of the change in his feelings and of what had brought it about, even when he'd had the perfect opportunity. He was just as complicit in Derek's mistreatment as his father.

"If this wasn't revenge against Camria, what was it, then?" Callan insisted, changing the subject back where it belonged.

Bergen turned away, looking through the embrasure to below, his hands resting on the stone ledge. The wind tangled his short gray hair, tugged at the hem of his long cloak, and for a moment, Callan thought he wasn't going to answer.

"When the raiders' attacks on our coastline had renewed, there was little doubt as to who was behind them. I knew something had to be done. A conflict of this kind puts us at a great disadvantage, and we simply haven't got the means to canvass every mile of the seaboard. But it still wasn't cause to declare another war; at least it wouldn't be in the Queen's eyes. She was already displeased with Mulberny for using excessive force to resolve the dispute with Camria."

Bergen scoffed, making it very clear his definition of "excessive" differed greatly from Her Majesty's. "But force is all they understand. Any sort of lenience is perceived by the Agiennans—or whatever clan—as weakness, as an excuse to push on with more violence. I knew I had to do something that would give us a proper cause to retaliate."

"And the kidnapping and murder of the Duke of Mulberny's new son-in-law would be the *casus belli* that not even the Queen could contest," Callan said slowly.

All the pieces of the puzzle fell into place to create a picture horrifying in its simplicity. The Undin, owing fealty to no one but themselves and guided by nothing other than immediate gain, would have no qualms about taking the duke's money to make it seem like Derek had been abducted by the Danulf. And when his mangled body was found, the duke would have no choice but to seek revenge against the presumed perpetrators. The situation with Agienna was so volatile already, with both sides barely keeping their mutual hate in check, that nothing more would be needed to ignite the fires of another war.

"Had Aegir executed me, you'd have gotten your wish," Callan said bitterly. "All your plans would have come to fortunate fruition."

Bergen's fingers flexed on the weathered gray stone. "You were never supposed to be there. For gods' sake, Callan. Had I known you'd be foolish enough to go after this man—"

"He's my husband," Callan gritted out. "The one you made me marry. Did you really think I'd abandon him to his fate even if I didn't—even if I cared nothing about him? I had to go after him. Leandre was killed because she was of the same mind."

He was shaking with rage and raw grief—for his best friend who was now dead, for the love he'd deluded himself into thinking he could have. He took a deep breath, willing himself to calm down. It didn't work as well as he'd hoped.

"I see now it was a mistake," Bergen said levelly, but his clenched jaw told Callan his father, too, was struggling for composure. "I've miscalculated your...attachment. Believe me, learning of your torture at the hands of the Danulf animal—I've rued that decision a thousand times over."

Hearing the pain in Bergen's voice took some of the edge off Callan's seething anger. There was no doubt in his heart his father loved him, and the possibility of losing

Callan (especially due to his own machinations) had had a deep impact on him. Callan could see it in the new lines around his eyes, in the stooping of his shoulders. But Bergen's only regret was unwittingly endangering the life of his son; he had no remorse for sacrificing Derek to what he considered a greater good. And no matter how much Callan loved and respected his father, he couldn't find it in his heart to forgive him for that.

Especially not if he was scheming to do it all over again.

"You may have rued it, but it hasn't stopped you from making another attempt at his life, has it?" he said with a fierceness that surprised him. He'd never taken such a disrespectful tone with his father, neither as a child nor as an adult. But there was a first time for everything, it seemed—even disenchantment with one's own parent.

"How did you learn about that?"

"It doesn't matter. It's true, isn't it?"

Bergen's lips pressed into a hard line.

"Yes. It had to be done, this time with no risk to you. And when you told me he knows about your...affliction, well, it was all the more reason to go through with my plan. The danger of exposure is too great to let someone run around carrying that kind of information."

"'Someone'? It's my husband we're talking about!"

"A husband in name only," Bergen said with emphasis. "Or so I believed."

"Father." Callan caught Bergen's gaze and held it. "Tell Medwin to call off the assassins, or call them off yourself. I don't care how you do it. I love Derek, even if he wants nothing to do with me after this. Do you hear me? *I love him.* And if he comes to harm by your hand, I swear to all the gods of sea and earth you will lose me too."

Bergen's eyes blazed with cold fire. Callan knew better than anyone the duke was not in the habit of taking orders from anyone. The High Queen herself had a hard time imposing her will on him. It was a heady feeling, openly defying his father and liege lord for the first time in his entire life, not unlike leaping off the edge of a cliff. For a second, Callan was suspended midair, equally likely to be embraced by the depths or be shattered against the razor-sharp rocks below.

He squared his shoulders, bracing himself for the outpouring of his father's wrath. But the flash of fury was gone as quickly as it'd sparked, the fire quenched in the duke's eyes. Bergen turned once again to face the sea, not looking at his son.

"Fine," he said, his tone both clipped and weary. "If that is how you feel, son, far be it from me to stand in the way of your happiness. Just...make sure you're bestowing your affections on a deserving person."

"He is, Father," Callan said quietly.

Callan had more reasons than most to hate fate. It was always a force to be dreaded, to contend with, sometimes to morbid outcome. But perhaps it had given him a gift, without Callan realizing it.

Both Derek and he resented having been forced into an arranged sham of a marriage. Neither of them had been happy, standing there in the chapel, forcing the pledges of matrimony out of their mouths. Hell, he had explicitly banished Derek from his bed, unwilling to sully the memory of his first spouse by paying conjugal debt to another. But later...later everything had changed. Against all odds, they'd formed a tentative connection based on grudging respect as well as unexpected attraction. They'd saved each other's lives. They'd shared an intimacy that extended well beyond the bedroom. In fact, that was why Callan had ended up sharing his bed with Derek at all, and not for a moment had he regretted his decision. His memories of Idona had not faded, his sorrow had not diminished—but it'd grown bearable. It was as if Derek had infused his gray and bleak existence with all the exuberant colors Callan hadn't noticed before—the shimmering azure of a calm sea, the delicate pink of dawn, the rich reds and purples of the setting sun. With him, Callan didn't merely exist. He *lived*.

If there was ever a time to fight for his life, it was now.

"My lord!" came a cry as a guard burst out into the walkway, and they both turned in alarm. Callan stepped forward, his hand going to the hilt of his dagger in lieu of a sword.

"What is it?" the duke asked.

"Pardon me, Your Grace," the guard bowed, panting. "Agiennan ships have been spotted off Shantor Island."

The island, no more than conveniently situated rock, marked the boundary of Mulberny's territorial waters. A watchtower, built centuries ago, housed a tiny alternating garrison and an aviary, to warn the mainland in case of an intrusion.

"What clans are the ships?" Callan asked, although he already knew the answer.

"Most of them are Danulf, my lord. But there are other ships, too—Herig, Sebald, Urfan."

"Well," Callan said, meeting his father's eyes. "Looks like you've gotten your war after all."

Chapter Seventeen

DESPITE THE BRASH words he'd flung at Callan earlier, Derek was perfectly aware that running off probably hadn't been the best idea.

Disappointment and righteous indignation were perhaps enough of a driving force to have him storm out of the castle, but he had to admit he'd be a much easier target for hired assassins traveling the high road, even escorted by his retinue. On the other hand, his best bet would be to take his brothers and his men and leave before Duke Bergen had the chance to hear of their departure and instruct his minions accordingly. He didn't know if Callan had informed his father of their conversation already, nor had he asked him to keep it a secret. It was painfully obvious where Callan's loyalties lay, and it wasn't Derek's place to split them further.

Therefore, as much as he might want to, he couldn't count on Callan's discretion. He had to hurry. But as he shoved the few personal possessions scattered around his room into his saddlebags, Derek hesitated, gazing out of the wide-open window.

The skies had grown darker, and the sun had all but disappeared behind heavy clouds pregnant with rain. Crisp, fresh blasts of cold air billowed the curtains, yet his lungs felt constricted, as if a thick, viscous...something filled his chest, binding his heart with poisonous tendrils.

He drew a deep, panicked breath, clutching at the bedpost for support. A ragged, convulsive gasp tore out of him, and the tears he'd been fighting so hard to keep back came right out with it. The carved wooden post shook under his hand, or maybe it was his hand that was shaking; he couldn't tell. He wanted to wail in frustration, like a child railing against the unfairness of life.

And it wasn't fair. Love shouldn't hurt so much, make him so utterly wretched, without the dubious solace of assigning guilt. Unlike his father, Derek couldn't blame other people for his own misfortunes. He couldn't even blame himself for falling in love with Callan because, in a sense, it was as unavoidable as him experiencing yet another loss. Even now, knowing the outcome, he'd do it all over again, because loving Callan had become as much a part of him as his own name.

He didn't know how long he stood there crying. Too long, considering the urgency. Eventually, the tears let up, though the ache remained. There was nothing to it, he told himself. The air crackled with the anticipation of rain as darkness rapidly descended.

A storm would make it difficult to follow them, however uncomfortable the journey. Derek wiped his face one last time, grabbed his bags, and quietly closed the door after him.

Muffled shouting and running sounded farther down the wing. For a second, he froze in apprehension, but the noise seemed to be moving away from the family quarters. Whatever it was, it probably had nothing to do with him.

Derek hurried down the staircase and into another corridor, heading to the guest rooms assigned to Ivo and Macon, but stopped in his tracks as a female voice called out his name. He turned and found himself face-to-face with Callan's sister.

Adele wore a simple day dress with a gray mourning ribbon tied around her forearm in Leandre's honor, but her hair was done in an elaborate arrangement of braids that made her look too sophisticated for her age.

The sight of the ribbon sent a pang through Derek's heart. He'd taken his off when they'd ridden out to patrol the coast what seemed like ages ago and hadn't put it back on. Perhaps he should—but to honor the memory of the brave woman who'd almost become his friend, the one who'd given her life to save him, rather than his abusive father, who'd never cared for anyone but himself.

"Derek," Adele said, and then her gaze fell on the bags he was holding. A frown creased her forehead, and her eyes, which were up until a second ago wide with alarm, narrowed. It reminded Derek so much of Callan that his heart twisted. "You're leaving?"

There was no escaping the direct question or hiding his state of distress, puffy eyes and all. Derek couldn't lie to her; although of sweet and gentle disposition, Adele was just as shrewd as the rest of her family. And besides, he liked her too much to deceive her. She reminded him of Ayleen—or at least a more grown-up, accomplished version of her.

"Yes," he said, dropping his voice. "Please don't tell anyone."

"What? Why? Does Callan know?"

"He knows. We...had a falling out."

"You cannot be serious—"

"It's what he wants," Derek said hastily, forestalling her incredulity. "It's what we both want."

"I don't know about you, but this is decidedly *not* what he wants," Adele said with a vehemence that surprised him. "Don't you see he's in love with you?"

Perhaps at one point Derek had let himself believe it. But whatever feelings Callan might have harbored for him, they weren't strong enough to weather the current storm.

"I don't think it's—" he began cautiously.

"It is true!" Adele insisted. Her cheeks were flushed with either anger or frustration, or perhaps both, and her tone, usually mild and lighthearted, had suddenly taken on the note of steel Duke Bergen used when addressing his troops. "I've watched you together this past week. I've seen how you look at each other. I might not have ever been in love myself, but I know it when I witness it."

Derek swallowed. He really didn't have time for this—nor, frankly, the emotional fortitude.

"Adele, please. I'm sorry; I have to go. I'm sure Callan will do perfectly well without me."

"You haven't heard, then?"

Derek's stomach lurched unpleasantly.

"Heard what?"

"Irthorg is under attack. Or it will be, soon. The Agiennan ships are coming."

Derek swore under his breath. So that was what all the running and shouting had been about.

"Where's Callan?"

"He'll be in my father's chambers. They're holding a council."

It took him all but a heartbeat to come to a decision.

"Here," he said, dropping his bags at Adele's feet. "Tell Ivo to put these back in my room."

"Good luck!" Adele called after him, but Derek already tore up the stairs leading to the duke's study.

WHAT AM I doing? Derek ran through the narrow corridors of the old keep, ignoring the stabs of pain in his ankle and drawing the startled glances of the passing servants. It wasn't as if his presence was in any way required. The Mulbernians had plenty of experience waging battles against the Agiennans, perhaps too much experience. Callan didn't need Derek there to hold his hand, and the duke would certainly oppose whatever help he might offer.

And yet... Derek couldn't in good conscience leave now, when war was about to break, if it hadn't already. He felt partially responsible for it having started, though he'd had no say in the matter. Callan had done everything he could to stop it, and Derek had been right there by his side. Despite their falling out, abandoning Callan now would feel like a betrayal.

He recalled Leandre's anguished cry as she fell off her horse, Mathis's gasps of pain, and the sticky warmth of his blood on his hands. So many other people were going to suffer, lose their lives and their livelihoods for no better reason than their rulers' pride and obstinacy. If there was any chance of him stopping a war, he would take it—politics and heartbreak be damned.

Everyone raised their gazes from a map they'd been studying when he all but burst into the duke's study. The room was brightly lit, both by the huge fireplace and a multitude of candles that dispersed the darkness now that the window was shuttered against the biting wind. It was a large space, but it felt crowded with all the people gathered around the table, including Bergen and Callan. Derek recognized Rema and Gella; the others must have been the duke's own lieutenants. To his surprise, Lady Elsie was also there, her delicate hand resting on the edge of the map. A strange expression flickered in her eyes as she looked at him, but he had no time to focus on it.

"Derek." Callan took a step toward him. "You're still here."

Derek's heart did a flip. He'd tried so hard to reconcile himself to the idea that he wouldn't see Callan again, or that if he did, Callan would treat him with cold scorn. Yet here he was, his breath catching at the sight of Callan's effortless beauty as if for the first time. Like a precious gem, it couldn't be marred by dirt, bruises, or despair, because the inner shine was always going to come through—as it did at this moment, with Callan's eyes lighting up with relief and tentative hope.

"Yes," Derek said.

"But—"

"You two may have your lovers' quarrel after we're done," the duke interjected dryly, glancing at Derek with an unreadable expression. "He's here, so he might as well be of use."

Derek walked up to the group as Callan fell in beside him, close enough to feel the warmth of his body, but not touching. Despite his earlier determination, Derek was slightly shaken and unsure as to what he was supposed to do. The grim set of the faces of the seasoned warriors around him reminded him too acutely of his own youth and inexperience. Perhaps he'd been deluding himself as to his ability to make any sort of difference. *Why do you think you can succeed where so many have failed before you?* a voice that sounded suspiciously like his father's whispered in his mind. What could he possibly contribute? And if he did, why would anyone listen to him at all?

He swallowed against the slimy bitterness in his throat, self-doubt less an option now than self-pity.

"How many ships?" he asked Callan in a low voice, focusing on the map of Mulberny's rugged shoreline instead of looking at him. This tension between them was a living, breathing thing, coiled like a poisonous snake ready to bite, but there was no addressing it in their current situation.

"About a dozen or so, fast approaching," Callan replied. "We've dispatched scouts up and down the coast in case there'll be more landings."

A strong gust rattled the window shutter, and Derek nearly jumped at the noise.

"How can they even set sail in this weather?" he wondered. "Aren't they running the risk of crashing ashore?"

"They use their magic to navigate troubled waters when they can," Callan said. "Considering the scope of this attack, I'd say they have several witches with them."

Witches. Magic. The words resonated deep inside him, triggering a reaction Derek didn't fully understand. It was like a half-coalesced thought slipping away from his grasp the harder he tried to pin it down.

He was still mulling it over as Bergen dictated dispatches—to Bryluen, Venara, and Shylor, where most of the Mulbernian troops were currently stationed after the Battle of Laurel Falls—to be sent out immediately to call on reinforcements and to man the outer defenses. Despite his resentment toward the man who'd almost sacrificed him on the altar of his formidable will, Derek couldn't help but admire the duke's efficiency. He was clearly in his element, single-handedly coordinating a military campaign with an authority that suffered no opposition.

On the other hand, Callan was uncharacteristically reserved, offering little to no input. He blended into the background, listening intently but without comment, his expression that of grim resignation bordering on defeat. Derek stomped down the ridiculous temptation to move closer to comfort him.

"We are being forced into a defensive position, which puts us at a disadvantage," Bergen said, addressing the other soldiers. Some of them, including Lady Elsie, nodded in agreement. "But we must turn the tide on this. Aegir is launching this attack as a preemptive strike against our potential initiative; even if the Council of the Chieftains is backing him, which I doubt, he hasn't had time to properly prepare for it. He's counting on a swift victory, but we shall not be caught unawares. If we want to gain the upper hand, we should settle for nothing less than a complete annihilation of his forces."

"Can't it be avoided, though?" Derek asked. He flushed as all eyes turned to him, regarding him with various degrees of disparagement, but made himself push through. "Clearly, it was an ill-advised decision. Aegir is driven by grief over his daughter and anger at the man whom he believes to be responsible for her death having slipped through his fingers. But surely, others in his camp must realize this is verging on suicide. If they could be reasoned with—"

"Even if they were inclined to talk, there's no chance of arranging a parley, is there?" one of the duke's older lieutenants, Xarin, said. "It's too dangerous to send out a ship or a boat in such weather, even if we were to disregard the risk of them sinking it. And once they reach the shore, there will be no talking, I assure you."

Derek felt Callan's gaze on him, heavy and scalding, but he refused to meet his eyes to find out the intent behind it.

"The time for negotiations is over," the duke said firmly before Derek could counter, cutting off all further debate on the matter. "We will meet them here." He tapped on a point on the map just south of Irthorg, and everyone tore their gaze away from Derek, both to his disappointment and relief. "Where the beach allows for easier landing. Every minute is of the essence. We ride in half an hour. Dismissed."

Derek stepped out of the way as people piled out of the study in a hurry to see to their respective duties, watching them helplessly with mounting frustration. It seemed no matter how hard he tried, he couldn't do anything right. He knew all too well that when men were raring for a fight, words of prudence carried little impact. It was too late, unless—

"Come." Callan's hand was like hot iron, burning his skin through his clothes. He jerked at the touch but let his husband lead him away from the duke's study into a small drawing room nearby. The fire in the hearth was too feeble to either warm or illuminate the space properly, so everything was half-shrouded in shadows. Callan's tall frame seemed to blend in with them as he leaned against the door, out of the reach of light.

"Listen, Derek, before I go, I should tell you—"

"There's no time." Derek cut him off in part because he was afraid to hear what Callan had to say and in part because he couldn't waste precious moments on rehashing a conversation that'd make them both miserable. "We need to stop this war from happening."

"I don't think we have any choice in the matter."

"But what if we did? If there was a way to stop the bloodshed before it began, would you take it?"

"Of course," Callan said without hesitation. "Of course I would. Gods, Derek. You know I've never wanted this to happen. My father thinks force is the only language the Agiennans understand, that this is the only way to deal with the Danulf once and for all. Perhaps he's right, but in my heart, I don't believe it."

The desperate urgency in his voice pierced right through Derek's soul. Somehow, over the course of the last few weeks, Callan had become not only his lover, but his closest friend, the one he could confide in, the one he could comfort when things got rough, and it all being taken away from him hurt more than he ever thought possible. Derek yearned to reach out to him, to take his hand and kiss him and promise him it would be all right.

And how silly was that? Callan was the one who'd made it clear Derek was little more than a burden he'd come to tolerate. Surely any such displays of affection would be unwelcome. Callan needed Derek's comfort as little as he needed Derek himself.

He bit his lip and remained in his place, the distance between them a physical ache.

"I want to protect my people," Callan continued, visibly getting a hold of himself and striving for calm. "I will fight for them as I've always done. But having to fight now, after both sides paid such a high price for peace, is a failure whether we win or not. If there's a way to avoid another war...yeah, I'd take it."

Derek drew a deep breath. That was what he was hoping to hear, but he knew what he was about to propose might elicit a whole different reaction.

"In that case, I may have a solution. I'm not sure if it's going to work—and I'm rather certain you're not going to like it. But we might not have another option."

Callan pursed his lips. "Go on."

"You said there are witches aboard these ships using magic. Well, we have magic at our disposal too."

"I don't know what you mean," Callan said, his tone instantly becoming wooden.

"Yes, you do," Derek insisted.

"I doubt I can call upon the wolves to attack the Agiennan longships," Callan said caustically, dropping his voice as if he was afraid someone was going to burst in and accuse him of witchcraft at the mere mention of it.

"No. But your abilities aren't limited to the wolves alone, are they? Remember what Logitt said about mindbending. The magic runs in the blood, taking different forms, different talents."

The Agiennan witches used it to tame the waves and sharpen weapons and see through birds' eyes while Callan, like his ancestors, communicated with wild animals. But these were all facets of the same ancient magic, as old as the Outer Isles themselves. Magic wove through the generations, even when people spread across the sea and made other lands their home.

"I don't understand," Callan said with a touch of exasperation. The shadows hid his face completely, and Derek found it easier to talk when he couldn't see the hard gleam in his eyes.

"You could connect to the other witches' minds the same way you can connect to the wolves. Make them speak to us. Make them see."

Callan recoiled as if Derek had struck him.

"I can't," he said, his voice hollow.

"You can. You just don't want to."

It was harsh, and perhaps it was unfair—if "fair" was a consideration in their current crisis. It hurt Derek to say it because Callan must have been hurt by it, and as angry and grief-stricken as he was over their breakup, he didn't wish to cause Callan pain. But it was the truth, and he could think of no other way to drive the point home before it was too late.

"You don't know what you're asking of me," Callan said after a long pause.

"I do know."

"No. You heard all the rumors when you arrived here for the wedding. People saying that I'm a murderer, that I'm cursed. Well, I'm not cursed. I *am* the curse."

Callan bit his lip and averted his eyes. His expression was so vulnerable that Derek involuntarily held his breath so as not to shatter it.

"I'm the reason people around me get hurt," Callan continued. "Maybe it's some kind of punishment for my gift, and if I dare use it again—"

"No." Derek stepped up to Callan and took his hand, realizing with a sort of jolt how comfortably familiar his touch had become in so short a time. "Listen to me, please. None of the tragedies that have befallen you are your fault. I know you're afraid that the magic will drive you mad. I know you're so afraid of exposure you'd rather people believe you a murderer than a witch. But I also know *you*. You're brave enough to face those fears if it means stopping more innocent people from being killed."

Callan took a step forward, and the light of the fire reflected in his eyes, the irises so wide they appeared completely black.

"Why do you care? This isn't your fight. You were ready to leave not an hour ago."

Derek bit his lip. It was a good question. Why should he care, really, for the fate of a fiefdom that had been so hostile to his own, whose ruler was hard set on having him killed for the sake of his own political stratagems? Why should he care for the clans of the Outer Isles, who'd shown him nothing but violence and hatred? They could very well fight it out among themselves, as they'd been doing for generations.

But during his short stay in Mulberny, Derek had grown attached to its people in a way he hadn't thought possible. He was their ruler and their champion by marriage only, and a spurious marriage at that, but the tenuousness of his authority didn't make him any less responsible for their safety. He remembered his own prideful promise to Callan, that he wasn't the sort to let his spouse shoulder all the burden, and realized he was going to hold himself to his promise.

"Sometimes we leave because we care too much to stay," Derek said quietly. "And yes, I *was* going to leave. But I'm here now, prepared to do whatever it takes. Are you?"

Callan's lips hardened into a grim line.

"All right. Let's do this."

Chapter Eighteen

THE COURTYARD WAS in a frenzy, with restless horses, shouting men, and running servants. Heavy rain slicked the cobblestones, and the smell of wet leather hung in the air.

About one hundred and fifty people were ready to ride out to meet the Agiennan fleet. It wasn't a large contingent, but the duke wouldn't leave the castle and city unattended, and he counted on reinforcements from the country estates joining them along the way.

Callan's troop was gathered closest to the gate, with the duke's personal guard beside them. Farther down, Callan glimpsed the Camrian soldiers under Hamlin's command in a tight circle around Derek and the two young lordlings. He'd have preferred they stay behind, but Derek apparently had no qualms about bringing the boys into battle.

Callan shook his head. Derek seemed awfully sure his plan would work, but Callan wasn't quite as certain. No plan, no matter how skillfully and well laid, had ever survived the clash with reality. So many things could go wrong, especially when their desperate scheme hinged on something as volatile as magic.

Magic. He still couldn't believe he was seriously considering calling on it, but when Derek pleaded with him, his eyes dark with emotion, Callan knew he couldn't refuse him. He couldn't refuse Derek anything.

He still hadn't had the chance to apologize to him, and there might be no other opportunity for him to do so. But hope was a weed that thrived on the most barren soil, and Callan still clung to it, weak as it might be.

Duke Bergen, sitting ramrod straight in the saddle, nudged his horse toward the gate, and Callan signaled his troop to make way and then follow him. He'd barely exchanged a few words with his father after their conversation on the battlements. There was still a lot more left to say, but all fateful decisions and resolutions would have to wait for later along with everything else.

The streets were all but deserted as they rode through the city. The people had been instructed to stay indoors and bar their doors and windows as a precaution. In an emergency, if the city walls were breached, the castle could provide refuge for those in need, but that hadn't happened in the last hundred years or so, not even during the last war. Callan hoped it wouldn't be needed again.

Once they were out of the narrow streets and past the main gate, the company picked up speed. The wide band of the south road hugged the rocky beaches, so close to the edge of the water the sound of the waves mixed with the rush of the heavy rain all around them. The storm lay on the sea like a thick blanket, shrouding the waters in almost complete darkness. Spotting ships at a distance would be all but impossible in these conditions, even if they'd guessed the chosen landing site correctly.

Nonetheless, the troop kept a steady pace as the ground became more level and the shoreline curved into a sort of a wide bay. It was too shallow to serve as a natural harbor for tall ships, but several fishing villages clustered along the stretch of beach, some boisterous enough to have grown into small towns, with newly built roads connecting them to large settlements farther inland boosting local trade. Their lights flickered in the distance like tiny swarms of fireflies huddling together in the darkness.

An outpost lay at the far south end of the bay, complete with its own quay, but it was too far away still to be seen from their current location. A messenger had been dispatched there earlier, so the garrison would soon be on high alert and joining them.

A cry went up at the lead, and gradually the entire troop came to a halt. Followed by Rema, Callan spurred his horse, rushing to join his father at the head of the column. The duke's guards gathered around him were little more than shadows, their black cloaks and the dark coats of their specially chosen horses making them all but invisible if not for the occasional glint of moonlight on polished armor.

"What is it?"

Bergen thrust a spyglass into Callan's hand.

"See for yourself. They're here."

Callan lifted the device and looked out over the waves. The rain obscured his vision, but finally he saw it—the regular shapes that were slightly darker than the background, moving toward them. Sails.

He gave the spyglass back, nodding grimly.

"This is where we make our stand," the duke said, raising his voice and addressing the troops. "The Agiennans think they can sneak up on us, like thieves in the night, and slaughter us in our sleep. Let them come, but they shall go no farther. We made the sea run red with their blood before, and by gods, we will again!"

Callan didn't join in with the cheers that went up around him. Instead, he hung back as the main force divided, readying for a sort of a pincer maneuver that would effectively cut the attackers off from the nearby villages.

"My lord? What is our position?" Rema asked. Their short curly hair was plastered to their forehead, but the rain didn't seem to otherwise bother them.

"Join the front line but keep an eye on the Camrians." Callan glanced at the jumble of men and horses behind him. "Just...make sure Derek stays safe."

Rema frowned. The way their eyebrows drew in consternation reminded Callan acutely of their mother, Priestess Nehewia, when she'd listen to Callan's succinct wartime confessions before sighing and offering her succor and blessings. He'd stopped seeking the comfort of those conversations as he'd gotten older and more jaded with divine providence, but sometimes he missed her soothing words and guidance. In a way, she'd been a mother to him, too, after the Unnamed Goddess had claimed his own.

"What about you?"

"There's something I have to do," Callan said.

"Do you want me to accompany you?"

Callan nudged his horse closer and clasped Rema's arm.

"No," he said. "But thank you. I want you to know it has been an honor serving with you."

Rema nodded, their dark eyes mirroring Callan's own grim resolution.

"Likewise. Good luck, my lord."

Callan dismounted and threw his reins to Rema before weaving his way toward the low sand dunes topped with swaying grasses. Wet sand crunched under his boots, and the rain trickled down under his collar. His cloak was already so soaked it offered little protection from the elements.

He could see something was wrong even before he got to the water's edge. The storm raged above, but the sea was unnaturally calm, as if it were a warm summer's night instead of the middle of autumn, the gentle waves urged forth by a strong, pleasant breeze.

The Agiennan witches' magic was at work, which meant they were drawing close. He didn't have much time.

Closing his eyes, Callan reached within, striving for the eerie, focused tranquility he'd previously only associated with priming for battle. The heightening of the senses shifted his perception, making his mind cling to the minute changes around him—the smell of salt so strong it tickled his nose, the distant neighing of the horses and the human voices, the fall of someone's footsteps on the sand.

He spun around, hand on the hilt of his sword, and came face-to-face with his husband.

"Derek." Callan made a step toward him but stopped, conscious of everything that lay between them. His chest expanded with something he was afraid to examine too closely but felt suspiciously like hope. "What are you doing here?"

"You really don't know?" Derek said.

His face was a pale smudge in the darkness, framed by strands of soggy hair, and his eyes appeared almost black.

"I think I do," Callan said, his voice barely more than a whisper. If he raised it just a fraction, it would crack. "But I'm afraid I'm wrong. Surely I can't be that fortunate."

"Fortunate?" Derek arched an eyebrow. "You're about to single-handedly engage an enemy fleet. That's hardly the definition of 'fortunate.' I'd say it's downright unlucky."

"Not single-handedly," Callan pointed out.

Derek pursed his lips.

"No," he agreed.

"Derek, I'm so sorry." The bubble of calm that surrounded Callan threatened to burst at the onslaught of emotion, and, at the moment, he didn't care if it did. "I was wrong to doubt you. Elsie brought proof of what'd happened. You were right all along, and I...I just couldn't..."

"You couldn't believe your father didn't live up to your expectations of him," Derek said quietly. "I can understand that."

Callan took a deep breath. "Is it too late to ask for your forgiveness?"

Is it too late for us? he wanted to ask, but he was dreading the answer even more than the inevitable confrontation between the enemy forces and the feral power that flowed and ebbed deep within, still blissfully quiescent.

Derek closed the short distance and took Callan's hand, the touch sending a wave of heat up his arm despite the clamminess of his skin.

"It's not too late," he said, looking up at Callan. Rain streamed down his cheeks in tiny rivulets like tears. Maybe some of it was tears; Callan certainly knew the moisture in his own eyes had nothing to do with the downpour.

A wry smile tugged at Derek's lips as he pulled Callan closer. There was no doubt as to what was about to happen, but the touch of Derek's lips against his still came as a shock, sending ripples through his awareness.

Abandoning any pretense at composure, he drew Derek into a fierce embrace, wrapping his arms around his shoulders. The kiss deepened, a hungry and desperate clashing of teeth and lips and tongues, and they were both drowning in it, locked together in their descent into the abyss that held everything still left unsaid—shame, regret, desire, faith.

"I'm sorry," Callan gasped when they finally tore apart long enough to catch their breath. "I'll never doubt you again, I swear."

Derek rolled his eyes but didn't hurry to break away.

"Don't make promises you can't keep," he said, his tone deceptively light, in contrast to the tension that lurked in the corner of his mouth and in the rigid line of his jaw. "But I know you mean it. I just... I don't want to have to leave you ever again."

"I don't want you to leave." Callan ran a hand over Derek's drenched hair and down his cheek, uselessly wiping away the wet streaks. "I love you. With all the heart I've got left."

"I love you too." Derek gripped his other hand, lacing their cold fingers together. "I'm here for whatever comes. Are you ready?"

Callan nodded. They started toward the beach, their hands still clasped. The rain lashed down hard, but with the high winds blowing far away, they were trapped in the eye of the storm, inside a cocoon of relative calm. Lightning struck somewhere above the sea where the storm still raged, illuminating the outlines of ornate bows and long hulls swaying with the motion of the waves.

"Damn, they're close," Derek said, not bothering to keep his voice down. "I hope we're not too late."

Callan didn't answer. It was now or never. As the distant thunder rolled overhead, he closed his eyes and inhaled the crisp night air.

The pungent, sweet smell of the storm mixed with salt reminded him of that terrible night when he lost Idona, and everything changed. He could almost feel the dark water closing above his head, filling his nose and mouth, threatening him with a crushing embrace. Pain surged again, rising up from that deep place where he hid it from the world.

He wasn't sure about this plan at all. But he owed it to Idona to make things right again for her family, as well as his own. And he'd sworn to Derek he wouldn't doubt him again. He was damned if he was going to break his promise. He'd learned to trust Derek—with his life, his heart, and now with the lives of his people. And he had to keep his end of the bargain, taking strength from both his grief and his love.

Callan reached within, to that place where serenity warred with turmoil, while simultaneously casting his consciousness across sand, water, and sky. With wolves, he'd known exactly what he was looking for, but with people it was so much harder. He could sense the minds of every person around him, each a shining star of sentience and individuality, drawing his attention every which way. There were so many of them, all different but similar at the same time. They didn't share the group awareness in the same way a wolf pack did, and for a moment, Callan panicked, not knowing where to focus. How was he supposed to find the right people in this jumble of thoughts and emotions? He would sooner get lost in them, spread too thin with the effort, than pick out the ones who would hear him.

His connection to his own body was so tenuous he couldn't readily perceive its reactions, but he must have swayed, because the person next to him gripped his hand harder, steadying him. The person—the man—was shining more brightly than any others, maybe because his mind was turned toward him. Callan easily read every emotion in that soul laid bare before him. He wanted nothing more than to bask in the bright warmth pulling him like a beacon, a lighthouse in a storm. But he couldn't abandon his mission. For now, the man had to be his anchor, not his haven. Callan had to venture far, extend himself even more.

He reached out farther, and... There. The ones he'd been searching for were distant, almost dull compared to the mass of swirling light somewhere behind him, but he could still feel them clearly.

"Can you hear me?" he whispered, gently touching the tiny stars. They were silent, oblivious to his presence, but one or two stirred at his words. There was something different about them, too—a sort of aura he hadn't noticed before. He zoomed in on them, focusing all his intent, groaning with the effort. His mind seemed about to snap, stretched as it was to its limits.

"Can you hear me?" he repeated, and this time, he felt them respond. It wasn't in words, precisely, but their attention was certainly on him, wary and prickly hostile. The witches of Agienna; the people who used forbidden magic without a second thought. But there was something familiar about them, too, something instantly recognizable, just as it had been with the wolves. A sense of kinship.

"You know who I am. I'm here to right a wrong before it's too late," he told them.

He didn't know which one of the tiny specs was Logitt. The prospect of falling under her scrutiny again filled him with uneasiness. But he didn't want to hide anything anymore. He laid his mind bare before his enemies as proof, as a gesture of good faith. No more secrets, no more lies, no more grudges.

"If you care for the prosperity of Agienna more than you care for the destruction of Mulberny, you'll listen to me," he continued. "It is time to stop the bloodshed, the cycle of death. Let us find the balance that will bring us peace—together."

There was a slight shift in their silence, a reluctant interest mixed with indignation, and Callan hurried to press on that interest before the effort of communicating prove too much for him to handle. Already, he was distantly aware of his hands shaking, his body breaking out in sweat despite the chilling wind. He wouldn't last much longer under the strain.

"I'd offer you a new truce, but what I really want for us is a new way to coexist. One that is fair, one that would allow you to sail the seas freely yet ensure the safety of our coast. One that would unite us again as neighbors and brothers instead of tearing us apart. All I ask is for you to listen before you strike—and I swear I will listen too."

The silence was so complete that for a second, he was sure they'd shut him out. But no—the witches were still there. Considering. Wavering.

"Please," he whispered, but didn't have the chance to add anything else. His consciousness was stretched to the limit, like a rope pulled too taut, and that rope finally snapped. Callan reeled with the unexpected force of the backlash, falling into blackness dotted with colorful lights dancing in front of his eyes. A wave of bile rose in his throat, and he crumpled to his knees onto the wet sand. His ears rang so loudly it took him a while to register the sounds of dry heaving, and longer to realize he was the one making them.

Slowly, his scattered mind came back into focus. The wind, stronger now, was blowing in his face, and someone was holding him, murmuring soothing words in his ear. No, not someone. Derek. He leaned instinctively into his embrace, the warmth of his body comforting even through layers of soaking-wet clothing.

"Are you with me?" Derek asked, a touched hesitantly.

It made Callan wonder what he'd looked like during the past few minutes.

"Yes."

"Good." Derek squeezed his shoulders a bit harder, and then let go, sitting back on his haunches on the sand. "Did it work? What did they say?"

"Nothing." Callan took a deep breath, trying to cool his burning throat. "I didn't have the chance to get their answer."

"I guess we'll know soon enough." Derek helped Callan to his feet and drew him in for a quick, hard kiss, even though Callan's lips probably still tasted like acid.

"You two have picked the worst possible time to go frolicking on a beach," a dry voice called from somewhere atop the sand dunes.

They turned just as Duke Bergen walked down the gentle slope, followed by a dozen guards.

"Father," Callan said, stepping forward. "What are you doing here?"

"Same as you. Meeting my enemies face-to-face." The duke tossed his head impatiently. "Our forces are ready to flank them while we draw them in."

"My lord!" One of the guards pointed toward the sea, and everyone turned their heads that way.

The dark curved shapes cut through the white foam, the sound of oars breaking the surface now distinct against the distant howling of the storm. With a low thud, the bow of the foremost ship hit the swash.

Moonlight briefly reflected off the blade of Bergen's sword as he unsheathed it.

"The Unnamed is waiting. Let's see who gets to meet her first."

Chapter Nineteen

"NO, WAIT!"

Derek stepped in front of the duke and his men, raising his hands in a pacifying gesture as useless as it was desperate. Loud splashes behind him indicated the Agiennans were already on the move. Beside him, Callan wheeled to face them. Unlike his father, he didn't reach for his sword, and Derek swallowed hard. Poised as they were, Callan and he were trapped between a rock and a hard place, with nowhere to retreat even if they wanted to.

"Please, just wait! Give them a chance to say their piece."

"What are you talking about?" the duke asked irritably, but at least he halted, and so did the troop behind him. In the back row of their black-clad silhouettes, Derek saw Hamlin's bulky figure and, beside him, Ivo and Macon's pale faces.

Damn it. He'd given in to his brothers' pleas to accompany him but had told them, in no uncertain terms, to stay back. They were going to have words—assuming they'd last the night.

"I talked to them." Callan's voice was clipped, and he was watching the dark shadows that amassed at the water's edge rather than looking at his father. "I offered a truce. They've yet to give their answer."

"You did what?" For a second Bergen was taken aback, the moon reflecting in his widened eyes. But he quickly regained his composure, his posture tensing as murmurs rose from the men around them. At the back, Ivo frowned, looking from Derek to Callan to Bergen, but Derek had no time to spare for his brother's feelings at the moment.

"He did what he knew to be right," Derek said, loudly enough to be heard above the startled whispers Callan's declaration had caused, but he was addressing the duke alone. "Your son has stood by your side his whole life, never wavering, never questioning. Can't you do the same for him just this once? Before you all go brandishing your swords and axes, stop for a second to hear what the other side has to say."

"Well, we're about to find out one way or another," Callan said dryly.

Several torches flared below them, illuminating the crowd of Agiennan warriors. The ominous glare painted the wicked blades of their axes red, as if in anticipation of what was to come, but like the Mulbernians, they hung back instead of rushing into an attack. A few figures detached themselves from the throng and made their way toward their party.

"My lord—" one of the duke's lieutenants began, stepping forward, but surprisingly, Bergen silenced him with a wave of his hand.

"Do you know what you're doing?" he inquired of his son.

"Not really." Callan glanced at him briefly and then turned back toward the shore, squaring his shoulders. "But I'm going to do it anyway."

The speculative murmurs hushed as the Agiennans approached and halted only a few yards away from where Callan and Derek were standing. The soldiers shifted uneasily at the sight of their sworn enemies coming so close to one of their commanders, but no one dared engage them without a direct order—which the duke had yet to issue, despite his earlier rancor. For a second, Derek let himself entertain the wild notion that the Agiennans were actually there to take Callan up on his offer and negotiate, until he saw who was heading the impromptu delegation.

One of the Islanders carried a torch, so their faces were clearly visible—and recognizable, despite the swirls of red and blue paint that decorated them. Aegir, flanked by his warriors, fixed his gaze on Callan, who met it steadily.

Derek suppressed an urge to stand closer to him. The air, already crackling with the storm's energy, was heavy with a tension dangerously close to bursting into flames, and every unnecessary movement could ignite them. Instead, he focused on Aegir's followers, most of whom had the look of older, seasoned fighters. The patterns on their gear and the plaiting of their hair differed widely enough for Derek to conclude these were the representatives of other clans, perhaps even the members of the council Aegir had mentioned during their captivity on Cirda. That, at least, would explain why they hadn't been attacked yet. Unchecked, Aegir would be unlikely to exercise such restraint in the presence of the man he'd sworn to kill.

"We received the message," one of the older clansmen said, his voice low and gruff. "Who delivered it?"

"This one." Logitt pushed through the row of men and women around the chieftains. Her hair hung around her face in long wet strands, making her appear like an ancient heathen goddess wreathed in seaweed. She pointed at Callan, her eyes glinting eerily in the firelight. "The witch of Irthorg is coming into his own, it'd seem."

Callan flinched. Angry whispers rose behind them; the Mulbernians didn't take well to the accusation. Their indignation was aimed at the Agiennans, but Derek didn't want to think about what would happen once they realized the truth of Logitt's proclamation. Callan was respected, but not universally loved, and there were enough vicious rumors circulating about him already.

"Witch or not, he's made a promise," Derek said, facing the clansmen. "Are you willing to discuss it?"

"I recall him swearing you off to make us spare you, yet here you are by his side. Deception is in his blood as much as magic. This is nothing more than an *egondar* trick," Aegir sneered, not taking his eyes off Callan. If looks could kill, Callan's blood would be drenching the already wet sand, along with every last Mulbernian's. "We're wasting our time, listening to their lies."

"We know your mind, Aegir," one of the other chieftains said, lifting her hand in warning. "You've brought us here. Now we want the mainlanders to speak. If this is some kind of a ruse, I swear to Dagorn they'll pay for it." She turned to the duke. "What is your proposal, Bergen son of Jennia?"

Dead silence fell on the beach, broken only by the distant wailing of the wind and the rhythmic breaking of waves against the shore, an eternal heartbeat of the world. Every eye turned to the duke, who was still standing only a few feet away from his unwanted guests, still clutching his sword, the flickering light catching on the hard planes of his face. Derek sucked in a breath, but his heart thumped too wildly to calm it.

"I'm not the one you should be asking," Bergen said finally. He pointedly lowered his weapon and gestured toward Callan. "I grant my son full authority to negotiate."

Derek's knees went weak. Whatever bad blood there was between himself and his father-in-law, at this moment, he was ready to forgive him his own attempted murder—not that Bergen seemed to be clamoring for absolution.

Callan drew a deep breath. If the unexpected show of support from that particular quarter surprised him, he didn't let on. *You can do this*, Derek urged him silently. *This is your moment to mend everything.*

Even though his husband couldn't possibly have heard him, he flashed Derek a quick smile before facing the chieftains.

"I've seen enough fighting." Callan's voice was soft, but it carried above the noise. "When I married Idona, I thought it was all behind us. I believed we could finally have peace, after all these years. Her death dashed that dream, but it's not too late to find it again—in honor of her memory as much for the sake of all of us who are still living."

Aegir grimaced at his words but said nothing. The other chieftains remained impassive.

"But I understand you're not here to listen to pretty words," Callan continued. "So here is my proposal. Mulberny will bestow the Outer Isles sailors the right of unrestricted passage through its waters all along the coast for the purposes of trawling, exploration, and travel. You'll be free to trade at any Mulberny port without additional levies or tithes, other than the usual commerce taxes."

The chieftains exchanged glances. The current treaty greatly diminished the scope of Agiennan seafaring, effectively limiting it to the passages between the Isles and the North Sea—if anyone was either bold or foolhardy enough to venture into the uncharted icy waters. As far as Derek knew, the abrupt cutoff of old trade routes in the aftermath of the war was the main reason for the swift decline in Agienna's welfare.

"And in return?" another chieftain demanded. Derek couldn't tell which clan he represented, but he was arguably the oldest one among them, his white hair done in a multitude of tiny braids that crowned his head like a snowcap.

"You must swear off plundering the Mulberny coastline. No more raiding. No more wars. Stop accosting our villages and our ships—and this goes for all of the clans. There can be no hiding behind rogue pirates or sending the Vanir to do your dirty work." Callan glanced at Aegir before letting his gaze sweep across the array of unreadable faces before him. "What I want is real peace, not a temporary patchwork solution we can slap on our problems for a few more years."

"This is a fucking insult," Aegir sneered. "This whelp presumes to *allow* us the freedoms that had been ours for generations! Our longships had been coming and going as they pleased all along these shores long before this land had a name. We don't need their handouts. I say we kill them all now and restore what rightfully belongs to us!"

His words caused a reaction among the Agiennans, but Derek didn't wait to see whether the murmurs were in agreement or in negation. He had to act before Aegir could inflame his listeners further, banking on mutual animosity.

"There's another thing." Derek was surprised to find how firm his voice sounded, despite the sudden dryness that seized his throat. Everyone's gaze shifted to him, and he had to consciously push down on his fear that once again his input would be ignored or dismissed as unimportant. But he couldn't back down now. Callan had risen to the challenge, and Derek was going to rise right along with him, relying on the compulsion of urgency to get him through where his sense of self-worth fell short. "As the Count of Camria, and Lord Callan's husband, I will pledge shipments of grain from my fiefdom be delivered to the Outer Isles all through the winter if this new truce holds. Camria can afford it for now."

"You think you can buy us off with bread?" Aegir's voice was dangerously low this time, barely audible above the crash of the waves. Derek couldn't decipher his expression, but his sudden eerie calm was a lot scarier than his late father's rage-induced fits.

"Of course not! It's not meant as a bribe, but as an aid. Before coming to Mulberny, I had no knowledge of your plight." Derek gestured widely, taking in everyone around him as a subject in his statement. "But now that I do, it's the least I can do to help. I'm making the offer in good faith, not as an insult. Please, I..."

He trailed off, too conscious of the attention his words had garnered, both from the chieftains and the Mulbernian troops. Logitt was watching him, her frail figure shrouded in thick furs. The glimmer in her eyes mesmerized him for a moment, so much that a touch on his arm made Derek jump.

"Thank you," Callan whispered. His hand slid down Derek's arm, and their fingers intertwined. His smile lit his eyes from within, washing Derek's whole soul in a warm glow. They could get through anything as long as Derek got to be on the receiving end of that smile every day for the rest of his life.

Aegir was watching at them as well, his gaze shifting from Callan to Derek and back again.

"When I first heard you'd killed my daughter, I vowed to take your life in return." Aegir's voice was still dangerously quiet, and though he was looking at both of them, there was no doubt as to who he was addressing. "Gods help me, I've tried. I came here tonight with this very purpose. But now I see I was wrong. You don't deserve that."

He advanced toward them, and Derek instinctively stepped back, pulling Callan along with him.

"That would be too easy," Aegir continued, apparently oblivious to how the rest of the warriors tensed all around them, hands going to their weapons. "Your death would be redemption, not punishment. I want you to suffer. I want you to feel what's it like to lose—"

Without finishing the sentence, he charged at Derek. A long serrated blade flashed in his hand, and time slowed even when everything seemed to happen at once. Callan lunged in front of him, moving like a shadow, but Aegir sidestepped him and ducked, angling the knife at Derek's ribs. Derek recoiled, stumbling backward, and collided with a hard body behind him. That someone grabbed him by the forearm and yanked him out of the way, sending him crashing into Callan. They both tumbled hard with the impact, sprawling on top of each other on the sand.

His own shocked face reflected in Callan's wide eyes. Derek rolled away just in time to see Aegir and Bergen locked in a deadly embrace. The knife that was meant for Derek had gone into the duke's abdomen all the way to its bone handle. Bergen stumbled and went down on one knee, his hand still gripping the hilt of the sword that jutted out of Aegir's back. For a split second everything froze. Then Aegir made an awful gurgling sound and crumpled to the ground.

Shouting erupted all around them, punctuated by the clamor of weapons being drawn. Callan scrambled to his feet, standing above the two fallen men, his arms extended to the sides as if he could keep the two warring sides at bay by sheer force of will.

"No, stop! Stop!" he bellowed.

A bolt of lightning speared the sky and hit the beach about half a mile to the north, followed by a roll of thunder. Derek didn't know if it was a coincidence, or if Callan drew on his magic again, or if this was Logitt's doing, but either way, it worked. Everyone ducked instinctively, cowering from the stroke of blinding brightness just before steel could meet flesh.

Derek crawled toward the duke, the rush of blood in his ears as deafening as the thunder. His hands shook as he half lifted the older man's shoulders. He spared a glance at Aegir, but his body, slumped over the duke's leg, was immobile.

Blood trickled down Bergen's chin, but he was awake, his breath coming in loud rasps. His bony fingers closed around Derek's wrists, digging in painfully.

"You saved my life," Derek whispered. "Why?"

Bergen closed his eyes briefly, but his gaze, when he opened them again, was steady.

"Couldn't let Aegir...hurt my son. He loves you...too much."

Derek swallowed hard, his mind racing. The din of raised voices and Callan's angry shouts as he desperately tried to stave off the impeding battle drifted in the background while Derek frantically searched for a response. But before he could say anything, one of the duke's lieutenants, Xarin, crouched beside them.

"My lord?"

Bergen's grip on Derek's hand tightened further as he pulled himself into a sitting position, grunting with pain. His forehead shone with sweat, despite the cold.

"Please, don't—" Derek began, but Bergen silenced him with an impatient glare and turned to Xarin.

"Stand...down. All of you, now."

"But, sir—"

"I said, stand down!"

Xarin's mouth tightened, but he nodded and sprang to his feet, calling out the order. Derek thought he could hear the Agiennan chieftain—the woman who'd spoken to them first—issue her own commands in a language he couldn't understand, but he didn't dare look up to see whether she was following Bergen's suit or not. His hand hovered above the handle of the knife, which glistened with blood, but the duke shook his head.

"Don't." He was pushing the words out now, each followed by a wheezing sound. "It's over."

"Father, no." Callan lowered himself beside them. Derek started to rise to give them a moment of privacy which he knew would be their last, but Bergen held on to him, so he had no choice but to stay in place. "I'll summon the physician."

"Too late...for that. I've been in your way...long enough, Callan. The Unnamed has had her sacrifice. It's time...for the young blood to lead the way. To leave...the wounds of the past behind." Bergen looked at Derek. "And you...promise me...you'll make my son happy."

"I promise," Derek said around the lump in his throat. "I will."

Bergen's eyes rolled back. The grip on Derek's wrist slackened. A shudder went through the duke's body, and then he was still.

"Father!" Callan shook Bergen's shoulders, but it was clear no answer would be forthcoming. The expression on his face was one that Derek knew only too well, one he'd hoped never to see again—stricken and lost, his cheeks streaked with tears and rain. Derek reached out to him, his own breath catching with resurfacing grief, but Callan wheeled around as a stooped, dark figure approached them.

"You. Do something! Help him!"

Logitt shook her head. Her gaze traveled from Bergen's face to Aegir's lifeless form, the tip of the duke's sword protruding out of his back at an awkward angle. Derek knew he didn't imagine the flicker of sorrow in her eyes.

"No magic can cure death," she said. "Be at peace. They died like just as they wanted; now you have to live the same way."

She turned away and hobbled back down the shore toward the ships. The crowd of Agiennan warriors, held back by their chieftains, parted before her and closed in her wake until she was out of sight.

"I'm sorry," Derek said, biting his lip. Considering Duke Bergen had caused Count Johan's demise, perhaps Derek playing an inadvertent part in his death served some kind of poetic, fated justice, but the notion brought no solace, only more heartache. "Callan, I'm so sorry."

Callan's exhale sounded more like a sob, but he shook his head jerkily.

"It's not your fault. He did what he believed was right. That's what we all hope to do, in the end."

He got up and helped Derek to his feet. They were standing on a narrow strip of sand between two tidal waves of tightly pressed human bodies, ready to crash into each other. Shouts and angry murmurs sounded on both sides but subsided when Callan addressed the Agiennan leaders again.

"This changes nothing. My offer to you still stands."

"You will let your father go unavenged?" the older chieftain asked. He leaned on the long handle of his battle-ax, but his posture betrayed no frailty. "Then you're either a coward or a saint."

"I'm neither," Callan said. "The one responsible for his death is with the Unnamed now. The blood spilled tonight was enough to quench my thirst for revenge, should I have wished for it."

The raw pain Derek had witnessed a few moments before had been wiped clean from Callan's face, replaced by his usual mask of calm iciness. The burden of responsibilities suffered no reprieve, however deep the grief. It was a lesson Derek had hoped Callan wouldn't have to learn for a long time yet, but fate was as impatient as it was cruel. Derek wanted nothing more than to hold his husband's hand and offer him comfort, but this was neither the time nor the place for gentleness.

"We are neighbors," Callan continued. "I was told we are brothers. Brothers sometimes fight and do awful things to each other, but they cannot escape the bond of blood. Let it be something that unites us rather than tears us apart."

"We hear you, son of Bergen," the tall woman said, once again hushing the men behind her. "I'm Gunnara, chieftain of the Herig clan. Aegir was my uncle, and since he had no direct heirs, I now speak for the Danulf as well, until the Council of the Chieftains chooses a new leader. Call your men off. We shall discuss your proposal and give our answer in the morning."

"Give me your word that you will not wage an attack until you give me your decision, face-to-face."

Gunnara nodded. "I swear it. There will be no more killing tonight."

"It's a trick." Xarin spoke up once Gunnara and the rest of the Agiennans who followed her were safely out of earshot, gathered by their ships. "They will betray your trust if you're not careful, my lord." Glancing down at the tangle of bodies behind them, he amended, "Your Grace."

"Perhaps. But I'm willing to take that chance." Unlike Xarin, Callan didn't look back, but his hand sought out Derek's, their fingers lacing together, sharing a spark of warmth despite the clamminess of their skin. Derek squeezed his husband's hand, hoping to convey through the brief touch everything he couldn't put into words.

"Set up camp for the night. Arrange for my father to be taken back to Irthorg and surrender the Danulf chieftain's body to his kin." Callan raised his face up to the sky. The moon shone brightly, gilding a path on the water for a few brief moments before the clouds shrouded it again. "Tomorrow we'll see how the dice fall."

Chapter Twenty

THE NIGHT STRETCHED on and on, seemingly reluctant to end and leave him in peace. Contrary to what his father's lieutenants might have thought, Callan wasn't entirely comfortable with the immediate proximity of a potentially still-hostile army right on his doorstep. He went about allotting patrols and scouts that would range all the way to the fishing villages along the bay, to make sure their dwellers were undisturbed, and arranged for a messenger to be dispatched to Irthorg with the grim news.

He hated not to be the one to inform Adele of what had happened or be there for her during that outburst of initial shock, but at least it would prepare her for the inevitable before the cortege with the duke's remains arrived at the castle. For all her delicacy, Adele was a strong soul, maybe much more so than him. But everyone deserved to have a shoulder to cry on when they were notified of their parent's death.

The thought reminded him of Derek—the tenderness of his touch, the softness of his voice, the sharpness of his gaze. The memory of Derek's hand in his, that small solace amid strife, filled his already battered heart with bittersweet longing. Callan wanted nothing more than to hold him in his arms again and be held back as he allowed himself to give in to his misery, even if it was only for a short while.

But he hadn't seen Derek since they'd broke off with the Agiennans on the beach. They'd made their camp in a field close to the main road, high enough above the shoreline to have a vantage point to the moored Agiennan ships. Having come prepared to engage in battle rather than spend the night, the troops had no tents, so most of them huddled around campfires, keeping an uneasy watch on similar fires that had sprung up at the water's edge. Rest seemed a lifetime away at this point.

Cold, tired, and soaking wet, Callan had finished making a final round, inspecting the perimeter of the camp, when a hooded figure stepped in front of him from behind the line of tethered horses. Callan reached for his sword, but the newcomer threw his hood back, revealing a pale, youthful face.

"Ivo." Callan relaxed marginally, but the sight of Derek's younger sibling did nothing to alleviate his mood. "What are you doing here?"

"I wanted to speak with you."

"With me? Where's your brother?"

The inquiry came out harsher than he'd intended, and Ivo raised an eyebrow at his tone. The drizzling rain plastered his usually wavy hair to his head, and he was shivering despite his thick wool cloak with its goldwork collar, but neither his voice nor his expression had lost any of their ingrained cynicism.

"Which one? Macon is probably asleep in our camp, and by all accounts, you should have much better knowledge of Derek's whereabouts than I."

"What is that supposed to mean?"

"You're the one married to him, aren't you? Against his will, I might add." Ivo's fingers clutched the edge of his cloak tightly, but his gaze, directed straight into Callan's eyes, was unwavering.

"I never forced him. Into anything."

"Maybe not. But your father did. Pushing for this marriage and this ridiculous agreement only to use my brother as a sacrifice for his schemes. Arranging for him to be kidnapped and killed to stoke the fires of his revenge. Derek told me everything just now," Ivo added, probably reading Callan's expression correctly. "I knew it was a mistake from the very beginning. I tried to warn him. But he's always been too high-minded for his own good."

"Unlike you?" Callan said before he could stop himself. He didn't know where Ivo was headed with this conversation, but he had no patience to continue it.

"Unlike me," Ivo agreed easily. "But very much like you. You too have a very similar sense of what is right and proper. And that's why I'm sure you will do the honorable thing."

"And what would that be?"

"Letting him go." Ivo raised his hand before Callan had the chance to scoff at him. "Hear me out. You know Derek was practically coerced into this marriage. We've drafted a petition for the High Queen to annul it."

Callan's stomach lurched. "We?"

"My family. Derek included. Look," Ivo said, taking another step toward him. "I know you and he have shared...something. But you cannot expect him to stay with you now. Not after what the duke did—and not after what you've revealed yourself to be."

Callan went very still, his throat so dry he couldn't form coherent words. It was as if for a moment he forgot how to breathe. A dull ache spread in his chest, a hopeless anticipation of loss.

That was exactly what he'd always been afraid of. He could endure the personal repercussions of exposure; he was no stranger to acrid whispers and judging glances, and he cared little for what others thought of his character. But no one else around him deserved to be ostracized for Callan's sins—or what society perceived as sin.

"You're a witch, Callan," Ivo said into his silence. "Which may be fine for the Outer Isles, but witchcraft is a dangerous thing to be accused of in Ivicia. Once the Queen hears of it, she won't hesitate to dissolve this marriage— and do much more besides."

"Is that a threat?" Callan found his voice again, but it sounded hollow rather than infuriated.

"All I'm saying is you should release him before someone else does it for you," Ivo said.

"What if 'he' doesn't want to be released?" Derek stepped up to them from the shadows. The horse closest to them in the line snorted and tossed its head, spooked by the sudden movement.

Callan's heart leapt before he could stomp down on the surge of irrational hope.

"What do you think you're doing here, Ivo?" Derek said, rounding on his brother.

"What you should have done a long time ago." Ivo raised his head defiantly. "Mulberny has been our enemy all along. It's high time to disassociate yourself from this wretched fiefdom."

"Whether or not I should is not your decision to make," Derek said.

Callan had never heard him use that kind of tone before. He was, of course, aware of his husband's title, but he hadn't actually thought of him as a count until now.

Now, he could well imagine him issuing commands or conducting hard negotiations in that voice. It certainly made Ivo shift uncomfortably.

He recalled Logitt's earlier words. It would seem "the Witch of Irthorg" wasn't the only one coming into his own. The Sparrow of Camria was showing he had talons too.

"I care about you. I care about our family. I'm only trying to help," Ivo said.

"If this is your idea of help, then I don't want it." Derek turned to Callan, his eyes bright in the faint, distant glow of the campfires. "I did plan to ask for an annulment. But it was before I got to know you. Before I fell in love with you. I want to be with you, now and always, whatever the future brings. The question is...do *you* want that too?"

Callan crossed the short distance between them. They were standing so close Callan felt Derek's breath on his skin, coming out in small white puffs, instantly dissipated by the falling rain. He smelled the moisture in his hair, almost heard the blood rushing in his veins.

"You already know the answer," Callan said. "I do."

"I'M SORRY ABOUT that," Derek said once they escorted Ivo back to the Camrian side of the makeshift camp. Macon was already asleep, but Hamlin kept watch by a fire and nodded when Derek ordered him not to lose sight of his brothers.

"Your brother was just trying to protect you," Callan said. "And he wasn't wrong. When the word reaches the High Court that I'm a witch—"

"We'll worry about that when it happens," Derek said firmly. He took Callan's hand and led him away from the edge of the camp. "It's all a terribly stupid superstition anyway. Magic is not evil in itself; what matters is how you apply it. You have done nothing but try to do right by everyone, friend or foe. Maybe it's time for people in this realm to confront their prejudices and bigotry."

Callan couldn't help but smile.

"You always know what to say. Aren't you a bit too young to be so wise?" he teased gently. The bitterness of unshed tears still burned at the back of his throat, but now, with Derek walking by his side, their hands tightly clasped together, he could breathe through it.

Derek was silent for a few moments. The night closed around them as they walked farther away from the light of the campfires.

"I've never thought about myself as wise," he said finally. "And neither did anyone else."

"I think so," Callan said, squeezing his hand. "I think you're smart, and brave, and selfless. I think I'm lucky to have you in my life."

"My only regret is that our marriage was possible because your first one had ended," Derek said softly. "That my happiness came at the expense of someone else's."

Not so long ago the mere mention of Idona would have felt like a stab to the heart, but now, it only brought forth a kind of quiet sadness. Perhaps somewhere amid Callan's attempts to make peace with the world he'd made peace with himself, too, putting some of the old pain to rest.

"It doesn't work like that," he said. "You didn't take her away from me. In fact, you came along when I needed it the most. And I think...she would have liked you. I have to believe she would wish this—us—for me."

Derek squeezed his hand.

"Thank you," he whispered.

"Where are we going?" Callan asked after a few more minutes of trudging through wet, windswept grassland.

"Remember when we talked about slipping into the woods alone, just you and me?"

Callan stopped. "I don't...I can't do this tonight. Not when my father—"

"That's not what I meant," Derek said gently. "But it seems to me we both need a few minutes to ourselves. We might not get them again for a very long time."

They proceeded to a tiny copse just by the side of the main road. It wasn't a wood by any means, only about a dozen trees, their trunks gnarled and bent by the strong winds. The fires of both camps flickered in the distance like tiny dots, separated by a dark swath of sloping beach, and farther away the lights of the fishing villages grew fewer as the night waned. From there they couldn't hear the whinnying of the horses, or the rasp of blades being sharpened, only the rustling of grass and creaking of the tree branches. If it weren't for the freezing cold seeping under their soaked clothes and chilling them to the bone, it'd be almost peaceful there, now that the storm had passed.

It was too wet to sit comfortably on the ground, so they stood, leaning against one of the thicker trees, looking down at the shoreline, distinguishable only by the reflection of the moon on the water.

Derek snuggled closer, and Callan threw his arm around his shoulders, pressing against him.

"We can't stay here for long," Callan said, even as he wished for the opposite.

"I know." Derek shifted, putting his head on Callan's shoulder. "Do you think they'll take you up on your offer?"

"It could go either way. Aegir's death certainly made a mess of things."

Derek scoffed. "You mean Aegir made a mess of things. That was madness. What was he trying to accomplish?"

"It was a desperate last act." Callan closed his eyes briefly, letting the salty breeze wash over his face. "An effort to stop his world from changing as much as it was an attempt to mete his final revenge on me. For what it's worth, this is not the end I'd wish for him."

"He was your enemy."

"He was a bereft father. I think we can all understand how devastating grief can be."

"Yes." Derek's breath was tickling the lobe of his ear. "All too well. If you let it fester, it becomes poison, a fire that has to be fed with other lives, other dreams. It will consume you and everyone around you. You made the right choice down there, letting go of the anger."

Callan swallowed. His father's face surfaced in his mind, haggard with strain and agony. Children losing their parents was the way of the world, but he hadn't been ready for that at all. Whatever disagreements they might have gotten into, whatever sacrifices Callan had to make to appease Bergen's ambitions, whatever unspoken things had passed between them, Callan had always known he was loved—and had loved his father in return.

Tears burned his eyes, and this time, he didn't hold them back.

"He's really gone," he said, his voice thick. "It's so... I can't grasp it. He's always been there for me, and somehow I believed he always would be. Immutable, like a rock."

Like the cliffs of Irthorg that withstood the fury of the sea year after year, generation after generation. It was a silly, childish notion to entertain in a family that'd seen its fair share of death and suffering, but Bergen had been one to defy the odds until the very end.

"I'm sorry."

"But you're also right. I've had enough of anger," Callan said, closing his eyes against the blur of tears. "I can't let it take up all the space inside me anymore. I have something else with which to fill it now." He turned his head, making Derek draw back and look up at him. "I love you, Derek. So much."

"I love you too," Derek said softly. His eyes shone in the moonlight, their color hidden by the darkness but their keen intelligence and loveliness impossible to disguise. "My beautiful, feral wolf."

"My fearless sparrow," Callan whispered and leaned in to taste the salt on Derek's lips.

THE DARKNESS AROUND them slowly faded to gray as they made their way down to the camp. With morning still a long way off, not even the chirping of birds broke the silence, but most of the men were already up, tending to the horses and heating up quick breakfasts.

"What a long night this has been," Derek said, looking up at the sky. Wet earth squelched under the soles of his boots. Even his gait felt weary. "But I'm not sure I want it to be over."

"Remember that first night on Cirda?" Callan asked. "I was sure I was going to die in the morning, my heart and lungs ripped out of me."

Derek shuddered. "Don't remind me."

Callan stopped, making Derek turn and look at him.

"But you came for me, and we lived through it. We lived through the next one, too, and the next. I can't promise you we'll live to see this dawn, but I have a hunch we'll pull through once again."

Derek smiled. "A witch's precognition?"

Deep shadows lurked under his eyes, his jaw sporting a hint of stubble. Callan was sure he presented an even worse sight, drained as he was first by the mental effort of contacting the Agiennans on the high seas, and then by the horrible shock of watching his father draw his last breath, but Derek didn't seem to mind.

"More like a foolish hope," Callan said. "Don't they say it's always the last to die?"

One of the watchers saluted them as they approached.

"My lords," she said. "Commander Rema was searching for you not a moment ago. They said it was urgent."

Callan and Derek exchanged a look and hurried to the temporary headquarters—which was no more than a sheet of waxed canvas stretched over high poles as a shelter from the rain.

Rema was already there, as well as several of Bergen's lieutenants, save Xarin, who'd departed to Irthorg with the duke's body earlier. Fully armed and geared, they were drawing lines in the damp sand, arguing about something, but all hushed and bowed when Callan entered the "tent" with Derek on his heels.

"Your Grace," Rema said with noticeable relief. "The Islanders are stirring."

All traces of fatigue drained from Callan's mind. Derek's sharp intake of breath indicated he was on alert too.

"Stirring how?" Callan asked, taking a mental stock and readying himself for impending combat. "Are they moving on the offense?"

"Too soon to tell," one of the older warriors said. "But if I were them, I wouldn't wait till dawn to strike a sleeping enemy."

Callan tended to agree with him. The Agiennans may have given him his word, but he knew as well as anyone that oaths had little to do with strategy. The fact that they hadn't yet attacked the Mulbernian camp was a good sign.

"Rouse the troops, but have them hold positions," he said. "No one does anything without my direct order."

"Yes, Your Grace."

"You should probably send your brothers back to Irthorg for now," Callan said, turning to Derek. "It would've been better if they'd never come, or left last night, but I admit I was too preoccupied to consider their safety. This might turn ugly, and I don't want them caught up in the melee."

"They're here for me."

"I know. But if things go awry, I'd rather not lose any more family members."

Derek pursed his lips but nodded in assent. Callan opened his mouth to summon a messenger but was stopped by a soldier ducking under the sagging canvas roof.

"My lords," they said, a little out of breath, and bowed when they saw Callan. "The Agiennan envoy wishes to enter the camp."

Callan and Derek exchanged a look again.

"Escort them here," Callan ordered. "Allow them to keep their weapons."

"Are you sure that's wise, Your Grace?" Rema asked.

"I'll risk it to respect their honor," Callan said. "Show them in."

The soldier bowed again and left. Derek's hand slid the length of Callan's arm, but he said nothing. A few tense minutes passed in silence until several Agiennan chieftains entered the tent, escorted by half a dozen of the duke's guards.

If tensions were high before, now the air could practically be cut with a knife. The envoy only included four people—Gunnara of the Herig; the older chieftain with the snow-white braids, whom Callan recognized as Siggeir of the Vanir; and the leaders of the Sebald and Urfan clans.

"I see you, elders," Callan said in Agiennan.

"We see you, Callan son of Bergen," Gunnara said, switching to the common tongue. "We have come to accept your proposal."

"I'm glad to hear it," Callan said.

In truth, he was struggling to hold his sigh of relief, as, he was sure, were all those present. Up until now, he hadn't quite believed his wild gamble would pay off. He'd been let down by hope too many times to have any faith in it. But perhaps that wasn't true anymore. Not when the most precious thing he could ever wish for was right there, within reach—and it wasn't a new political alliance.

"You've sacrificed your reputation and your blood for the chance of peace," Gunnara said. In the faint light of the slowly rising autumn sun, the lines in her face were more pronounced, a testimony to her age and experience. "We trust you to uphold your end of the bargain. The raids will cease, as you requested."

Callan's heart leapt at her words, but he'd had plenty of practice hiding his excitement when he had to.

"What about the Vanir?" he asked. "They're the ones who've been harrying us the most."

"I will vouch for the Vanir," Siggeir said, "if you'll vouch for Camria's aid."

Callan nodded. "I will."

"We both will," Derek said, coming to stand beside him. When the Agiennan elders' eyes all turned on him, he didn't flinch. His inflection was as soft as ever, but there was nothing soft about his demeanor as their gazes met in silent understanding—old enemies, new allies, joined with nothing more than good faith. Perhaps, in the end, it was all that was needed. "A word spoken cannot be undone."

Epilogue

DEREK LAY ON the bed in a casual sprawl. He thought, lazily, that he should probably get up and clean himself, but he couldn't be bothered, and there was something unexpectedly erotic in lingering in bed, the evidence of their mutual pleasure still clinging to their skin.

Callan's breath tickled his neck, and he turned his head to look at him. His husband's face was more relaxed than he'd ever seen it, as if some of the perpetual tension he always bore had seeped away into the sweaty sheets. Derek smiled at the thought that he could do that, that he could ease Callan's unseen burden, even for a little while. It felt almost better than the sex itself.

"I've never had anyone boss me around so much in bed," Callan said gravely, but laughter was sprinkled in his eyes. "And so early in the morning too."

"I'm sorry," Derek said smugly.

"Don't be. It feels good, giving your lover exactly what they want."

Lover. The choice of word was strange between husbands, but perhaps not so incongruous after all. It could have a thousand different meanings, but only one that really mattered at the moment. Derek lifted his hand to trace the line of Callan's jaw, the morning stubble prickling his fingertips.

"And what do you want?"

Callan leaned closer, the warmth of his solid body a lure Derek couldn't resist.

"I want to kiss you."

"Then kiss me."

The touch of their lips was unexpectedly light. Callan explored his mouth with a gentleness so unlike their earlier frenzy, and Derek responded with the same unhurried curiosity. With the flare of their lust effectively sated, they now took their time reveling in the simple pleasure of a shared kiss, tasting each other anew, as if for the first time.

They were both a little breathless when they broke off.

"What you do to me," Callan murmured in his ear, sounding rueful.

"Whatever you want me to," Derek said and was rewarded by an actual shiver that ran through Callan's body.

"We have to get up, unfortunately," Callan said, sitting up on the bed with a sigh and then lowering his legs to the floor. "I want to say goodbye to Adele before she leaves."

"Me too." Derek sat up as well, drawing the sheet over his rapidly cooling skin. "She is so excited about her departure."

Adele was set to begin her studies at the School of Musical Arts in Oifel. Ivo, who was currently visiting their mother in Camria, was to meet her on his way to the Royal Academy. Knowing her, all her trunks were already loaded and arranged just so by the new castellan's efficient hand at the back of the carriage marked with a wolf's head crest, and she was busy saying farewell to all her friends at Irthorg.

"She probably packed half the castle," Callan grumbled, getting up and walking over to the wardrobe.

Derek hid his smile as he watched his husband rummage around in search of a set of clean clothes, admiring the nice image his nakedness presented.

"It's your sister's first time away from home," Derek said. "Going to a new place, meeting new people—it's understandable if she's a bit overeager and wants to bring a few extra outfits. Especially considering how glamorous Oifel might seem to someone so young."

"The way you describe it makes me want to go along and watch out for her in the big city," Callan said, pulling on a pair of pants.

"Those are my exact thoughts about Ivo." Derek chuckled. "But we have to trust them to be sensible. They could use a certain amount of freedom after everything they've been through."

"That reminds me." Callan turned to him, and for a moment Derek almost missed what he was saying, distracted by the vibrant blue of his eyes catching the rays of an early morning autumn sun. "I have something for you."

"What is it?"

"Well, you see..." Callan walked back to the bed and sat down on the edge, pursing his lips. If Derek didn't know better, he'd say Callan was nervous. "I've never given you a proper wedding gift. And seeing as it's been close to a year already, I wanted to..." He trailed off again with a sheepish look on his face that sent Derek's heart aflutter in a decidedly undignified manner.

"Wouldn't you rather wait till our anniversary?" Derek asked, half-amused, half-touched by Callan's insecurity regarding something so apparently trivial.

"If I've learned anything during the last few years, it's that life is too fragile to postpone things." Callan shook his head. "No, I don't want to wait."

He took out a small velvet pouch from the pocket of his pants and handed it to Derek, who untied the strings and dropped the contents onto his palm.

"You shouldn't have," he said after the moment it took him to compose himself.

"You don't like it?" Callan asked anxiously.

"I love it."

A large green stone, polished to a high shine, was set in a silver signet ring that fit Derek's finger perfectly when he slipped it on. He traced the delicate carving of a sparrow and a wheat stalk on its flat surface with his thumb.

"I know it can't replace your father's ring," Callan said. "But I thought perhaps this one might bring you better luck than the old one had brought him. The stone was a gift from Gunnara—a beryl from the Outer Isles."

"Thank you," Derek said, his previous mirth giving way to a quieter, more profound sort of happiness. "It's beautiful."

Callan smiled, but apprehension still lingered in his eyes. Derek reached out to touch the hard planes of his face, just as gently as he had earlier in the warm darkness of predawn.

"What's troubling you?"

"There was something I've been meaning to ask you," Callan said, taking both of Derek's hands in his. His pulse was racing under Derek's fingertips. "How would you feel about starting a family with me?"

"You mean—"

"Yes. I've been thinking for a long time about having children. I know we still have unresolved issues to think about, with the petitions to rescind the witchcraft laws in Ivicia, but this is another thing I don't want to leave to perfect timing which may never come to pass. Is that...something you'd consider?"

Derek glanced at the side table where twin gray mourning ribbons lay entangled, ready to be worn around their sleeves. The period of mourning for the Duke of Mulberny was almost over, but Derek knew Callan wasn't wearing his solely to honor Bergen's memory. It was for all the friends and loved ones and even adversaries he'd lost along the way, for a past that couldn't be changed.

But the future was laid out before them with its endless possibilities, and it was up to them to shape it out of love and trust.

"There has been too much gray in our world for far too long," Derek said, looking up into his husband's eyes. "I'm ready for all the new colors we can bring into it."

Acknowledgements

Huge thanks to the whole NineStar Press team, and especially to Elizabetta and Raevyn, for believing in me and my stories.

About the Author

A voracious reader from the age of five, Isabelle Adler has always dreamed of one day putting her own stories into writing. She loves traveling, art, and science, and finds inspiration in all of these. Her favorite genres include sci-fi, fantasy, and historical adventure. She also firmly believes in the unlimited powers of imagination and caffeine.

Email: info@isabelleadler.com

Twitter: @Isabelle_Adler

Website: www.isabelleadler.com

Other books by this author

Staying Afloat Series
Adrift
Ashore

The Castaway Prince Series
The Castaway Prince
The Exile Prince

Fae-Touched Series
A Touch of Magic

Frost
Irises in the Snow

Also Available from NineStar Press

Connect with NineStar Press

www.ninestarpress.com

www.facebook.com/ninestarpress

www.facebook.com/groups/NineStarNiche

www.twitter.com/ninestarpress

www.tumblr.com/blog/ninestarpress

CPSIA information can be obtained
at www.ICGtesting.com
Printed in the USA
LVHW031458310120
645463LV00001B/167